MW01037169

Shoshone Trail II

Hans' Pass

Shoshone Trail II

Hans' Pass

by

David J Hawkes

BONNEVILLE BOOKS™
Springville, Utah

Copyright © 2002 David J Hawkes

All Rights Reserved.

No part of this book may be reproduced in any form whatsoever, whether by graphic, visual, electronic, film, microfilm, tape recording, or any other means, without prior written permission of the author, except in the case of brief passages embodied in critical reviews and articles.

ISBN: 1-55517-608-9
v.1

Published by Bonneville Books
Imprint of Cedar Fort Inc.
www.cedarfort.com

Distributed by:

Typeset by Kristin Nelson
Cover design by Adam Ford
Cover design © 2002 by Lyle Mortimer

Printed in the United States of America
10 9 8 7 6 5 4 3 2 1

Printed on acid-free paper

Library of Congress Cataloging-in-Publication Data

Hawkes, David J., 1956-
  Shoshone Trail II : Hans' Pass / by David J. Hawkes.
     p. cm.
  ISBN 1-55517-608-9 (pbk. : alk. paper)
  I. Title.
  PS3558.A8169 S48 2002
  813'.6--dc21

                    2002000400

Hans' Pass is respectfully dedicated
to my best friend, Hans Bayles

No Greater Love . . .

PROLOGUE

Sitting on the porch of her cabin, Sarah Stewart enjoyed the warmth of the weak spring sun. Uncomfortably she shifted position in the wooden rocker her husband, Moroni, had made for her. When she had told him she was expecting their baby, he had insisted on making the rocker. Brushing at a wisp of her long, blonde hair, she looked to the aspen-covered ridge for any sign of Moroni and her son, Sam. Nothing so far. Moroni and Sam had gone hunting elk early that morning and the day was now turning into afternoon. A faint smile on her face, Sarah let her thoughts run back over the last year.

It had been over a year ago that she and her first husband, Nils, along with their son, Sam, had been traveling toward Montana with several other families when tragedy struck. A renegade band of Blackfoot warriors had killed all of the people in the party, with the exception of Sam and herself. Destitute, she and her son had begun walking back to the Cache Valley settlements. In crossing the North Fork of the Snake River she had gotten soaked to the skin and, due to exposure, fallen ill. Then along came Moroni. Fondly she recalled waking from her fever-ridden sleep to see his face. After resting for a few days to recover from her illness, Moroni had taken her and Sam south to the Cache Valley settlements, arriving just in time for the terrible massacre of the Bear River band of Shoshone. Moroni had been a prisoner in the Indian camp when the soldiers attacked the village, and she had accompanied her old friend, Porter Rockwell, and the army. Following the battle, she and Moroni married. Then in the spring they had traveled to the banks of the Teton River. Here she, Moroni, Sam and Kate, their adopted Shoshone daughter, made their new home. It had taken Moroni, with Sam's help, most of the summer to build the cabin they now lived in. Strongly built to last through the harsh winters in this country, it contained three rooms plus a loft that Sam had claimed for his own. Moroni also built a matching barn from peeled logs to house meadow hay, horses, and the milk cow they had brought with them from Franklin.

Sarah straightened with a jolt. As she massaged her side where the baby she was carrying kicked her, Sarah wondered again if it was a boy or girl. *Well, it sure is active,* she thought. She let her eyes stray to the crib Moroni had lovingly crafted during the long winter. He had slaved over the crib for evenings on end, trying to make it perfect. Perfect. Yes everything was perfect now.

Several miles away, Moroni loaded the last of the elk meat on the bay gelding he had been riding. Giving the knot on the rope a last tug, he looked over at Sam sitting on the appaloosa.

"You look like you're riding a camel," Moroni said to Sam.

Perched high on the load of meat atop the horse, Sam grinned at his stepfather. "At least I get to ride."

"That's true," Moroni answered. "Just don't fall off."

Shaking his head, Sam clucked at the appaloosa stallion and turned him toward home. "Hey, Moroni, can I do the shooting next time?" he called back.

"I don't know, you're pretty young."

"Aw, come on. I've killed elk before, you know," Sam coaxed.

Giving a short laugh, Moroni replied, "Yes, you have. Sorry, I forgot. Tell you what: we don't need any more meat for a while, but next time you get first shot."

"Okay," Sam answered. "I can wait."

As he walked along, leading the bay and following Sam on the appaloosa, Moroni couldn't help but reflect on the past two years. He had changed so much, and grown, too. A year ago, he was alone, and now he had a family. And soon it would get even larger. Sarah was expecting the baby in a few weeks, and a month ago, a traveler going to the Montana gold camps had brought word that Sarah's father and his family were coming to live nearby. He didn't know if he should be happy about that prospect or not. Here they lived in the border lands. There weren't any white people living within a hundred miles—and those were the traders at Fort Hall to the south. Scanning the sky, Moroni couldn't detect any sign of a storm. An odd year, he thought. It was April and the snow had been gone for almost a month. Lost in his thoughts, he almost ran into the back end of the stopped appaloosa.

Alarm in his voice, Sam exclaimed, "Moroni, look at these tracks."

On the ridge overlooking Moroni and Sarah's cabin, a Sioux warrior watched and wondered. He had traveled through here last year and this white man's house had not been here then. Letting his gaze go to the horses in the corral, he wondered where the people were. Six horses in the corral. Two for each of them, he thought to himself. He was accompanied by two young men of the Gros Ventre. Normally, he and the two young warriors would be at odds, but they had a common bond. They were all outcasts from their own people; he for disobeying his war chief while on a raid, the two Gros Ventre for molesting a young girl in their own village. Watching the cabin for a few minutes, the Sioux wondered if he should just ride down and take the horses from the corral now, or if it would be wiser to wait for darkness.

"Brother, my stomach is empty," said the oldest and biggest of the Gros Ventre, named Buffalo Robe. "Let's ride down and ask for something to eat."

"All you think about is your stomach," the Sioux answered crossly. "We can steal those horses down there if we are careful."

The younger of the Gros Ventre, Bad Eyes, looked from the Sioux to his friend. "Horses would be nice, but some food would be good, too."

The Sioux grimaced at the thought of his companions. No

wonder everyone called them Big Bellies. Food was about all they thought of. Then the door of the cabin opened and a woman stepped outside. At once—despite the distance—he recognized the woman. And he, Hunts at Night, would have her hair!

Bending down and looking at the fresh unshod pony tracks in the soft spring earth, Moroni felt his hair stand on end. Pulling his knife out of its sheath, he cut the ropes holding the meat on the saddles of both horses. Helping Sam to the ground, he pushed the meat off and put Sam back in the saddle of the appaloosa. Then, mounting the bay, he led off toward home at a run.

* * *

Walking out of the cabin into the warmth of the sun, Sarah was about to sit again in her rocker when her heart skipped a beat. There on the ridge above the cabin were three Indians, and even from where she stood she could see they were painted for war. Stepping back inside, she spoke to her adopted daughter, "Katie, there are three bad men outside. Quick, out the back door and hide in yours and Sam's secret spot."

Obediently, three-year-old Kate scurried out the door and into the trees in back of the cabin. Once there, she squirmed her way into a cave she had found one day when she and Sam were playing. Never once did it occur to her that the men she was now hiding from were of her own race.

Looking out of the firing port, Sarah tried to see the three warriors, but they had disappeared. Her revolver in her hand, she walked to another port on the right side of the cabin. Peering out, she could see that the mares in the corral were acting up. The Indians were still around, and probably creeping up toward the corral in preparation to steal the horses. They would have a hard time doing that, Sarah knew, as the gate to the corral faced the cabin and the fence was stout enough that without an axe or saw the Indians weren't going to pull the corral down. There! A stealthy, brown form snaked its way along the ground in front of the corral. Now she watched as the warrior stood and started working the latch on the gate. Poking the barrel of her Colt through the gun port, Sarah aimed and fired. As the gun smoke cleared away she observed a limp form lying next to the gate and she watched as the two other Indians galloped their horses over the far ridge. Sarah felt a little queasy at the sight of the lifeless form, but there was no other way to protect their horses. Watching through the port for a few more minutes, she looked for any sign of life or the return of the other Indians. Satisfied that all was clear, she opened the door of the cabin and stepped out. Everything looked clear to Sarah, so with a lump in her throat, she walked to the body lying next to the corral. Halfway there, she paused to check for anything unusual. Nothing was, except that all the mares were at the far end of the corral staring at the dead Indian. Well, that was to be expected. Reaching the body, Sarah stopped and looked down. Then to her horror, the Indian's eyes opened. It was then she saw the wicked-looking club gripped in his right hand.

Hearing the muted thump of a pistol shot from the direction of his cabin, Moroni urged the bay even faster. A knot of fear in his throat, Moroni hoped he could make it home in time. But as the bay began climbing the ridge on the far side of the cabin, a cold dread gripped him. Cresting the ridge, with Sam mounted on the appaloosa right behind him, Moroni could see two Indians tying ropes onto the mares in the corral. Another was kneeling down next to the gate, a war club in his hands, Sarah at his feet. With a shout of anger, Moroni pulled his Henry repeater from the saddle boot and raced the bay down the ridge. Halfway to the bottom he began firing shot after shot at the Indians. One Indian toppled from his pony, to Moroni's satisfaction. Then the bay shuddered and went down. Kicking free of the stirrups, Moroni hit the ground hard, losing his rifle. As he got to his feet, he saw Sam, still on the appaloosa, go by him. Moroni staggered as an arrow hit him in the chest. Gritting his teeth, he pulled one revolver from the holster and shot into the warrior who was fitting another arrow to his bow. Then the warrior who had been standing over his wife mounted his horse and prepared to escape. Gasping for air, Moroni snapped a shot at the Indian and watched as the horse buckled and went down, throwing the warrior to the ground. His mind fogging, Moroni staggered toward the form of his wife lying on the ground, her head and face bloody. Reaching Sarah, he watched as the Indian whose horse he had shot scrambled to his feet. Shouting a wild whoop of victory, the savage climbed on the appaloosa behind Sam and begin whipping the horse through the trees back of the cabin. With a groan of fear and rage, Moroni tried to bring the pistol level, but he didn't have the strength. The revolver fell from his limp fingers and, dropping forward to his knees, he reached for Sarah's hand.

CHAPTER 1

Hidden in the cave that she and Sam had discovered, Kate huddled, her arms folded tightly before her. Unmoving and silent she had learned as a baby from her Shoshone parents that when hiding from an enemy, silence was the difference between life and death. But inside, Kate was in turmoil. Since being orphaned she had found happiness again as the daughter of Moroni and Sarah. Her white adoptive parents were vastly different from her Shoshone mother and father, but here, again, she had found love and security. Shivering slightly in the dampness of the cave, Kate felt fear—fear that she would again lose her family.

* * *

Sam held onto the mane of the galloping appaloosa. Watching the trunks of the budding aspen fly by for a few more moments, he began to struggle against the strong, bronzed arm that held him in place against the Indian's buckskin shirt. Gaining courage, Sam let go of the galloping horse's mane and tried to pry the arm loose. Wriggling and struggling, he felt the arm start to give. Then the horse swerved to avoid a fallen log and Sam felt himself flying through the air, still in the grip of the Indian. Then there was a sudden impact and darkness.

* * *

Fifteen miles to the southeast of Moroni and Sarah's cabin rolled a caravan of two heavily-laden wagons along with two dozen assorted cattle and horses. Mounted on a stocky buckskin gelding fifty yards in front of the lead wagon, Rolf Gunnarson raised a fist signaling for the wagons to stop. Peering about, Rolf cantered the buckskin further up the vague trail another hundred yards. Stopping short of the crest of the ridge where the faint trail passed over, Rolf slid from the buckskin and pulled a Spencer carbine from a scabbard hung on the left side of the saddle. Nearing age fifty, Rolf had surprisingly little gray in the blond braid that poked out from the battered black hat pulled low on his head. With his full beard and powerful physique, he could easily have passed for one of his Viking ancestors if he had been dressed in something besides woolen trousers, boots and elk-hide jacket. Letting the reins of the buckskin drop, Rolf knew the horse would stay ground-hitched until he called or came back. Using the sparse brush as cover, Rolf crested the ridge, then slipped a few yards down the far side. A greening chokecherry bush in front of him, he studied the lay of the country. As he surveyed the country before him, Rolf pondered his situation. He, his wife Greta, his daughter Melissa, her new husband, Hugh MacAskill, and his youngest daughter Jeni, were traveling north to homestead on the Teton river near his oldest daughter, Sarah, and her husband, Moroni Stewart. During the last year and a half he had learned from the contents of three letters as well as from talking with an old acquaintance, Porter Rockwell, of Sarah and Sam's near-death and rescue by Moroni. And following the winter massacre of the northwestern band of Shoshone near Fort Franklin in the north part of the Cache Valley, she and Moroni had been married. One of the letters from Sarah had informed him that she and Moroni intended to settle somewhere on the west slope of the Tetons. The last letter they had received had been just too much for Rolf. From the description that Sarah had written, she had, in Rolf's opinion described paradise. Early in the spring of 1864, he sold his farm in the Utah valley, and, with his wife and family started north.

Shifting his position slightly, Rolf let his gaze go to the Tetons touching the sky to the east. Yes, his daughter was right, this was paradise. And if he had followed the directions correctly, he shouldn't be more than twenty miles from Moroni and Sarah's place. But since morning he hadn't been able to shake an uneasy feeling. Although they hadn't seen any sign of anyone in five days, he still had a feeling of being watched. Hearing a faint sound behind him, Rolf glanced back to see his new son-in-law standing in the open behind him.

Rolling an eye at him, Rolf whispered, "You're showing yourself on the skyline, boy."

Broad of shoulder, bushy red hair and beard and standing an inch over six feet in height, twenty-year-old Hugh MacAskill grimaced at Rolf, then thumped over and squatted down beside him.

Patiently, Rolf explained his remark. "Son, if you stand in the open like that, especially on the skyline, you stick out like a sore thumb. What you want to do is sorta' slither over the crest, then set down behind a bush or tree or some other cover. Then you can take a look-see at the country all around without lettin' anyone else know you are about."

"You mean the red savages?" Hugh asked in a thick Scottish brogue.

Rolf nodded his head.

Still smarting from the rebuke, Hugh attempted to study the country around, but his mind wandered. It had been just two years since he had come to America. Before that he had lived in France, Spain, and Italy, doing the best he could to stay out of the clutches of the Queen's law. At age fifteen he had become an outlaw in his native Scotland. One night a squad of English dragoons had stopped at the small inn that Hugh's father owned. After a series of insults from the young Subaltern, Hugh's father demanded that the soldiers leave. But the officer demanded Hugh's pretty seventeen-year-old sister for the night. At the last remark, Hugh, his father, and older brother had fallen on the dragoons with pistol and sword. At the end of the wild melee in the close confines of the MacAskill Inn, Hugh found himself to be the only person still standing with a saber cut on his back and a pistol ball in his arm. He checked his family for any sign of life, but found none. With his father's claymore clutched in his grip, Hugh had staggered to the door of the inn and collapsed.

The morning sun was peeking over the eastern hills when a neighbor found him. Knowing that retaliation from the Crown would be swift and unmerciful, he had bound Hugh's wounds as best as he could and found him passage on a small boat to the continent. The years after that were a jumble of narrow escapes—he was living by his wits. Landing in San Francisco, he had wandered throughout part of California. After meeting several Mormons and listening to them and hearing about their persecutions, he felt drawn to them. Once in Utah, he had found work with Rolf as an apprentice gunsmith. It hadn't taken long after that for Hugh to catch the eye of Melissa, Rolf's middle daughter. After several months they were married, even though Hugh still had not been baptized a member of the Church. But neither Melissa nor Rolf had pressed him on the subject. The only comment Rolf had made was, "All in the Lord's time."

A proud young man who had made his way in the world for more than five years, Hugh couldn't understand why his father-in-law was always correcting him or questioning an action. Though Rolf never raised his voice and generally was right about what he said, Hugh at times felt resentful. Shifting around a bit, Hugh was about to make a comment when Rolf put his hand to his lips. "Shhh, there be something moving down there."

Shifting his gaze, Hugh could see nothing. A few more moments of straining his eyes and he was beginning to wonder if this wasn't another of the alarms that had punctuated the trip north, when out of the tiny grove of stunted aspen a file of horsemen appeared. Although they were several hundred yards away, Hugh could tell at once that the men on horseback were Indians—at least two dozen, and then the reality hit him. The riders were men, there were no women or children. A war party! Closing his hand on the action of the Spencer carbine he carried, Hugh watched as the file of Indians crossed the valley and splashed across a shallow stream. Then turning away from him and Rolf, they wound their way up the slope and out of sight. After the last of the riders had disappeared, Rolf leaned over and asked in a whisper, "Tell me what you have just seen."

"Um, well, we have just seen a war party of the red savages. They rode their ponies across that wee valley there an' disappeared over the other side."

Giving his son-in-law a long look, Rolf asked, "and how many were there? How were they armed? What tribe were they from? And how do you know if they were a war party?"

His face turning red at the questioning, Hugh began, "I dinna' count the heathen an' . . ."

"There were twenty-three warriors in that bunch; most armed with bows and lances, but I did see five rifles or muskets. From their dress I'd say they were Shoshone. Now, some of the Shoshone are friends to the whites, but after what happened down on the Bear River a couple of winters ago, some aren't, and in my opinion they have a right to hate us." Continuing, Rolf said, "I don't think they were a war party—no paint. But always remember this: Indians are opportunists and most don't think the way we do. You see, they are like we were until a couple of hundred years ago. The favorite occupation for a young man of the Shoshone or Ute, or most other tribes for that matter, was to make war on their enemy and steal horses. See, a young gal wants a man that can provide for her no matter if she is white or Indian. And in the Indian culture, raiding and stealing from your enemy is the best way to get rich. We don't look at it that way anymore, but how many of the rich and mighty families in England or Scotland got to be rich and mighty? They did it by being great fighters."

Hugh opened his mouth again, but Rolf cut him off.

"Hugh my boy, you are a fine lad, and I'm trying my level best to educate you in the ways here on the frontier. I'm trying to teach you the things you need to know to survive. This world here is a long way from Scotland or the continent or Salt Lake, for that matter." Then giving Hugh a wink he added, "I don't want Melissa a widow at eighteen."

"And I dinna' think I'll be doin' that," Hugh replied.

"Fine, I'll be staying here for a bit to watch and see if they double back. You slip back to the wagons and help the women-folk get the wagons and stock into the draw we passed."

Giving Rolf a quick nod, Hugh crawled back over the ridge and trotted back to where the wagons waited.

Once the wagons and stock were nestled in the deep, brushy draw, Hugh got the itch. He needed to move and look around. Making sure that the women were armed and on watch he told Melissa of his intent to scout their back-trail.

Concern on her face, Melissa asked, "Hugh, are you sure Pa would want you to do that?" From the look on her husband's face she instantly regretted her question.

His face crimson, he retorted, "Melissa, me lass, I'm a high-lander. And I can sneak aboot as good as any old red Indian." Then, turning, he stalked away.

Hugh preferred to scout on foot and had left his horse back at the wagons. Taking long strides, he gazed at both sides of the trail. Nothing. There was nothing but the deep wagon tracks in the soft soil along with the hoof pockmarks from the stock.

"Tracks," he muttered to himself. 'We be leavin' a trail a blind man could follow. Looking at the torn-up trail, Hugh remembered a spot in the trail several hundred yards back where the ground was rocky and relatively dry, even with the spring rains that had been falling. Moving along quickly he soon reached the rocky spot of ground. Studying the trail he could see that their caravan had left little apparent sign of their passing. Leaning his rifle against a clump of sage, he set about erasing the smudges on the rocks and other tracks. Just as he was sifting some dirt and crumpled leaves over the last of the tracks Hugh heard behind him the soft thud of a hoof, then a clink of metal. Turning, Hugh's heart stopped a beat. There in a line facing him were the Indians he and his father-in-law had watched not over an hour ago. A grinning warrior wearing a wolf-hide jacket held Hugh's Spencer carbine pointed at his chest.

CHAPTER 2

As consciousness returned, Sam felt the swaying movement of a horse. Cracking an eye open he could see last Fall's blackened aspen leaves moving by as the horse under him wove its way through the grove of trees. Still weak and unable to move, he watched as the ground sloped. Then he felt the warmth of the sun on his back. Shifting his gaze ever so slowly he could see the back of another horse ahead of the one he was tied to. But seeing only a leather-clad leg hanging from the saddle on the horse, he couldn't make out who it was. Then he remembered. He remembered the swift ride back to the cabin, the shots, the sight of his mother on the ground with blood all around, his stepfather, Moroni, with an arrow protruding from his chest, and then the Indian climbing on the appaloosa in back of him and the wild ride—and falling. Feeling sick to his stomach, he retched. Spitting, Sam attempted to clear the vile taste out of his mouth, when a rough hand grabbed his hair and pulled his head around. There in front of him was a painted face, dark eyes glaring at him.

"You live?" It seemed to be a question.

"Uh huh," Sam groaned weakly.

For a moment all he got was a grunt in return. Then the hand jerked on his hair again. "You mine now. I kill Mama. Soon I kill you!"

Now Sam remembered, this was the young warrior who had tried to kill him and his mother when they had been lost two Falls ago. As the savage had attempted to brain his mother, Sarah, with a vicious-looking war club, she had shot the warrior's horse. Then Gall, the warrior's leader had ridden up and shamed the young man by calling him Horse Ears. Still weak from the blow to his head and hearing the Indian announce the death of his mother, Sam's stomach rebelled again, this time spewing its contents all over the deer-hide leggings the warrior wore. With an oath, the warrior, now known as Hunts At Night, smashed Sam on the side of the head, plunging him into darkness again.

The warmth of a fire and the smell of roasting meat brought Sam to consciousness this time. Shifting himself, he found that his hands and legs were bound. His head still throbbed, but wriggling himself around he managed to get to a sitting position. In the gathering twilight he peered around the campsite. He noticed several chunks of meat sizzling on green sticks over a low fire. In a corner was a thick bedroll of blankets. The smell of the meat set his stomach to growling. Gazing at the meat, he was formulating a plan of getting a chunk to eat when a moccasined foot sent him sprawling. Rolling up against a tree, he looked up into the sneering face of his captor.

"You want meat?" the warrior asked.

"Yes," replied Sam.

"Hah, you no get. You mine now." Then turning, the warrior sat next to the fire. Picking up one of the half-cooked chunks of meat, he began to gnaw on it.

Watching the Indian eat the meat made Sam nearly faint with hunger. But steeling himself, he turned his eyes away and began to think of his situation. He had no idea where he was. He wasn't even sure if he had been unconscious for more than a day. His head hurt and he felt weak from hunger as well as the blow to his head. Shivering slightly, he looked back at the Indian noisily gulping the last piece of meat down. Sam wondered what had caused the beast to seek vengeance on him and his mother. Had he found out where they had settled?

Wiping the grease from his hands on his buckskin leggings, the warrior looked at Sam and grinned. "You hunger?"

"Yes," replied Sam again.

"Hah, that bad. You no git food," said the warrior.

Looking the warrior in the eye, Sam lifted his chin and answered, "Fine then, I'll go hungry."

"You baby? You cry?" sneered the warrior.

"Wolf Chaser, the son of Gall, does not cry."

"Bah!" exploded the warrior. "We see you cry." Then pulling a wicked-looking knife from a sheath, he advanced on Sam.

Watching as the warrior came toward him, Sam stared fiercely back at the Indian. "You don't scare me none, Horse Ears," he said, as the warrior picked him up by the front of his shirt.

"My name not Horse Ears!" shouted the warrior, spraying Sam with spit. "I am called Hunts At Night."

"Horse Ears," Sam replied, in a calm voice.

Screeching a war cry, the Indian threw Sam to the ground. Sitting astride him he tore the boy's shirt off. Then with his knife, he carved a tiny square of skin from Sam's chest. His chest heaving with anger, Hunts At Night waved the bloody piece of skin in Sam's face. "You call me Horse Ears, I cut you."

Finally getting up, he tossed the piece of skin into the fire and walked into the darkness.

His chest stinging from the cut, Sam nearly cried out from the pain, but he wouldn't give the Indian the satisfaction of seeing him cry. Taking deep breaths, he willed the pain on his chest to go away. After a few moments, Sam struggled to a sitting position. Looking around at the small campsite again, he watched for any sign of Hunts At Night. Nothing. Just the small campfire and the bedroll. Then in the flickering firelight he spied a chunk of fat and gristle Hunts At Night had discarded while eating. Looking around once more, Sam wriggled over to where the cast off meat lay in the leaves. Lying on his side, he managed to get the leftover meat into his mouth. Then quickly he made his way back to the stump he had been lying against. Chewing slowly, Sam nearly gagged, but he knew that he had to choke down the chunk of gristle. He had to have the nourishment it would give him. Swallowing the last particle of meat, Sam's stomach growled—from hunger or protest from the greasy meat he had swallowed. He wasn't sure. But at least for the moment he felt a little better. A cold breeze filtered through the budding aspens, and, shirtless, Sam shivered. Inching closer to the fire he let its warmth soak into his tired and sore body. Straining a little, he tried the rawhide strings that bound his hands and feet. Too tight. How was he going to get out of this mess, he wondered? Hearing a soft footfall, Sam glanced up to see Hunts At Night. In his hands he held two roughly-made saddles. Dropping them near the bedrolls, the Indian glared at Sam. Then, undoing the blankets, he lay down and seemed to fall asleep. Shivering again, Sam wished for just one of the blankets. Spying the remnant of his wool shirt, he scooted over and picked it up with his teeth. Then wriggling back to the dying fire he spread the torn shirt out and curled up on it. Filled with despair, Sam thought about his situation. Would anyone know what had happened to him? Was his mother truly dead? And what about Moroni? He knew his grandparents were on their way up from Salt Lake City. But when would they arrive, and when they did, what would they find at the cabin? Blinking back a tear, he knew he couldn't just give up. Someone would come, he knew it. Besides, he was Wolf Chaser, the adopted son of Gall. Feeling stronger, he slipped into a fitful sleep.

CHAPTER 3

A pair of eyes looked down at the scene before them: a spacious log cabin and barn with a large corral made from peeled pine logs. In the yard between the cabin and barn lay two dead horses and several human forms, one of which looked to be a woman with long, blonde hair. Shouldering a large pack, the man behind the eyes began to trot down the slope toward the cabin and barn. Rounding the corner of the barn, the man stopped and stared. Next to the corral gate lay the woman, a crumpled heap of blue blouse and buckskin skirt. Further out in the yard lay an obviously-dead Indian warrior next to one of the dead horses. At the corner of the cabin lay another warrior. This one had apparently dragged himself to the corner of the cabin after being shot, but the corner was as far as he had made it before expiring. Next to the woman lay a white man, dressed in buckskin trousers and a blue army-style shirt, his hands extending toward where the woman lay. Walking quickly to the woman, the leather-clad man knelt at her side. To his relief, she was still breathing. Looking closely at the wound on her head and the deep stab wound in her upper arm, he clucked his tongue and gently picked her up and carried her into the log house. Laying her on a blanket-covered bed in the bedroom, he touched her forehead, and after saying a few soft words, hurried back outside. Kneeling at the white man's side, the leather-clad man looked closely at the arrow buried deep in the chest of the unconscious man. Grasping the arrow he pulled gently, but he could tell it was probably hooked to a bone deep in the man's chest. Muttering softly to himself, the leather-clad man grasped the arrow and shoved the arrow the rest of the way through his body. Then, pulling out an oddly-shaped steel knife, he deftly cut the head from the arrow and pulled the wood shaft out. His eyes searching the yard for a few moments, the leather-clad stranger picked up the unconscious man, and with effort, carried him into the log home.

The man and woman both resting, the stranger stirred up the fire in the cast iron stove and placed a pot of water on the top to heat. Surveying the inside of the log home, the man looked for something he could use as bandages. Finding some clean cloth, he began tearing it into strips.

Finished caring for the man and the woman, the stranger wearily walked to the door of the cabin and looked outside. *There should be two more,* he thought to himself. But where were they? For several moments he looked out at the greening hillside opposite the cabin and wondered why tragedy had to visit so often in such a place of beauty. Heaving a sigh, he was about to enter the doorway again when he heard a soft footfall around the side of the cabin. Turning quickly, the stranger waited . . . then, to his surprise, a small Indian girl peered around the corner of the cabin at him.

A smile quickly spreading on his face, the leather-clad man went to a knee and spoke softly to the child, "Katie, do you not remember me?"

Tears forming at the corners of her eyes Katie ran to the stranger and threw her arms around him. Through the sobs she managed to choke out, "Wise one, some bad men have hurt Mama and Papa and stole Sammy."

Holding the sobbing child close, the man known as Hawk stroked Katie's hair and said softly, "Your mama and papa will be fine. Now you must be brave and tell me what happened."

Wiping at the tears, Katie told Hawk of Moroni and Sam

going hunting early in the morning. While they were gone, of she and Sarah had seen the Indians attempting to steal the horses. Obediently, she had hidden in the cave until she had heard the shots. Then, unable to stay hidden any longer, she had peeked through some brush at the fight. On seeing her adoptive parents go down and Sam being kidnapped, she had again run to the cave and hidden there.

A gentle smile on his face, Hawk wiped at Katie's tear-stained face and told her, "Little one, we will have to be strong in the days to come. Your mama is going to have a baby and both of them will need care. Will you help me?"

Her eyes large and round, she nodded her head, "Oh yes, I will help you. But what about Sammy?"

The smile fading just a bit from his face, Hawk said softly, "We will have to hope that Sam will be all right. Your mama and papa need us right now."

Soberly, Katie bit her lower lip and nodded her head.

* * *

A white light penetrated Moroni's senses. Holding up a hand to ward off the light he could see a man walking toward him. A sudden thought came to him at that moment: *I must be dead!*

Then the man was standing next to him. His eyes accustomed to the light, Moroni looked closely at the man who was now smiling at him. It was Charlie! His body feeling as if it was about to burst, he looked at the smiling brother he had lost during the first day of battle at Shilo.

"Charlie!" Moroni called.

"Hello, brother," Charlie said, with the ever-present grin that was his trademark. "I can see you've been busy."

His eyes trying to penetrate the light that surrounded him, Moroni asked, "Where are Father and Mother? Are they coming?"

Laughing, Charlie shook his head, "Oh Moroni, don't be in such a hurry."

Feeling unsure of what was going on, Moroni asked, "Well, aren't I dead?"

Still laughing, Charlie shook his head. "Not yet, brother. It's not your time." A sober expression coming to his face, he added, "Not unless you take the wrong path."

"The wrong path?" asked Moroni, not understanding.

His arms at his sides, Charlie smiled warmly at Moroni and said, "My brother, you have a great mission in life. Even I do not comprehend or see it all at this time, but you are not dead nor will you die unless you take the path of unrighteousness. You will have many who will aid you in your mission in life and if you follow the spirit you will know what is right and what is wrong."

"I see," Moroni said, feeling let down. Then, reaching out to his brother, Moroni said softly, "but I don't want to leave you."

Still grinning, Charlie moved back a step. "Moroni, there are others in the mortal world who need you." His eyes burning with an intensity that Moroni had never seen before, Charlie went on: "Moroni, your life will affect thousands. What you accomplish on earth will serve as a beacon and an example to a multitude of others."

Confused, Moroni shook his head. "But I don't understand."

"You will, my dear brother, you will. But remember, you must always choose the right. It will be hard at times and it is known that you live in a violent time. Remember to trust in God; he can deliver you when all else fails. Now, I must go."

A feeling of sorrow and despair came over him as he watched Charlie fade away. Moroni held his hands out and called, "Please, Charlie, don't leave."

Then as the light faded into darkness, he could hear Charlie call out, "Don't worry, brother, I will always be with you."

CHAPTER 4

His mouth dry as an alkali desert, Hugh stared into the dark eyes of the warrior under the wolf hide. In a holster on his belt he had a Colt revolver, but he knew without a doubt he would be dead long before he could ever get it out and fire at the twenty or so warriors arrayed before him. Running his tongue over his dry lips, he was about to say something, when he saw the warriors' eyes flicker. There was something behind him. Hearing the jingle of a bit, then a hoof-fall of a horse, Hugh could only wonder at how many Indians were at his back. Staring into the eyes of the warrior in front of him, Hugh felt the hair on the back of his neck stand on end, as he heard the double-click of a rifle being cocked behind him. He nearly fainted with relief when he heard his wife's voice, "What is it you want with my husband?

Grinning from ear to ear, the warrior in the wolf hide answered, "Your man has lost his rifle. I have found it for him. Then perhaps I will show him how to rub out signs from his trail."

Taking a step back, Hugh stole a glance at his wife, Melissa. She was mounted on his horse, a sturdy bay, and in her hands was a Colt revolving shotgun. Off to the side he could see Melissa's younger sister, Jeni, a heavy Sharps buffalo rifle in her hands.

Holding out the rifle, the warrior took a step toward Hugh. "Here is your rifle." Then, casting a wry grin at Melissa he added, "Do not shoot me, warrior woman. I am called No Arrows of the Shoshone and I have always been a friend of the whites."

Taking his Spencer back from No Arrows, Hugh nodded his head and said, "Thank ye. Ye be a fine red savage."

At the mention of red savage, Melissa and Jeni blanched, but No Arrows only chuckled. "Perhaps you wouldn't think I am such a savage if you got to know me better."

Embarrassed, Hugh stammered, "I be sorry for callin' ye a savage. I dinna' think of me manners."

"It does no harm," replied No Arrows. "Tell me, what are you people doing in this part of the country?"

"Me brother-in-law has settled up this way a bit an' me wife, her father an' mother and daughter Jeni have decided to move up here next to 'em."

His eyes going to Melissa then to Jeni, No Arrows asked, a faint smile on his face, "Is your brother-in-law Moroni Stewart?"

"How would you know what his name is?" asked Jeni, the Sharps trained on No Arrows. "And how did you learn such good English?"

"Ho, little one," No Arrows replied holding out both hands. "I learned to speak your language from the Crier—his white name is Nick Wilson. Many years ago he lived with Washakie and was one of my best friends. From your looks you have to be a sister to Sarah, Moroni's wife."

Her turn to be embarrassed, Jeni lowered the muzzle of the heavy rifle. It was true, most people believed her to be the exact replica of her older sister, with her long blonde hair, fair complexion and blue eyes. Melissa, on the other hand, had her mother's looks. Dark eyes and hair, with olive skin that told of her Spanish ancestry. "I'm sorry, sir. We just didn't know who you might be."

Laughing, another younger warrior dismounted from his paint pony and said, "From a red savage to a 'sir.' You have come a long way in a few minutes, my uncle."

At the joke, all present became more relaxed.

"Will you come back to our wagons and share a meal with us?" asked Melissa.

Looking back at the twenty-odd warriors, No Arrows said, "You want to feed these warriors?"

A smile on her face, Melissa answered: "Father and Hugh killed a couple of elk last night. I'm sure we can feed you all. And besides, we want to know how you got to know Moroni and Sarah."

"Then we would be honored," replied No Arrows.

Following the evening meal, Rolf and Hugh as well as No Arrows and his nephew, Strikes Hard, sat near the flickering fire and talked. Holding a cup in his hands, Rolf asked, "Have Moroni and Sarah picked out a good spot to live?"

Nodding, No Arrows replied, "A fine place. Running water nearby and plenty of timber and, in the summer, excellent grass. The winters are bad in that spot."

"But Moroni cut much grass and put it in the barn," said Strikes Hard.

"That is true, he is a wise man. He stores much and is always prepared," agreed No Arrows.

"How far are we from their place?" asked Rolf.

Looking at the wagons, No Arrows shrugged and replied, "One day if you travel fast."

Now Melissa and Jeni walked up and sat on a log pulled up next to the fire.

"How is it you are traveling in this country?" asked Jeni. "Where are your people?"

Nudging a stick further into the fire, No Arrows answered her question. "Our people are to the south, near the Soda Springs. Washakie has several bands of men scouting the country around. He is afraid that some Indians are going to be causing trouble again this year."

"How did you get to know Moroni and Sarah?" asked Melissa.

Laughing, No Arrows said, "Well it is a long story but to make it short, it was when Moroni shot my young nephew here. Then I whacked Moroni on the head and captured him."

Rolf said nothing, but Hugh sat bolt upright and stared from one warrior to the next. "He shot ye? An' then ye clubbed the mon on the head and ye still be friends?"

"The best," commented No Arrows.

Strikes Hard, holding a straight face, pulled up his buckskin hunting shirt. Pointing to a puckered scar on his side, he added, "See, that is where he shot me."

Mouth hanging open, Hugh looked first at his father-in-law, then to the two Indians. "What do ye think I am? A bloody fool?"

Howling with laughter, Strikes Hard fell backward off the log he had been sitting on.

Red-faced, Hugh stood and said, "I dinna' think it's funny, mon. If a mon shot me, I'd do me best to kill him."

A smile on his face, No Arrows said gently, "Peace, my red-haired brother. Strikes Hard laughs at himself as well as you. You see, when he was shot by Moroni, he and several other warriors were doing their best to kill Moroni and Sarah. I was there as well, and when Moroni offered peace, these young, foolish warriors tried to kill Moroni. Moroni is a very hard man to kill. After shooting my nephew, he also bandaged his wound and helped him to recover. I hit Moroni on the head to save his life. After that, we were all in the camp on Bear River when Connor attacked."

"I know that story," broke in Jeni. "Sarah wrote and told us all about it." Then looking closely at the scar on Strikes Hard's side, she added, "You all were saved by God as far as I am concerned."

"Port told us a little bit about the *massacre*, as he called it," said Rolf.

Sober now, No Arrows nodded his agreement. "Yes, it was a bad thing. Some of the soldiers had bad hearts and killed women, children, anyone they saw. Many good people were wiped out that day."

"And some bad ones too, my uncle," said Strikes Hard. "It was not a bad thing that Bear Hunter, Tall Bull, and some like them are dead. They would have continued to kill whites and others until they, too, were killed."

"What you say is true, nephew." Looking up at Rolf and Hugh he added, "That is why we ride through this country. Washakie is worried that some of the other Shoshone as well as other tribes may be causing trouble again this year and he would like to put a stop to it."

"How can he do that?" asked Melissa. "He's just one of the many chiefs."

"Ah, but he is one of the most respected and feared chiefs, too," said No Arrows. "He has already had a parlay with Plenty Coups of the Crow and Four Fingers of the Blackfoot tribes. They have agreed to try and keep their young men from warring against each other as well as the whites. Washakie believes that the only way to survive the next ten years is to be a friend to the white man."

"You say Washakie has talked with the Crow and the Black-foot?" asked Rolf leaning forward.

"Yes, I know it is hard to believe the Shoshone and the Crow as allies, but we know it is the only way to survive," answered No Arrows.

"But what about Pocatello?" asked Rolf.

Shrugging his shoulders, No Arrows said, "I don't know. Pocatello is still angry over what happened at Bear River and some of his men want to keep raiding the weaker parties that travel to Oregon. And then there is Buffalo Horn. He had sworn never to give in to the whites, but from what we can find out he has moved west toward Fort Boise. Whirlwind is a Piegan Blackfoot who has told Four Fingers he is a woman to want peace with the whites. He has drawn away many of the young men who seek glory and scalps. So I'm not sure what will happen. I'm afraid that Washakie knows he cannot have war between the factions of the Shoshone just as Four Fingers knows he cannot fight Whirlwind. It would destroy the tribe."

"You forgot the tribes to the east, uncle," commented Strikes Hard.

"Ah yes, we have the Sioux, Cheyenne and others," said No Arrows with a sigh.

"What about them?" Asked Melissa.

"I am afraid before there is peace in this country there will be much blood spilled," said No Arrows. "There is already trouble along the Gold Road from Laramie to Montana. Red Cloud of the Sioux has said he will close it to the white man."

"Can't someone talk to the Sioux and reason with them?" asked Jeni.

"That is not always so easy as it sounds, my daughter," said Greta, coming up to the fire. Sitting next to her husband she changed the subject, "Have you seen Moroni and Sarah lately?"

"Not since last fall," replied No Arrows.

"Were they well?" asked Greta.

"Yes, they were fine, and Sarah was expecting a child this spring."

Clapping her hands together, Greta exclaimed, "Wonderful!" Then, her eyes narrowing, she asked no one in particular, "Why didn't she tell us in her last letter?"

Clearing his throat, Rolf said, in an attempt to keep the peace, "Perhaps they didn't know at that time." But looking at his wife, he could tell he hadn't pacified her.

Seeing that her mother was beginning to get into one of her moods, Jeni asked No Arrows, "If you don't mind me asking, how did you get your name?"

No Arrows was about to answer when Strikes Hard interrupted him: "I will tell the story. My uncle does not do his deeds of bravery justice. It was six years past. Our band of the Shoshone was camped on what you whites call the *Sweetwater*. We were preparing for a buffalo hunt when we were attacked by a strong war party of Sioux. I was just a young boy at the time, but I can still remember my uncle leading the charge to repel the Sioux. As many of the men were scouting for the main herd of buffalo on the other side of the village, most of the warriors who rushed to defend our people were the very young and the old. But my uncle, riding on an old horse, almost singlehandedly drove off the raiders. He fired arrow after arrow at the Sioux until he used all of his, then he gathered up some from a wounded warrior and shot all of them. When he had used all of the arrows, he rode the old horse in among the Sioux and began lashing them with his bow. At this, the Sioux retreated, and upon seeing the return of our hunters, left us for good. When Washakie heard of this deed, he jokingly asked my uncle why he whipped the Sioux with his bow. He answered that he had no arrows left, and that is how he got his warrior name."

Looking closely at the warrior known as No Arrows, Rolf, as well as his family, had a new appreciation for the young warrior. "Tell me, No Arrows, why is it you are not married?" asked Rolf.

A faraway look came into the warrior's eyes at this question. "Three years ago my woman died. I have not found one to take her place."

Embarrassed, Rolf said, "I am sorry. I did not know."

With a wave of his hand, No Arrows replied, "It is done.

Now, I would guide you to Moroni's place if you would like. My nephew and I will go with you, but the rest of the men will have to continue on."

"We would be most grateful," answered Rolf.

"It is late," said No Arrows. "We will be ready to travel at first light."

"Agreed," said Rolf watching No Arrows walk off into the night followed by Strikes Hard.

CHAPTER 5

Breathing deeply of the crisp morning air, No Arrows urged his horse to the crest of the next low ridge. Pausing near the top, he stood in the crude stirrups of his saddle and looked over the ridge. Wearing an elk-hide jacket over a cloth shirt and buckskin leggings, he wore nothing that would reflect light or draw attention to him. A round hat made of marten pelts was perched on his head, but as the spring sun began to warm the air, he contemplated taking it off and stowing it away in the small pack on his horse. For several moments he looked at the country around him. Rolling hills with sage and spring grass in the bottoms and aspen timber crested the ridges. No enemies in sight. That was good. At first light he had ridden away from the wagons of Rolf and his son-in-law hoping to scout a good trail for them to follow on the way to Moroni and Sarah's cabin. He, too, was looking forward to visiting with his friends. It had been a long winter and he wondered if Sarah had given birth yet. A lance of pain ran through his heart as he thought of Small Grass. She had been gone three years now. She had been giving birth to twin sons when a raiding party of Sioux and Cheyenne had swept down on the village, and a raider's war club had ended her life as well as his sons'. For several months his heart had been black. And during his period of mourning he had held a wish for death in his heart. And so he had ridden alone against the Cheyenne and the Sioux. During those months he had killed over two dozen of his tribe's enemies. Then on his last raid, he cornered a young Cheyenne woman, and intending to kill her and take her scalp, he had thrown her to the ground. As his war axe was descending, he noticed her round stomach.

At that moment he had seen the face of his lovely Small Grass. As the young woman watched in wonder, he stood up, threw his bloody axe into the grass, and sadly mounted his pony and rode away, not even caring if others of the Cheyenne caught him and killed him. Since then he had lived a somewhat solitary life even though some of his own tribe thought him a brutal person. One of Washakie's most trusted war leaders, he had served as a messenger for the Shoshone chief, traveling from band to band. In that time he had found a friend in Moroni Stewart. A smile on his face, he hoped that all was well with Moroni and his family.

No Arrows was about to urge his horse up over the ridge and down onto the brush and sage flat when he noticed two coyotes slink away from a low spot. Then several magpies gave off their yakking cries and flew away from the same spot the coyotes had come from. His eyes narrowing, No Arrows watched the spot for several more moments. The coyotes had stopped a few yards away from the low spot, and the magpies were perched in some stunted trees still fussing about. No Arrows had survived far too long to do something foolish like ride boldly over the ridge to see what the coyotes and birds stirred up. Dropping from his horse, he tied it loosely to a greening tree and slipped silently over the ridge.

Worming his way through some stunted brush, he crept closer to the spot that the birds and the coyotes were watching. Drawing up in a clump of budding chokecherry he again studied the low spot. Nothing. No Arrows watched the coyotes for a few moments. The dog coyote was pacing back and forth while the female patiently sat on her haunches and watched whatever was in the depression. No Arrows watched and listened for several minutes. Then from the low spot waddled a bear. A grizzly. Pausing at the lip of the depression, the huge bear sniffed the air and stared at the coyotes. Whuffing, the grizzly ambled down the stream course and out of sight. Sniffing the air, the coyotes watched the spot where the bear had disappeared. Then with a faint wag of their tails they slunk back down to the depression.

For another half hour, No Arrows watched the depression. Then, rifle in hand, he went forward at a crouch. Nearly to the place, the coyotes either heard him or smelled him, and with their tails held between their legs they scooted from the low spot. Another few steps and No Arrows was able to see what the bear and the wild dogs had been feeding on. What remained of four quarters of elk meat lay around the shallow wash. Cautiously, the Shoshone warrior slipped into the wash and studied the rotting meat. One thing for sure was that the meat had been packed on a horse for a while before being dumped on the ground. Why was that? His eyes scanning the surrounding area, No Arrows, an expert tracker, took everything in. Then his gaze was captured by the frayed rope that had at one time held the meat to a saddle. A saddle? What caused him to think that? Walking quickly around to the far side of the wash, No Arrows could see in the soft earth the tracks of two horses and a man. One look at the tracks and there was no doubt in his mind that the track belonged to his friend, Moroni. The man's tracks were of the hard-soled, knee-high moccasins his friend favored. With a feeling of dread, he knew that there were few things that would cause his friend to dump meat on the ground like this. No Arrows looked for any sign of danger on the horizon. Then, hoping that no enemies lay in wait, he began to run toward where his horse was tethered.

Cresting the slight rise where his horse was, No Arrows sprang into the saddle and urged the buckskin into a gallop. Whipping the horse along, he kept an eye out for any sign of danger. He spied the brown tops of the two wagons as he rounded the hill. Urging his horse even faster, he soon could see Sarah's father, Hugh, Strikes Hard, and his warriors traveling together at the front of the wagons. On seeing him coming at a gallop, his men fanned out, knowing that only danger would bring him back to them at the pace he was traveling. In a few moments his warriors had encircled the two wagons and the small herd of livestock. Drawing near, he watched Strikes Hard stand in his stirrups looking to see if danger was following him. Good, thought No Arrows, they are alert and prepared for trouble. Thundering up in a cloud of dust, No Arrows looked first at Rolf, then his nephew, and explained what he had seen.

"You're right," said Rolf, tugging at his beard. "Something has happened."

"Shall we ride?" asked Strikes Hard, checking his rifle.

"I think some of us should ride ahead, but we should leave a strong force with the wagons and stock in case someone is watching for the chance to attack," said Rolf.

"Agreed," replied No Arrows. "I will have ten of my men ride with me and the rest will stay here."

"I'll ride, too," said Rolf. Then looking back to the lead wagon, he called to his wife, "We're riding ahead. You and the girls keep a sharp eye."

"What aboot me?" Asked Hugh, trotting his horse up.

"One of us needs to stay with the girls," replied Rolf, looking his giant of a son-in-law in the eye.

His face flushing, Hugh was about to make a reply when he noticed a look he had never before seen in Rolf's eyes. "I'll keep a sharp eye," he said quietly.

Putting his hand on Hugh's arm, Rolf replied, "Thank you." Then turning his horse, he spurred it along the faint trail toward Moroni and Sarah's.

For an hour the group rode swiftly along. Their weapons in their hands, the band rode, expecting trouble, and, in the hearts of most, hoping that Moroni, Sarah and their children would be found safe.

Riding into a thick forest of budding aspen, No Arrows held out his hand. "Just over the ridge and down into the shallow valley is where Moroni has built his home."

Nodding once, Rolf replied, "It looks to be fair land, but we best be careful. If the boy has had trouble, he might be a little on edge. I don't want anyone to get shot by mistake."

Nodding his agreement, No Arrows let Rolf lead the way over the ridge. Topping out on the aspen hillside above Moroni's homestead, Rolf could see the cabin and barn laid out two hundred yards beneath him. From what he could see, nothing was amiss. There were half a dozen horses in the pole corral and a black and white cow resting in the grassy meadow near the barn. Then his eyes caught what looked like a dead horse on the packed earth of the yard. His eyes searching the rest of the homestead, he detected the sprawled form of a person near the corner of the cabin.

"There's been trouble," he muttered to no one in particular.

"Yes," replied No Arrows quietly.

"I'll ride down first," said Rolf. "You and your men watch and stay out of sight. If I turn around and wave, everything is all right, but if I come a foggin' back up this hill, give me some covering fire."

"It will be as you say," replied No Arrows. With hand motions he spread out his men along the ridge under cover of the trees.

Giving No Arrows a glance, Rolf clucked to his horse and slowly rode over the lip of the ridge and toward the peaceful-looking homestead below him. Weaving his way down the gentle slope through the scattered aspen, Rolf's eyes took in everything. The scene before him looked so peaceful with the exception of the dead horses and two dead Indians. His Spencer in his hands, he watched for any sign of movement, but there was none. Urging his horse to a trot, he rode around the back of the barn and dropped to the ground next to the peeled-log walls. He placed his hat on the horn of his saddle, and on cat feet he went to the corner of the barn and peered around to the yard and the cabin. For several minutes he watched and listened. Hearing or seeing nothing, he was about to move forward when from inside the cabin came the faint wail of a baby. His eyes riveted on the two-story log structure, he waited for several heartbeats. Then, unable to stand it any longer, Rolf clutched his rifle in both hands and began to run for the closed door. Moving swiftly across the packed earth of the yard, he moved silently up on the wide covered porch. He was about to charge through the door when to his surprise, it opened, and framed in the doorway was a man Rolf took at first to be an Indian.

A smile on his bronzed face and his blue eyes twinkling, the strange leather-clad man said, "Welcome, please come in. You have a new grandson."

CHAPTER 6

His mouth hanging open, Rolf didn't even have the presence of mind to point his rifle at the stranger standing in the doorway of his daughter's home.

"A grandson? What do you mean?"

"Are you not the father of Sarah?"

Unable to reply, Rolf merely nodded his head.

"Then come in and see your daughter and new grandson."

Looking around, Rolf said, "There's some friends of mine up on the ridge, I better wave and let them know everything is all right."

"Friends?" The stranger asked.

"Some Shoshone we met on the way up. A couple of them, No Arrows and a young nephew of his, are with them."

A broad smile creasing the stranger's face, he chuckled, "I know them well. Go to your daughter and I will see to No Arrows."

Nodding obediently, Rolf walked into the spacious cabin and looked for his daughter. Hearing a faint cry he walked through the open door of a back room and there he saw Sarah lying back in bed holding a bundle.

Seeing her father enter the room, Sarah's eyes filled with tears.

"Oh, Papa," she blurted out.

Going quickly to his oldest daughter, Rolf knelt at her bedside and put his arm around her shoulders. Noticing her wince when he did so, and seeing the white bandage wrapped around her head, he pulled himself back. "What has happened?"

Through the tears, Sarah told her father of the attack by the three Indians and regaining consciousness to find that Moroni had been badly wounded and Sam gone.

"Papa, Moroni is in the other room with Katie. It doesn't look good—I don't know . . ." Unable to continue, Sarah closed her eyes and began to sob.

Again holding his daughter close, Rolf managed to reply, "He'll make it, Sarah. Somehow we'll make it through."

Nearing dusk, Hugh wiped the dirt from his shirt and, shouldering the shovel, began to walk back to the cabin. Earlier, Rolf had asked him to bury the two dead Indians. Knowing it was best to do the job asked of him , he picked up a shovel from the barn, took the two bodies out to a slight knoll in the meadow, and buried them. Looking around the small valley in which the homestead lay, he knew he had never seen such a beautiful place. Seeing the lush deep grass and timber on the ridges, Hugh figured he had found heaven. Hitching his belted revolver around, he took long strides back toward the log home. *What a thing*, he thought to himself. If they had only been two or three days quicker, Sarah wouldn't be recovering from a nasty cut on her head and a stab wound in her shoulder. And her husband, Moroni, wouldn't be on a pallet with a bad wound in the lungs. The boy Samuel wouldn't have been kidnapped by some red heathen. Shaking his head, Hugh knew that very few ever recovered from a wound in the lungs.

Reaching the log barn, Hugh marveled at how his brother-in-law had managed to put together such a well-built place in such a short time. Putting the shovel back in the corner near the open doorway, he was about to walk toward the house when the Shoshone warrior, No Arrows, came from the interior of the barn.

"The barn, it is well built?" asked the Shoshone.

"Aye," replied Hugh. "I don't know how the mon was able to build such a home and barn in such a short time."

Chuckling, No Arrows patted the log wall. "He had a lot of help. About thirty of my people camped here last summer and we helped."

His eyes going to the cabin, then back to the barn, Hugh nodded his head, "You did a fine job."

"Thank you. Moroni said he was going to hire us out to build cabins and barns down in the Cache Valley settlements and become rich."

A faint smile on his face, Hugh nodded. "There aren't many places this fine in all of the west."

"I would build a hundred places like this and give them away if Moroni would recover," No Arrows said with a wistful look on his face.

Clapping the Shoshone warrior on the shoulder, Hugh nodded his agreement. "Come, let's go to the house and see what's for supper."

Sitting next to the iron stove that was used for cooking as well as heat, Rolf took apart one of Moroni's revolvers and began to clean it. It seemed that at times like this when he needed to think, he would always find a gun in his hands— working with it, cleaning it, improving it. Looking up from his work, he looked at the form of his new son-in-law on the low bed. He looked to be a good man. Heaving a sigh, he hoped Sarah wouldn't lose him, too. She was still so weak from her wounds and from having the baby, he didn't know if she would survive his death. Sitting in her rocker, she held her new son close and never let her eyes stray far from Moroni. Greta and Jeni hovered around both of them, offering their care in any way they could. But Rolf was gravely concerned. His daughter wasn't acting her usual lively self. Biting his lower lip, he began the task of reworking the first of Moroni's two revolvers. He would get well and be able to use them. Rolf wouldn't contemplate anything else.

From the position of the stars, Rolf figured it to be after midnight. Unable to sleep, he had quietly pulled on his heavy elk-hide jacket. Picking up his Spencer, he had slipped out of the cabin. In the yard and next to the barn he could see the blanket-covered forms of the Shoshone warriors. He knew he shouldn't be nervous with the Indians sleeping in the yard, but something disturbed him nonetheless. Stepping down off the wooden porch, he walked around the side of the cabin and looked toward the river. In the stillness he could hear the gurgling as the water flowed over the rocks. For a time he stood quietly and listened. Then with a start he felt a presence next to him. Peering to his right he could see the form of the strange Indian he had first welcomed at the door on his arrival.

"I am sorry if I startled you," the stranger said.

Shrugging, Rolf replied, "You're the one they call Hawk aren't you?"

"Yes. That is what they call me."

"Thank you for what you have done for my family. I don't know what would have happened if you hadn't come along."

"I wish I had come along sooner," Hawk said with a sigh.

"As do I," commented Rolf.

"But we can't always be in the right place at the right time."

Looking at the face of Hawk, faintly lit by the starlight, Rolf could see the drawn look on the face of the strange man. "Are you all right? You look pretty tuckered out."

A faint smile came to Hawk's face. He looked at Rolf. "I will be fine." Then, grasping Rolf's arm he added, "I must go now. Have faith."

With no sound, his vague form disappeared into the darkness. For several minutes, Rolf stood rooted in place wondering who the man was. Turning to walk back into the cabin, he heard the sound of a horse approaching. Kneeling, so he wouldn't provide any enemy with a large target, he strained his eyes to see who was approaching. Then into the yard trotted a powerfully-built appaloosa stallion still saddled for the trail. For several heartbeats, suspicious for any sign of treachery, Rolf watched the big horse as it cantered into the yard. As the horse came further into the yard, the sleeping Shoshone came from under their blankets and robes prepared for battle. Watching the horse canter up to the porch, Rolf was grateful to see that the Shoshone were not surprised. Stopping at the log porch, the big horse seemed to look inside. Rolf walked to the horse and picked up the trailing reins. Speaking softly to the appaloosa, he looked at the saddle and wondered if this was the horse he had heard about.

Then Strikes Hard was at his side. "It is the horse of Moroni," he said quietly.

A quick grin coming to his face, Rolf said, "Then if we back-track him we will find Sam."

Nodding his head, Strikes Hard answered, "The tracks will take us back to where the horse has been."

"You will ride with me at first light?"

"I will," replied the young Shoshone.

CHAPTER 7

The rain continued to beat down as Rolf, No Arrows, and a dozen of the Shoshone warriors threaded their way through the aspen thicket. Pulling his slicker closer around him, Rolf peered through the gray curtain looking for Strikes Hard and another of the Shoshone who had ridden ahead earlier in the morning. A grimace on his face, Rolf knew they had no chance at all of following the tracks of the stallion now. Shortly after leaving the homestead, the clouds had moved in, and just short of noon the rain began. At first it had just been a sprinkle but now it had turned into a downpour. But still they had to look. Hopefully in this weather and after losing the stallion, Sam's captor would hole up or at least be moving slower. Pushing his way through the thicket, Rolf looked through the rain across a wide sage-filled opening. For several moments he studied the opening, looking for any sign of movement on the far side of the aspen and fir timber. He was about to urge his horse forward when No Arrows pointed with his steel-tipped lance. "The young one is coming," he said softly.

Then through the pouring rain, Rolf could see the soaked figures of Strikes Hard and the other warrior. Riding his paint gelding next to Rolf and No Arrows, Strikes Hard wiped at the water running down his face and shrugged his shoulders. "There is no more sign. Rabbit and I have searched and we cannot find the tracks of the stallion anymore. The rain has wiped them out."

Knowing that any further search at this time was futile, Rolf's shoulders sagged. How could he go back and tell his daughter they couldn't find her son? A sick feeling in the bottom of his stomach, Rolf nodded his head. "Thank you, my friends. We have done all we can do in this weather. We will search when the rain stops."

Then turning his horse, he began the long ride back to the homestead.

Propped up on her bed, Sarah looked over at the unconscious form of her husband and felt a pang of despair. Earlier, she had insisted that her father and Hugh move her bed into the front room next to the low bed that Moroni rested on. Now it seemed like all she did was watch the rise and fall of his chest and hope that soon he would open his eyes and look at her. Biting at her lip, she said a silent prayer that he would be well. He just had to. How could she end up a widow again? Closing her eyes, she thought back to that day nearly two years ago when she had opened her eyes to see him bending over her. A tear running down her face, she knew she would never forget his smiling grey eyes and his insistence that she call him "Moroni" because "Mister Stewart" made him feel old. Hearing movement in the room, she looked up to see her sister, Jeni.

"How are you feeling?" Jeni asked, kneeling next to Sarah.

"All right, I guess. I'm just worried about Moroni and Sam."

"Moroni will be fine," Jeni said with a faint grin. "Ma says she knows his kind and they are just too hard to kill. And as for Sam, I'll bet Pa and those Shoshone will be back with him any time."

"I sure hope so," replied Sarah wistfully.

Jeni was about to make another comment when their mother and Melissa came into the room.

"Your new one is asleep," Greta said in a low voice. Then massaging her back she asked Sarah, "Have you decided on a name?"

Tears springing to her eyes, Sarah nodded, "Yes, Moroni

and I decided on *Charles* if it was a boy."

"After his brother who was killed in the war?"

Sarah nodded, "Yes, I know Moroni would want it."

"Then Charles it is," announced Greta with a smile.

"Oh Ma, I'm so worried," whispered Sarah.

"About the baby? Well he looks to be about two or three weeks early, but as far as I can tell he's healthy as a horse."

"Not the baby. Moroni and Sam."

Her eyes showing the concern she was feeling, Greta put her hand on Sarah's bandaged forehead. "Sarah, it's all in the Lord's hands now. All we can do is pray."

"I just wish Hawk hadn't left. He could have made sure of Moroni and . . ." Sarah's words trailed off into sobs.

"Daughter, please put your trust in God. He knows what is best," said Greta, stroking Sarah's hair. "Now you need to get some rest or we'll be worrying about you."

Leaning back and closing her eyes, Sarah tried to relax. How could she have been so foolish? Why hadn't she just stayed inside the cabin instead of going out to look at the Indian she had thought was dead? With a shudder she remembered the paint-streaked face and the hate-filled eyes as the Indian she recognized as Horse Ears swung his war axe at her. Why hadn't she just let Gall kill him? Then, feeling ashamed, she knew why—it would have been murder. But what was the difference between that and what the young Sioux had done to *her* family?

Standing watch in the loft of the log barn, Hugh looked through the grey curtain of rain for any sign of movement. With the clouds lying low on the mountains and the cold rain, it reminded him of many a day in the highland home of his youth. Shivering slightly in his wool coat he could almost hear the mournful wail of the pipes. It was at times like this when he wondered what his life would have been like if the British soldiers had passed by that night. But now here he was on the edge of the known world, as far as he was concerned, keeping watch for hostile Indians or any other kind of danger. But, Hugh realized he was better off. Never before had he seen such opportunity. Nowhere on the continent or in Scotland was there such a good chance to better oneself or to reach out and grasp a dream. No, if he would have stayed at home, he would have become a soldier like his father had been, and possibly lost a hand like his father—or his life like many other men who went off to the wars. No, he was much better off here. Now he had a kind of freedom of the like he had only dreamed. With a grin, he sent his gaze back to the cabin. He had found a wife that was too good for him. What luck to have met Rolf and become his apprentice as a gunsmith, and to have caught the eye of his daughter, Melissa. Melissa was more like her mother than Sarah or Jeni. With dark eyes and black hair, she resembled Greta, as Sarah and Jeni with their nearly-white blonde hair resembled their father. Melissa, with her quiet, thoughtful demeanor was so different from Jeni's outspoken and forward ways. No wonder the girl hadn't caught herself a husband yet, Hugh thought to himself. Back in Utah, she had bested most of the lads in about anything they did. Shaking his head, he knew that no boy or man likes to be outshot or outridden by a mere slip of a lass. Moving to the other side of the barn, Hugh was about to look through another of the small windows in the loft when a brown form detached itself from the far corner. Wheeling, rifle at the ready, Hugh was surprised to see a bearded white face grinning at him.

"Skeered ya, didn't I boy?" chortled the buckskin-clad man.

His Spencer at the ready, Hugh stared at the bearded man, tall and rail-thin with a long, grey beard, bushy eyebrows and piercing black eyes that seemed to laugh at him.

"What are ye doin' here?" asked Hugh, the muzzle of his rifle trained on the strange-looking apparition that had seemed to appear from thin air.

"A Scot. Wall hang me," exploded the thin old man, slapping the wet buckskin of his leg.

His eyes narrowing, Hugh asked again, "I said, what are ye doin' here?"

A snaggle-tooth grin showing through the bushy beard, the old man replied, "Gitten' outa' the rain, boy. This here barn looked to be jist the place an' I didn't want to announce myself to them folks in the house there so I jist holed up here."

Noticing the huge, long-barreled rifle the man carried as well as two pistols and a long, bone-handled knife, Hugh figured that if the man had wanted to kill him he would have done it long since. "We've had trouble here. Me brother-in-law is wounded fearfully and me nephew has been took by a red savage."

"Do tell," commented the old man with a sly grin.

Flushing, Hugh nodded his head. Then hearing one of the horses in the corral whinny, he spared a glance out of the window. There on the far side of the meadow he could see Rolf and the Shoshone riding back toward the homestead.

"Here comes me father-in law. We'll have some answers from ye now," Hugh said, jutting his chin out.

"Answers," cackled the old man. "You ain't asked me no questions! Why would you be a wantin' answers from me, anyway?"

Feeling foolish, Hugh glared at the man and asked, "Well, what be your name?"

Still grinning at Hugh through his beard the man said, "Well now, that's a mite more neighborly. My name is Rufus. Rufus Ordoway."

"Hugh MacAskill," replied Hugh.

"MacAskill," commented the old man, a different light in his eyes. "Well, Hugh MacAskill, let's go see your father-in-law and mayhap you can feed me some o' them vittles I can smell cookin' and you can offer me some o' that coffee I can smell a boilin' and we'll palaver some."

A strained look on his face, Hugh just shook his head. "Come on with ye then. But one wrong move and I'll set those red Indians on ye."

"Set the red Indians on me!" cackled the old man as he followed Hugh down the ladder and into the bottom of the barn.

CHAPTER 8

Seated in the warmth of the cabin, Hugh looked closely at the old man who had identified himself as Rufus Ordoway. Watching the steam as it filtered out of Rufus' buckskin clothing, Hugh wondered at how old the man might be. From the craggy looks of what he could see of his face and the gnarled hands, Hugh figured he must be as old as the mountains. Seated at the table, Hugh watched as Rufus wiped at the last bit of stew with a chunk of bread, then stuffed it into his mouth. Although he fancied himself a healthy eater, never in his life had he seen food disappear like he had today. The old man had eaten four helpings of the stew his wife and Greta had prepared, along with what he estimated was a whole loaf of bread.

Following Rolf's return, the Shoshone had camped in the barn with the exception of No Arrows and Strikes Hard, who had come into the cabin with Rolf and Hugh. Inside the cabin, Greta and her daughters had spent quite some time preparing a meal for everyone, knowing that on the return of the search party they would need something hot, after being out in the cold rain all day.

Leaning back against the log wall, Rufus eyed the blanket-covered form of Moroni. "Is he the one what got stuck?"

"Yes," replied Rolf.

Rufus' eyes lingered on Moroni then went to the rest of the people in the crowded room. Finally, he nodded his head. "Thanks for the vittles. It was mighty tasty."

Her dark eyes going to Rufus then to her husband, Greta acknowledged Rufus, "You are most welcome." Then taking the plate from him she added, "You didn't say where you had come from."

Running his fingers through his beard, Rufus grinned and replied, "Nope, I sure didn't."

Exasperated with the round-about answers that he and his family seemed to be getting from the mountain man, Hugh was about to make a sharp comment when Rolf interrupted him.

"You seem to have traveled far."

"Uh huh," replied Rufus.

"It seems odd you don't have any horses."

Stretching himself, Rufus looked at Rolf and grinned through his beard. "Ain't odd, it's a fact. That be why I'm here. Bout a week ago I had stopped to look this crick over and if there was beaver there I was goin' to set traps. Well, I found this spot where there was some beaver doin's and after checkin' things out, I figgered there weren't no injuns about. Next thing I know three 'o them was a ridin' off with all my horses and plunder."

"We can lend you a horse if that's what you need," Rolf said.

"I'd take that and thanks be to you," replied Rufus.

"Any idea who the thieves were?" asked Hugh.

A grin on his face, Rufus nodded his head. "Yup, I figger it was them what you planted over by the crick."

"How do you know that?" asked Hugh, surprise in his voice.

"Because one o' the horses that boy there kilt was mine."

Speaking for the first time, Sarah said, "the one that got away is Sioux."

Turning his gaze to Sarah, Rufus looked at her for a moment, then asked, "How do you know that?"

"I have met him before. This was the second time he has tried to kill me."

Blowing through his mouth, Rufus looked more closely at Sarah. "You be a lucky one then. Next time you see that boy you'd better leave plenty of daylight between you or you might go under."

Her face drawn and pale, Sarah nodded, "I plan to."

Sarah was obviously not feeling well. Greta got to her feet and took Sarah by the arm to lead her into the bedroom.

Stopping at the doorway, Sarah straightened her back and looked Rufus in the eye. "That Sioux took my son. Will you help us get him back?"

Grinning nervously, Rufus sensed the intensity on Sarah's face and in her eyes. Licking his lips he bobbed his head once. "Wal' since you be a-givin' ol' Rufus a horse I reckon I can help out a little here."

A slight nod of her head and Sarah allowed her mother to help her into the bedroom.

"She's got sand, that one," Rufus said quietly.

"She's been through a lot," replied Rolf, getting to his feet and feeding several more chunks of pine into the stove.

"Hardship is what puts steel inter' a body," said Rufus. "I figger she'll do."

Getting up from his place against the log wall, No Arrows nodded to Rolf and Hugh. "My nephew and I will be out in the barn. Thank you for the food." Then with a glance at Rufus, the two Shoshone went out into the wet darkness.

Noticing the odd expression on Rufus' face, Hugh asked, "Do ye ken those men?"

Looking at Hugh, Rufus smiled and nodded. "I do. I stole two horses from old No Arrers there back about two year ago."

"You stole horses from him! What for?"

"I needed the horses, boy! I was near afoot and in sore need of some fresh pack animals."

"I wonder why No Arrows dinna' say anything to you?"

A rueful look on his face, Rufus replied, "The following month he stole them back and took one o' mine too!"

Laughing, Rolf glanced at Jeni, then Hugh, "I guess No Arrows figured he just borrowed the horses to you, then got them back with interest."

* * *

Morning dawned overcast but the rain had stopped. Looking out through the open window, Sarah felt drained but better. Putting her hand up to the bandage that covered the wound on her head, she knew that if she hadn't jerked back against the grip the Sioux had on her arm, she would now be dead. Hearing a sound behind her, she looked to see her father sitting at the table with one of Moroni's revolvers disassembled before him.

"Don't be dwelling on it," Rolf said quietly as he went about his work.

"I know, Papa, but I just can't help it," Sarah sighed as she closed the window and sat next to her father.

Holding the cylinder up to the light, Rolf glanced at his eldest daughter and smiled faintly. "He looks to be a strong man. I believe he'll pull through."

Glancing at where Moroni lay unconscious, Sarah bowed her head and said nothing.

"I know you're worried, but he doesn't have a fever and there is no bleeding. And his breathing seems to be fine. I really believe he will be all right."

Heaving a sigh, Sarah nodded her head and said nothing but continued to watch her father as he began to rework the first of Moroni's revolvers. For a fleeting moment she felt like a little girl again as she watched her father work at his trade as a gunsmith. Then her thoughts were interrupted by a call from outside. Getting up, she walked to the door and looked out.

Her eyes going to the far side of the barn she could see Strikes Hard and half a dozen of the Shoshone riding toward the cabin. As they grew closer, she saw that the spare horses the warriors led were burdened down by what looked to be several elk as well as the quarters of a moose.

"It looks like the hunters were lucky today," Sarah

commented as the Shoshone tied their horse up at the corral and began to unload the meat.

"We'll need the meat," Rolf commented to his daughter knowing that if they continued to feed the Shoshone, their food stocks would become perilously low.

"I wonder where Hawk went to?" Sarah asked absently.

"Perhaps he went looking for Sam," replied Rolf, continuing to work on Moroni's Colt.

Turning back from the door, Sarah nodded, "I just wish I knew if he was still alive."

CHAPTER 9

It had been three days since his capture, and during that time Sam had been thrown on the back of a horse every day at daylight. All day long his captor led his horse and three others at a trot. With little rest and even less food, Sam felt as if he could go no further, but he knew to quit was to die. His thighs and legs were chafed and sore from the thumping ride on the bony back of the pony he had been tied to every day. And his stomach felt as though it were feeding on itself. Nearing darkness, Sam hoped Horse Ears would stop, but still the young Sioux kept pushing onward. As they splashed across a small stream which was running high due to the rain of the past few days, Sam saw Horse Ears stiffen, then slip from his horse, his old musket in hand.

Still mounted on the pony, Sam peered ahead into the thick lodgepole-pine timber that Horse Ears had crept into. Licking at his lips, Sam hoped that the Indian had seen a deer or an elk. If he made a kill, hopefully the renegade would share a little bit of it with him. His mouth began to water as Sam wondered what an elk steak would taste like, when he heard the thump of the Sioux warrior's musket. Leaning forward, Sam strained his eyes to see into the gathering gloom of the thick pine jungle in front of him. Then to his utter surprise he saw Horse Ears sprint out of the timber and leap onto his horse, and to Sam's horror right behind the Indian was the biggest bear he had ever seen. A grizzly! With his eyes distended with fear and a wild cry on his lips, the Sioux whipped his horse around and urged it back across the stream. As his own horse shied violently and screamed in fear, Sam caught a glimpse of the raging bear as it pulled one of the pack horses down. His own pony following the others, Sam held a fleeting hope that the bear would be satisfied with the horse it had killed and not follow.

For several miles, Sam gripped the mane of his stampeding pony and hoped he wouldn't fall off. Then to his relief, Horse Ears slowed his own horse and grabbed the trailing rawhide ropes of the remaining pack horses as well as Sam's. His heart still thumping from the scene of the charging bear and the wild ride, Sam was surprised to see the expression of stark terror on the face of his captor. Unable to contain himself, Sam giggled.

His face contorting in rage, Horse Ears lashed out with his hand and knocked Sam from his pony.

"You no laugh!" raged the Sioux.

His lip split open by the blow, Sam staggered to his feet and looked up at the Indian. "You looked pretty scared there."

Leaping from his horse, the Sioux struck Sam again.

Lying on his side, Sam could see that the Indian was still terrified and now becoming angry at what had happened, and Sam was sure that Horse Ears was even more infuriated because he had seen him running from the bear with one thing in mind, and that was to save himself. Holding still and not meeting the Indian's glare, he knew it best not to taunt him anymore. When he saw that Sam had not responded to his hate-filled gaze, Horse Ears kicked Sam in the side with a moccasined foot and stalked back to his horse. It was then Sam saw that the Indian had lost his musket. For several moments Sam watched as Horse Ears checked his remaining pack horses. Once he was satisfied the packs were straight, he mounted his horse, and, motioning Sam to mount, he started off again into the gloom.

For several more hours they had ridden north until Sam

was sure he couldn't go any farther. But as they rode an idea had been forming in Sam's mind. Finally stopping next to a gurgling stream, Horse Ears yanked Sam from the pony he had been riding and began to unsaddle the horses. Massaging his thighs, Sam watched as the Sioux took a strip of dried meat from a leather bag and began to chew on it. His stomach growling at the sight of food, Sam closed his eyes and wished for just a small piece. For several minutes, Sam sat in silence listening to the sounds of the stream, the horses as they cropped the new spring grass, and the noises of Horse Ears gnawing on the strip of meat.

Shivering in the night air, Sam opened one eye and looked at the Indian sitting wrapped in his blanket still worrying at the meat. "What you gonna' do when my bear catches up?"

Pausing in his feast on the meat, the Indian turned his black eyes on Sam.

"You lost your gun. What you gonna' do when my bear gits you?" asked Sam again.

Getting to his feet, Horse Ears walked to where Sam sat huddled and kicked him. "Bear no yours. Next time I feed you to bear!"

A grin spreading on his face, Sam sat back up and said, "Then let's go back and see the bear." Then, his mind racing, Sam shook his head, "No, we won't have to do that. I'll bet that bear of mine is following us right now."

"Bah!" exploded the Indian. Whirling, he stalked back to where he had been sitting. With another piece of dried meat in his hands and his blanket wrapped around him, Horse Ears sat chewing the meat and glaring at Sam. For several moments Sam and the Indian sat staring at each other in the moonlight. Then one of the horses threw its head up and snorted.

A grin on his face, Sam winked at the startled-looking Indian and whispered, "Here he comes."

A look of terror on his face, Horse Ears dropped the strip of meat to the grass and, springing to his feet, gathered the horses in. Throwing the packs on the pack horse he quickly put his rough saddle on his. Then with a grunt he motioned for Sam to get on the pony he had been riding.

"Why should I?" Asked Sam. "I told you, it's my bear and he's comin' to rescue me."

Snarling, the Sioux kicked at Sam and hissed, "Get on horse."

Reluctantly, Sam got up and walked toward the standing horse. As he did so, he spotted the strip of meat still lying in the grass where the Indian had dropped it. Pretending to stumble, he went to his knees and as he did he clutched the meat in his hand. Just then one of the remaining pack horses snorted and shied. His eyes distended, Horse Ears grabbed Sam by the hair and threw him onto the back of the horse, then mounting his own, he kicked them into a gallop.

It seemed to Sam they had pushed on for hours in the darkness. But he had scored a victory of sorts—he had kept his grip on the strip of dried meat, and as they had ridden through the night he had devoured it. Now he was getting sleepy and he was finding it hard to stay on the back of the trotting horse. By the aid of the nearly full moon overhead, Sam knew they had broken out of the scattered timber and onto a sage-covered flat. Riding out onto the flat in the silver light of the moon, Sam could see nearly as well as in the day. Several hundred yards out on the flat, the Indian stopped and paused, looking back. For several minutes they waited. Sam was nearly asleep on the back of the horse when Horse Ears growled something unintelligible and again pushed on across the flat. It seemed like an eternity passed to Sam before they splashed across a shallow stream and wound their way up a slight ridge. Pausing on top of the ridge, Horse Ears again watched their back trail. Seemingly satisfied this time, he dropped to the ground and yanked Sam from his horse. Getting his feet under him, Sam watched as the Indian pulled the saddles from the backs of the exhausted horses. It took several minutes for the Indian to hobble the horses, then he turned his attention to Sam. Taking a rawhide rope from his saddle, the Sioux tied a loop around Sam's neck and the other end around his own wrist. Wrapping up in his blanket he lay down and went to sleep. For several moments Sam wondered what could or would happen next. Shrugging his shoulders, he scraped together some dry grass and, plopping down on it, fell instantly to sleep.

Feeling the warmth of sunlight on his body, Sam rubbed his eyes and sat up. He could see the three horses grazing on the new grass among the sage. His hands going to the rawhide rope around his neck he wondered where Horse Ears was. Standing, Sam noticed they had camped on a slight, pine-covered ridge that separated the broad sage-covered flat. Seeing that the rope was tied securely to one of the pines, Sam walked as far as his leash would let him and peered over the other side of the ridge. Where had the Sioux gone? Looking once at the horses, then at the packsaddle and the crude saddle that Horse Ears rode on, a plan began to form in Sam's mind. If he could just get to the packsaddle, he hoped he could find a knife or something to cut the securely-tied rawhide rope. After another quick look around, Sam stretched himself out to the limit to see if he could reach the rawhide panniers where the Indian kept his goods. But he was too short by about three feet. Searching around he found a long, crooked pine branch. Reaching out with it, he hooked the branch on one of the leather loops that held the pannier in place on the forks of the packsaddle. Holding back a whoop of joy, he pulled the heavy rawhide sack to him. Pulling open the flap, Sam peered inside. A leather sack filled with dried meat caught his eye first and, stuffing a large chunk in his mouth, he began to chew hungrily. Another coil of rawhide rope was inside, several pairs of moccasins, a coil of sinew with a large metal needle stuck in it, an elk-hide shirt and a worn old blanket, but no knife! Nothing to use to cut the rope. Disappointed, Sam stuffed several strips of the dried meat in the pockets of his tattered pants and packed all of the items back in the pannier. Picking up the branch again he was preparing to reach for the other pannier when the snort from one of the horses drew his attention. Looking across the sage flat he could see Horse Ears coming toward him at a hard run. He held his bow in his right hand and a quiver containing only a few arrows flopped loosely on his back. Sam could tell the Indian was in a hurry. Then looking past the running warrior, he saw the reason why. About three hundred yards behind him was a huge bear. Rolling along in a swinging gait, the bear stopped and sniffed at the air. Even from a distance, Sam could tell it was a grizzly. The long, wheat-colored hair and the hump on its shoulders positively identified it as one of the big bears. Amazed at the sight before him, Sam wondered why the bear was following Horse Ears. Could this be the same bear from last night? These thoughts and a hundred others flowed into Sam's mind as the panting Indian staggered into camp and began throwing saddles onto the horses. Seeming to ignore Sam, Horse Ears slipped the panniers in place on the pack-horse, and after tightening the cinch on his own horse, he motioned for Sam to get on his horse.

"Hey, you still got me tied to the tree," Sam said, a disgusted look on his face.

Casting a fearful glance in the direction of the still advancing bear, the Sioux slashed at the rope with his knife, picked Sam up by his tattered shirt and tossed him onto the back of his horse. Then gathering up the lead ropes of the horses, the Indian led off at a gallop.

For more than an hour, Horse Ears galloped the horses in a

westerly direction, only stopping when they crossed a wide, rock-bottomed stream. Stopping in the middle of the knee-high water, Horse Ears let the horses drink. Thirsty, Sam dropped from his horse and stood in the cold water scooping up and drinking handful after handful.

Seeing Sam standing in the water, Horse Ears, with an infuriated look on his face, shouted at Sam, "Get on horse!"

Insolently, Sam scooped up one more mouthful of water, then getting a grip on the mane of his horse swung astride. Noticing that there were only four arrows in the quiver on the Indian's back, Sam grinned and said, "Boy, if you shot my bear with them arrows he's really gonna be mad."

Flashing Sam a look of pure hatred, Horse Ears cuffed him across the face and hissed, "Shut mouth or I feed you to bear."

Glaring back at the warrior, Sam forced the grin back on his face and said, "If you are so sure that he's not my bear, then just let me go."

Growling an oath, Horse Ears swung his horse around, and yanking at the lead ropes of the others, plunged across the stream. Holding to the mane of his horse, Sam had no alternative but to follow.

CHAPTER 10

He could hear voices, and the sound of shoes walking on a wooden floor. Attempting a deep breath, Moroni felt as though his chest would burst. Just for a moment he listened to the voices and tried to place them. Through the haze came the voice of his wife, Sarah, softly singing. A low sweet lullaby. He felt so weak. Concentrating all of his strength he forced an eye open. A lamp flickered on the table in the center of the room, and sitting in the rocker next to the table holding a bundle of blankets was the perfect image of an angel. With her long, blonde hair swirling around her shoulders, Sarah was rocking back and forth ever so slowly, softly singing. Her attention focused on the blanket wrapped bundle in her arms, she didn't see Moroni as he kept his gaze on her. What had happened? Why was he confined to a bed and why was he so weak? Then the memories flooded back. The wild ride and the Indians stealing the horses and the picture of Sarah lying on the ground with a warrior bent over her. Closing his open eye, Moroni slowly ran his thick tongue around his mouth. Then forcing his eyes open, he tried to call out to her. All that came out was a dry rasp. At the small sound, however, her blue eyes flew to him. A tear squeezing from the corner of his eye, Moroni again tried to speak but nothing would come. Then Sarah was kneeling at his side, her head on his chest.

Sobbing, she ran her fingers over his face and asked, "Moroni, are you all right?"

His mouth incredibly dry, he couldn't speak. But mustering a little more strength he nodded his head just a bit. The tears flowing down her face, Sarah pressed her cheek to Moroni's face. For several minutes she held him as if he were a line to life. Then the bundle of blankets that she cradled in her free arm wiggled and made a tiny noise.

Leaning back up, Sarah wiped at the tears and beamed a smile, "I guess you haven't met your son yet."

Peering at the bundle, Moroni saw a red, squinting face and a tiny fist. His son! Working his mouth, Moroni looked into Sarah's eyes and tried to tell her how much he loved her, but nothing would come.

Wiping at the tears with her hand, Sarah smiled and asked, "Can I get you a drink?"

Moroni's eyes lit up and he nodded ever so slowly.

Getting up from beside him, Sarah called to someone else in the room, "Mother, Moroni is awake!"

Again at his side holding a tin cup to his lips, she helped him drink a few sips. Never had anything tasted so good. Working his tongue around, Moroni managed to clear some of the dryness from his mouth.

"You're all right?" he croaked in a weak voice.

"I'm fine," she smiled. "Just a bad cut on my arm and a bump on the head." Then, her brow wrinkling, she asked, "How do you feel?"

"Just weak," Moroni managed to say.

Her eyes tearing over again, Sarah brushed at an errant lock of Moroni's hair. "We have been so worried. It's been over two weeks since Hawk found us and my mother and father came."

His mind whirling, Moroni couldn't quite understand. "How long, he rasped?"

Sarah put her hand on his cheek, "For a while I thought I was going to lose you."

Now a tall, dark-haired woman was standing next to Sarah.

"Moroni, this is my mother, Greta," Sarah offered. The

woman smiled and handed a bowl to Sarah. "Here, he should try and eat some of this broth. It will build his strength."

Nodding, Sarah took the bowl from her mother and began to spoon some of the hot soup into his mouth. With every spoonful, he could feel life come back into his body. His eyes locked on Sarah's, he eagerly took every spoonful until the bowl was gone. Feeling better, but drowsy, Moroni gazed around the room. He could make out the sleeping forms of several other people and boxes and trunks piled along the far wall.

Standing next to Sarah again, her mother took the empty bowl and smiled at Moroni, "glad to meet you."

Trying to smile back, Moroni whispered, "The pleasure is mine, but I fear it will be a while before I'm up and around."

Her dark eyes flashing a smile at Sarah, Greta said, "Well, he has his sense of humor back, so I guess he'll live."

"My son?" Moroni asked, his eyes searching.

With a bright smile on her face, Sarah walked to the low crib and picked up the sleeping baby. Coming back, she knelt down and again let Moroni see his son. Filled with wonder, Moroni could only stare at the small, sleeping form. For several moments he looked at the tiny little hands, the delicate eyelashes and the perfect face. Smiling up at Sarah, he asked, "His name?"

"Charles," Sarah replied.

His eyes filling with tears, Moroni nodded faintly. Feeling Sarah's hand take his, he tried to smile. So tired, he needed to rest.

Feeling the soft touch of a hand on his face, Moroni cracked his eyes open again. He'd fallen asleep, he knew that, but now sunlight streamed through the open door. Shifting his gaze he saw the slight form of Katie. Her dark eyes resting on him, she tried a tentative smile.

"Hello, little one," Moroni whispered.

"Papa," was all Katie managed, blinking back the tears.

Weakly, Moroni took his adopted daughter's hand in his. "I'll be fine," he whispered, trying to relieve the fear he saw in her eyes.

"Papa, the bad Indian took Sammy," Katie said softly. Then wiping at her eyes with the back of her hand, she began to sob.

Unsure of what Katie was trying to tell him, he just held his daughter's hand for a moment. Then Sarah was at his side.

"Where's Sam?" Moroni rasped.

Sighing, Sarah knelt and put her arm around Katie. "Moroni, he's been missing since we were attacked. Katie says the Sioux was holding onto him as he rode away. Your stallion came back the next night and they had hoped to backtrack him. My father, Hugh, and No Arrows have been searching, but they haven't found a thing. And the weather—it has rained off and on ever since you were wounded."

Seeing the pain in his wife's eyes, Moroni weakly reached his free hand for her. Despair welling up inside of him, Moroni felt utterly helpless. How could this have happened? He had always been so careful and now his family had nearly been wiped out and Sam was missing. Wiping at her eyes, Sarah sensed what Moroni was feeling. "Moroni, you can't blame yourself. How could you have known that he would be back? How could he have known where we lived?"

"But . . ." Moroni whispered.

"No buts," interrupted a large man with a graying blond beard. "I'm Rolf, Sarah's pa. Moroni, you can't blame yourself for what happened. A body has to take care of their stock and put in crops and hunt for meat. You can't just sit behind the walls of your cabin and watch for danger all day."

"I still feel guilty," Moroni replied.

"Who wouldn't?" Rolf continued. "Now you got to get on

with it. We haven't found Sam's body so I figger there is a good chance he's still alive. Sometimes, Indians take notions. They'll keep a captive and raise them up to be their own."

A note of hope in Sarah's voice, she added, "Moroni, No Arrows and a few of his men are looking north and Rufus Ordoway is scouting around to the east but the weather has been so bad most of the tracks have been wiped out."

Then Katie raised her head and wiped at her eyes with her tiny hands. "Papa, the holy one was here."

"Hawk?" asked Moroni.

"Yes," replied Sarah. "It was he who came first."

"Where is he now?" asked Moroni, coughing a bit.

"He left a couple of days after the raid," answered Rolf. "Said he needed to go and just took off in the middle of the night."

Closing his eyes for a moment, Moroni tried to digest all he had been told. Soon the feeling of despair was replaced by a fierce determination that began to well up inside of him. Focusing on Sarah, he said, "I need to get well."

Smiling through her own tears, Sarah nodded, "I know you will and I'll be here to help you."

His teeth flashing through his beard, Rolf nodded. *They will make it,* he thought to himself. *But there is much to do.*

CHAPTER 11

It seemed to Sam as if they were in a nightmare. No matter how far they ran or what they did, sooner or later the bear would catch up to them. Horse Ears wore a gaunt, haunted look and had developed a nervous twitch in his right eye. The horses were worn and tired and Sam was feeling the toll. It seemed as if Horse Ears had relented in his torture of Sam. Not only did he cease to beat him but he acted as if he didn't care when Sam would take an old obsidian knife he had found and use it to cut off his own chunk of partially-roasted meat. A better question in Sam's mind was, *Why was the bear following them? Or was it the same bear? Could it be that they would just happen to run into a grizzly every other day or so?* Sam didn't think so. It had to be the same bear. But why? Had Horse Ears hit the bear with one his arrows or with a musket ball and so angered the bear that it was following to seek revenge?

Half asleep on the back of the horse, Sam was nearly thrown when it stumbled across a rocky shelf along the rim of a ridge. Getting a firm grip on the mane of the horse, Sam took stock of his surroundings. They had been traveling east for the better part of two weeks now, and not only was the country drier, but at times they would see huge herds of buffalo. From what he had heard, this must be the country that the Sioux claimed as their own. But after what Gall had done to this warrior who had taken him prisoner, would he be welcomed back into a camp of the Sioux? Further to the east, Sam could see the purple haze of mountains rising in the distance. But now before them, in a small pine-ringed valley grazed at least a hundred buffalo. Pausing, Sam watched as Horse Ears gazed at the buffalo. Licking his dried lips, the Sioux was hungry for fresh meat.

Slipping from his horse, Horse Ears handed the lead rope of the pack horse to Sam.

"You stay. I hunt," he grunted at Sam. Mounting his horse he started slowly down toward the grazing herd of buffalo.

It seemed odd, but now, the young warrior almost treated Sam as a companion of sorts. Several times in the last few days Sam had been given the opportunity to escape his captor, but something had stopped him. What if he did escape? Would Horse Ears come after him? And if he did and caught up with him what would happen? What direction should he take? And, moreover, how would he survive? No, something was keeping Sam with the Indian. He wasn't quite sure what it was, but he knew he was safer with the Sioux than on his own. His thoughts kept going back to his mother and Moroni. Were they still alive? Sam knew with all his heart that if Moroni still lived he would find him sooner or later. Knowing his stepfather as well as he did, he knew without a doubt that Moroni would be coming. And so he bided his time.

Returning his gaze to the shallow valley where the buffalo grazed, Sam watched Horse Ears as he trotted his tired horse toward the beasts. A buffalo steak would taste good right now, Sam thought to himself as he watched the Sioux get closer and closer. Suddenly one of the buffalo threw up its shaggy head and saw the warrior nearly upon it. With a bellowing snort it raised its tail and began to run from the approaching hunter. The action of the first buffalo alerted the rest of the herd and they began to run from Horse Ears toward a shallow gap in the far ridge. Kicking his horse into a gallop, the warrior gave chase. Eagerly Sam watched as the scene before him unfolded. Gradually the Sioux drew closer to his quarry. Thumping the ribs of his tired horse, he began to ride abreast of one of the trailing buffalo. Fitting an arrow to his bow, Horse Ears leaned in and fired an arrow into the side of the running animal. Swerving away, he watched for the buffalo to weaken, then again he urged his horse in and again he fired an arrow, but the buffalo stampeded on. Drawing close again he shot another arrow into the buffalo. This time the shaggy beast turned sharply right into the path of Horse Ears and his laboring horse. His mouth agape, Sam watched the collision from his vantage point. There was a rolling swirl of horse, buffalo, dust and Indian before the herd thundered through the gap and out of sight.

For a moment, Sam wasn't sure what course to follow, but soon his hunger got the best of him. Kicking his own tired horse in the ribs, he yanked on the lead rope of the packhorse and started toward the tangle of horse and buffalo. He was half way there when, to his amazement, Horse Ears crawled from the wreckage. Staggering to his feet, Horse Ears walked to where the buffalo lay and with a sharp cut of his knife, slashed the throat of the still-living beast. Then lying down next to the spurting blood, he began to lap at it like a dog.

Sickened, Sam turned his head for a moment. He was thirsty, but he was nowhere near ready to do something like that. Drawing up to where the buffalo lay, Sam slipped from his horse and watched as Horse Ears got up from his drink and made a long slit in the side of the buffalo. Reaching inside, he felt around for a moment and then pulled forth a large chunk of the liver. Cramming as much as he could into his mouth, Horse Ears glared at Sam as he began to chew. Ignoring the Indian, Sam used his crude blade to cut through the thick hide and carve off a large chunk from the hump. Putting this into one of the empty sacks on the pack horse, he knelt again at the side of the buffalo and carved off more meat. Filling the sack, he still paid no attention to the warrior still gorging himself on liver. He turned away and led the two remaining horses toward a shady spot among the pines.

Walking into the coolness of the pines, Sam was surprised to find a tiny seep of water nestled in a clump of boulders. Nearly crying from thirst, Sam dropped to the ground and drank. Finished, Sam wiped his mouth, then staked out the horses where they could get at the sparse grass. Finding a good spot for a campsite, Sam knelt, and with expert hands started a fire with a bit of steel he had taken from one of the packs. Adding more wood to the fire, he propped one chunk of hump roast over the fire to cook. Using the obsidian knife, he began to saw the remaining meat into strips for drying. The meat on the fire began to sizzle, giving off a tantalizing aroma, and Sam, feeling faint with hunger, sliced off a strip and began to eat the half-cooked meat. Never had anything tasted so delicious! Savoring the taste he let his gaze wander to where Horse Ears was still squatting next to the dead buffalo and horse. Sam did not care what the Indian was doing as long as he left him alone. Now he busied himself with making a rack on which to dry the remaining meat. Using strips of rawhide, he soon had a crude rack placed near the fire. After hanging the strips of meat on it, he sat back to finish his roast.

Burning his fingers a little on the hot meat, Sam ate until he felt he would burst. Wiping his greasy hands off on a clump of grass he returned to the seep and drank. The water tasted a little brackish, but a thirsty as he was, he paid no attention. Returning to his drying rack, Sam checked the meat, then looked down at Horse Ears. The Sioux was cutting off huge chunks of bloody meat from the carcass of the buffalo and throwing them on a large piece of the hide. Satisfied with his pile of meat, the Indian gripped the edge of the hide and began dragging it toward Sam. When he reached Sam's campsite, he promptly tied his rawhide rope around Sam's neck again and fastened the other end to a tree. Then, as an afterthought, he plucked the obsidian knife from Sam's belt and tossed it out of his reach.

Feeling defeated, Sam folded his arms and said, "You don't need to thank me for doing all the work."

His eyes going once to Sam, Horse Ears growled, "You do slave work. Now shut mouth."

His shoulders slumping with dejection, Sam walked toward the thick pine when his tether was tied. *At least he gave me about forty feet of rope this time,* Sam thought to himself. Then shrugging his shoulders, he plopped down next to the tree and relaxed. For the first time in ages it seemed that he had a full belly and wasn't thirsty. Then thoughts of the bear jerked him erect. Was the grizzly still following them? Sam looked down across the wide valley expecting to see the familiar rolling form of the huge bear as it followed their trail. But nothing was to be seen except the bloody carcass of the buffalo and the dead horse. Leaning back against the trunk of the pine, Sam again relaxed. He felt so tired and sleepy. Wondering if he could get away with a nap, he looked in the direction of Horse Ears. To his satisfaction he saw the warrior sprawled in a deep sleep next to the saddles. Grinning to himself, Sam let his eyes flutter closed.

Waking with a start, Sam looked wildly around, fully expecting the grizzly to be roaring down on them, but all he could see were the grazing horses and the still-sleeping Horse Ears. Looking out to where the buffalo and the horse lay, a lone coyote sat on its haunches surveying the scene, trying to get up enough courage to sneak in and get a bite or two. Stretching, Sam got to his feet and softly walked closer to the Indian. He nearly giggled as he observed the warrior with his arms outflung, mouth open and snoring away. The sight of the Indian sleeping made Sam yawn. He was thinking about getting some more sleep of his own when the hair on the back of his neck stood straight up. Holding perfectly still, he wondered what had alarmed him. Looking toward to the valley he could still see the dead horse and buffalo, but where was the coyote? When Sam located him, he was slinking away to the north. A feeling of dread came over him. He peered around but could see no danger. Still, the feeling stayed with him.

"Hey, Horse Ears," he called in a low voice.

The Indian slept on.

A small pebble in his hand, Sam tossed it onto the sleeping Indian's chest, "Hey, wake up."

Rubbing the spot where the pebble had landed, Horse Ears leaned up and stared at Sam angrily. He opened his mouth and was about to make a sharp reply when his eyes widened in fear. The expression of terror on the Indian's face was all Sam needed. He scrambled for the pine tree where his leash was tied. Reaching the base of the thick tree his hair stood on end as he heard the blood-curdling roar of the grizzly. Though fear knotted his stomach, he glanced behind him. There, sitting in the middle of the camp was Horse Ears trying with shaking hands to fit an arrow to his bow. And twenty feet away charged the grizzly. Jumping, Sam gained the lowest branch of the pine just in time to hear the scream of fear and pain come from the Indian. Not daring to look at what was happening, Sam crawled several feet higher in the tree. As he climbed higher, he could still hear the roars of the bear as well as the screams coming from the throat of the Sioux. Panic-stricken, Sam kept climbing until he literally ran out of rope. Hugging the trunk with both hands, he finally gained enough courage to spare a look down at the devastation below him. The screams had stopped now, but still he could hear the growling of the huge bear. He was sickened. The grizzly had picked up the Indian by the head and was shaking him back and forth as a terrier shakes a rat. With bile building up in his throat, Sam leaned over and retched. Still clinging to the trunk of the tree, he closed his eyes and said a quiet prayer. Then taking several deep breaths, he opened his eyes again. The grizzly was now sitting on its haunches like a big shaggy dog staring at the mutilated body of the Indian. Holding his breath, Sam hoped that the bear would ignore him and leave.

For what seemed like a lifetime, the bear sat and stared at the obviously-dead Indian. Then with a mighty "whuff" it swatted at the body with a powerful paw, sending it spinning. Then Sam could make out the stub of a broken arrow sticking out of the ribs of the bear. It was the same bear, Sam realized. Holding perfectly still, Sam watched as the grizzly sniffed at the dead warrior, then waddled over to the still-smoldering fire. Its pig-like eyes gazed at the rack where the meat was drying. Finally its tongue flicked out and pulled off a strip. Swallowing the meat, the bear plucked the rack clean then began to nose around in the rest of the packs that lay on the ground. Suddenly the bear whirled and raced for the body of Horse Ears. Growling, he cuffed and bit at the body for several minutes, then, seemingly satisfied, waddled back to the camp. Plopping down near the smoldering fire again, it seemed to study the camp and its surroundings.

Finally the bear began to eye the two terrified horses. For a moment, Sam thought the bear might attack them, but then it turned its head and looked straight at him in the tree.

Chilled by the two dark orbs looking at him, Sam dared not move. Muttering like an old man, the grizzly walked slowly over to the base of Sam's perch and looked up through the branches at him. For at least a minute the bear stared at Sam.

Then, as if curious about the leather rope running up the tree, it gripped the rawhide in its teeth and tugged. The yank on the rope nearly dragged Sam from the branch he was sitting on. With sudden clarity he knew that if the bear wanted to, it could haul him from the tree like a hooked trout. Once on the ground his fate would be sealed. Then the solution came to him: slowly climbing down to the next branch Sam wound the excess rope around a branch that was at least eight inches thick. Crawling around to the other side of the tree, he gripped what little slack he had left in the rope and hung on. Again the bear gripped the rope in its teeth, and again it tugged. This time the rope was looped around the thick branch. Leaning back, the bear pulled harder. Still, the rope held. Pulling back with all its might, the bear hauled away. With a sharp crack the rope broke, sending the bear rolling down the slight incline.

Whuffing a bit, the grizzly stared up in the tree at Sam, the end of the rope hanging from its jaws. The sight was almost comical. Letting go of the rope, the bear shook itself as if to regain its dignity, then sauntered from sight into the pines. After unwrapping his end of the rope, Sam crawled higher into the pine and found a perch on a large branch that forked near the trunk. Not for a moment did he believe the bear had gone. Sam was tired and he knew that sometime during the night he would fall asleep. With a grim smile on his face, Sam used his half of the rope to tie himself to the tree. No use making it easy for the bear.

CHAPTER 12

Feeling a sudden lurch, Sam opened his eyes, his heart beating wildly in his chest. Gripping the trunk of the pine with both hands, he stared down at the ground thirty feet below. It was still dark, but the moon had come up, casting a silver glow over the area. Hearing a scratching noise, he looked down and watched as the grizzly clawed at the trunk of the tree he was perched in.

With shaking hands, Sam fumbled at the knots in the rawhide rope. Untying the rope, he pulled himself higher into the tree. Somewhere he had heard that a grizzly couldn't climb trees, but at this point he wasn't about to tempt the bear. Reaching as high as it could on the trunk of the tree, the bear dug its claws into the bark creating long gashes in the wood. Shuddering, Sam could only watch as the bear reached up again and again. Never uttering a sound, the bear clawed at the tree for what seemed an eternity to Sam. Then silently the bear dropped to all fours and waddled from sight deeper into the trees. Shifting himself in the branches of the pine, Sam looked and watched for any sign of the bear. Feeling sleepy, he again tied himself to the trunk of the tree.

Sam felt the warmth of the sun's rays and, shaking his head, he knew he must have dozed off. Searching the ground, he could find no sign of the grizzly except for the pile of shredded bark at the foot of his tree. His stomach growling, he looked longingly at the remains of the fire and the empty meat rack. He knew very well he couldn't spend the rest of his life in the tree, but he knew his life could end as rapidly as had the

Indian's if he were to be caught by the bear. Pulling the knots of the rope loose, he climbed lower in the tree. Waiting and watching for a few moments he looked and listened for any sign of the bear. Satisfied that the creature must be gone, for a while at least, he dropped to the ground. Tensely, he waited for the charge of the grizzly, but nothing came. His every sense alert, Sam crept to the cold fire and searched for the knife Horse Ears had been using. Thrusting the long, steel blade into his belt he picked up a few fragments of cooked meat. Brushing the dirt and ants off, he began to eat.

Glancing toward the tethered horses, he could see only the roan-colored packhorse. The other was gone. Watching the roan for a few minutes, Sam was satisfied the grizzly must be gone from the roan's sight and smell, anyway. Chewing on the meat, Sam went to where the broken body of the Sioux lay. Sickened by the sight, he averted his eyes and searched the ground for any weapon he could use. Seeing the elk-hide quiver lying a dozen yards away, Sam picked it up and examined it. Four arrows were left. Checking them for cracks or loose points, Sam wondered what had happened to the bow. A few more seconds of searching paid off and he found the bow. But the string had been broken in the melee. Hefting the stout bow in his hand, Sam wondered what he could use as a string. Perhaps a strip of leather from the dead Horse Ear's leggings? Shaking his head, Sam didn't think he had the stomach to touch the mutilated body of the warrior.

Quietly and quickly as he could, he piled the possessions of the dead Indian on a corner of the ripped blanket. Remembering how he and his mother had survived after living through the massacre two years past, Sam knew what needed to be done. Glancing again at the horse, Sam wished it had been the roan that had escaped. The reddish, roman-nosed beast was the most ill-tempered horse Sam had ever been around. Every time Horse Ears had packed the beast, he had been forced to tie a foot up or beat it with a club to get the saddle and packs on. Picking through the packs, Sam began to pile up items he could use: several pair of moccasins, a heavy, fringed-leather jacket as well as a lighter shirt made from tanned antelope, several balls of sinew, a steel hatchet, and an extra skinning knife. Finally a long blade that looked like a spear point. Examining the blade, Sam turned it over in his hands. His mind working, he knew this had some possibilities. Setting it by his side, he looked into a smaller leather sack. Recoiling in disgust, he tossed the sack over near the body of Horse Ears. Scalps. Apparently the warrior had been able to collect himself a few trophies from somewhere. With a shudder, Sam wondered where the warrior had gotten them. None of them looked like they came from a white person.

All of the usable goods piled into two leather sacks, Sam set them aside and looked out on the grassy valley floor at the dead horse and buffalo. Feeling his stomach growl, he wondered if there was any usable meat left on the buffalo. He knew well what would happen if the grizzly came back while he was out on the treeless flat. But he had to have the meat, and if he left it much longer it would sour. Watching the two carcasses for several minutes he could see a raven perched on the shoulder of the horse. The coyote still hadn't come back, but soon there would be all kinds of scavengers. Going to the pile of limbs he had dragged in for firewood, Sam picked out the longest and straightest. After knocking off the smaller branches, he hefted the ten-foot pole. It would make an excellent spear shaft. Sitting on a fallen log, Sam used his knife to notch the pole. Then with a long piece of sinew he lashed the lance blade to the pole. Holding the spear in his hand he tested it for balance. A grim look on his face, he wondered if he could kill the bear with it. No, he knew he couldn't. Not by throwing it, anyway. But under the right conditions . . .

Sam had been working swiftly for the better part of two hours now. He had carefully gone out to the buffalo, and using the piece of hide that Horse Ears had used the day before, had already dragged two loads of meat back to his campsite. Rekindling the fire, Sam had the drying rack full of meat again and had eaten his fill of hump roast. Wiping at the sweat, Sam paused for a moment. The early summer sun was fully up now and it was getting warm. It was slow work cutting the meat off the carcass and dragging it to his camp, but he didn't dare use the horse quite yet. When he went to use the foul-tempered beast, he wanted everything to be in his favor. He had, however, staked the roan on a new patch of grass and let it drink a little water from the old copper kettle that Horse Ears had found somewhere.

When the hide was piled high with meat, Sam bent his head, and with the lance resting on the pile of meat he began pulling toward the campsite. Dragging the load up the slight incline into the trees sapped his strength and he had to rest several times before he arrived at the fire. Breathing heavily from the exertion, Sam plopped down on the fallen log again and wiped the sweat from his face and chest. He had nearly a hundred pounds of meat now and on the first trip he had cut off a large square of the hide. Remembering how warm the buffalo robe was that his mother and Gall had given him, he hoped to tan the square of hide for use as a blanket. Then he could throw away the two old ragged blankets that had belonged to Horse Ears. Gazing at the roan, he could see it was grazing quietly. Would the grizzly come back now that its prime tormentor was dead? Shuddering, he knew what would happen if the bear came back. Closing his eyes, he could still hear the screams of Horse Ears as the bear had mauled him. And what to do about the body? Heaving a sigh of resignation, he knew what he had to do, but that didn't make the job any easier. Picking up the spare knife he walked out of the trees a short way and began digging through the tough sod. For a half hour he dug until he was satisfied the hole was deep enough. Going back to the Indian's body he used the rawhide rope to drag it to the grave. Finished with filling in the grave, Sam bowed his head.

"I guess you gave me no reason to like you much," he began. "But we are all God's children and I figger right now you are contemplating the error of your ways. Amen."

Walking back to the camp, Sam wondered if he should put a cross on the grave. But he shrugged it off. As far as he knew they only put a cross on the graves of Christians. His captor had been a heathen as far as he knew.

Back at his campsite, Sam fed a few more sticks into the slow-burning fire. After checking the meat on the rack, he assessed the heavy wood bow. What could he use to make a string with? And when he had a string, could he shoot well enough to kill anything with it? Plucking another piece of meat off the rack, Sam squatted down and began to slice the rest of the meat into strips for drying. Chewing on some meat, Sam laid out his predicament in his mind. First, he had no idea where he was. Second, how long could he hope to survive in this place, and third, where was the grizzly? Without a doubt he knew it would return. Resting his eyes on his lance, he knew his only chance was to kill the bear if it showed up again. He couldn't keep running into the trees every time it came and pillaged his food supply. He now had an idea forming in his mind. Last winter, Moroni had told him stories of how the Germans killed wild boar with a spear. Wrinkling his brow in thought, Sam pulled the lance over to him. He ran his hands over the two-foot blade, as he looked closely at the inscription on the bottom. Toledo. Sam had no way of knowing that the lance blade had once belonged to a Spanish soldier killed in battle with the Comanche. The lance blade had passed from one warrior to another, finally ending up in the hands of Horse Ears in a trade. Passing his finger over the blade, he found it was still razor-sharp and would do the job on the bear if he had the courage and good luck.

Sam searched the scattered pine forest around him for just the right tree. There! Taking the steel hatchet, he walked into the trees and chopped down a fifteen-foot sapling. Trimming off the branches, he notched the smaller end and lashed the lance head to it. Then halfway down the shaft of the lance, he lashed a crosspiece about four feet long. A whispered prayer on his lips, Sam wondered if this was what Moroni had described. A long spear with a crosspiece halfway up the shaft to keep the boar—or in his case the grizzly—from sliding up the shaft to the hunter. Leaning the heavy spear up against a nearby tree, Sam put more wood on the fire. Then, hatchet in hand, he walked to the seep for a drink. Satisfying himself, he watered the roan. And after making sure the horse couldn't get loose and grass was still within reach, he went back to his camp.

Yawning, Sam felt drowsy, but the fear that the bear would come at anytime kept him awake. Wishing he had his mother's revolver, Sam figured he could kill the bear with that if he could get the right shot. But with a wry grin on his face, he knew wishing wouldn't get him out of the mess he was in. Shifting himself to a more comfortable position, he felt his eyelids droop. Then back in the sparse timber the roan snorted. His hair standing on edge, Sam scrambled to his feet and grabbed the lance. The grizzly! No more than a hundred feet away the bear stood on all fours, its red eyes boring into Sam.

Mustering all the courage he could, Sam yelled out, "Go on bear! Leave me or I'll fix you!"

As if answering Sam's challenge, the huge bear lowered its

head and without a sound, charged. Sam's blood turned to water. He could only stare with wonder at the swiftness of the charge. He barely had time to grip the lance and point it at the bear, with the butt resting against the ground behind him. Gritting his teeth, Sam felt a jolt as the point of the lance pierced the bear's chest. With a bellow of rage and pain, the grizzly rolled to the ground. Sam, still clutching the shaft of the lance, was thrown to the ground. Snarling with rage, the grizzly regained its feet and tried to get at Sam. Holding to the wooden shaft of the lance, Sam hoped the wood would hold as the bear clawed at the pole. Pushing toward Sam, the bear drove the lance deeper into its chest. The snarl turning to a gurgle, the bear reached out with a massive paw and snapped off one side of the crosspiece. Then, with a massive effort the bear lunged forward again. This time Sam saw the point of the lance come out of the bear just in front of its hip. With wonder, Sam couldn't believe the bear was still on its feet, let alone still alive. Stopping for a moment, the grizzly stared at Sam with hate-filled eyes. Then, hearing the last snarl, Sam watched as the life in the bear suddenly ebbed, then faded. His legs unable to support him anymore, Sam abruptly sat down. With his head swimming, he ran a hand over his face. He'd done it! He killed the beast that had driven them clear across the country and occupied his thoughts during every waking moment. His knees still trembling, Sam regained his feet and walked to the dead · bear. One glance at the long claws and the teeth and Sam knew he had been protected. There was no way he could have killed the beast without help from on high. Going to his knees again, Sam bowed his head and said a quiet prayer of thanks. His eyes wet with tears he stared again at the claws.

"I ought to make me a necklace out of them claws or nobody will believe me," he announced to himself, the beginnings of a smile on his face.

CHAPTER 13

Four days had gone by since Sam had killed the grizzly and during that time he had improved his rude campsite. Nearer to the spring he had built a small lean-to from pine logs and part of the buffalo hide. The swelling was snug, and with a small fire at the front it kept Sam warm and dry, but he knew he couldn't stay there for long. He had dried a hundred pounds of buffalo, but the meat from the bear proved too greasy to dry properly. Not wanting to waste it, he had eaten some of it roasted over his fire. After skinning the bear he had dragged the hide from the grizzly as well as the square of hide from the buffalo near his shelter and attempted to tan both of them. Cracking the thick skull of the buffalo with his hatchet, he had smeared the brains over the staked-out hides and then let them dry. Now he was busy trying to soften the hides by pounding them with a wooden club.

Sweat pouring from his body, Sam leaned on the club and wondered if he was doing it right. Last summer when Moroni and some of the Shoshone had been engaged in building the cabin and barn he had watched some of the Indian women tan several of the hides the hunters had killed. He had even seen one woman chewing on an antelope skin, intent on making it soft and pliable. After talking the brains from the buffalo and putting them on the two hides, he knew there was no way he could ever chew on them. But after an afternoon of beating on the hides with the club, he thought he was making headway. Deciding he needed a breather he picked up the bow and the quiver with four arrows and walked to the edge of the timber. Shading his eyes with his hand, he looked out across what he came to think of as his valley. Nothing could be seen moving except the ravens picking over the carcass of the buffalo and the horse. Testing the rawhide string he had fashioned for the bow, he wondered if he could hit anything with his arrows. Thus far, he had been too fearful of breaking an arrow to test the bow, so he really didn't know how accurate he could be. *Tomorrow*, he thought to himself. Tomorrow he would make a handful of practice arrows and begin target practice. A sour look on his face, Sam realized he had been putting off several things for tomorrow, such as riding the roan and making a complete survey of his valley. Sucking on his lower lip, Sam knew he had to push forward, but for right now he was comfortable. He had food, water and a place to sleep. He was trying to put off the fact that sooner or later he would have to leave his valley, and when he did he would have to ride the runty, nasty little roan, and he would have to become somewhat proficient with the bow.

Back at his camp, Sam eyed the roan and wondered that if the mean horse threw him, would he be able to catch it again? That for now was his chief worry. He had hoped the little sorrel he had always ridden would come back, but the bear or something else must have chased it away. Deciding on a plan, Sam set his bow and arrows aside. And hitching up his worn trousers, he walked over to where he had picketed the roan. As he approached the horse, it eyed him balefully. Sam had saved a hackamore and the rude saddle that Horse Ears had used. Hopefully, with these aids he could ride the horse. With the hackamore in his hand, Sam walked closer to the horse, and, talking soothingly to it, he managed to slip on the rawhide headstall. So far the roan stood quietly. Placing a torn piece of blanket on the back of the horse, Sam waited for the explosion. Still, nothing. Whispering kind words to the horse, Sam heaved the saddle onto the back of the roan. This time the horse shied sideways a step, but still Sam hadn't seen the violent outbursts that he had seen on the trip east. Keeping an eye on the roan's head, Sam reached under the horse's belly and pulled the wide leather strap up, looped it around a rude metal ring on the saddle, and began to pull it tight. At this the roan hunched its back and snorted. Pausing for a moment, Sam spoke quietly to the horse. Again he pulled on the wide leather strap. Satisfied the strap was tight enough, Sam untied the long rawhide rope from the tree to which the roan had been picketed. Slowly, and still talking to the horse, he led it around in a circle. Surprisingly the horse followed without pulling back, bucking, or performing any of the other antics that marked the other times he had seen it saddled. Feeling braver, Sam tied the rope securely around his waist, and with the reins of the hackamore in his hands, he thrust a foot in the stirrup of the saddle and swung aboard. At once the roan put its head down and began to buck violently. His head snapping back, Sam grabbed for the forked elk horn that formed the front of the saddle. Getting a grip, he clenched his teeth and held on with all his might.

For several seconds Sam held his seat in the saddle of the pitching horse, but soon lost his grip on the elk horn and flew through the air. His arms and hands outstretched, he landed face first in the sparse grass and dirt. The wind knocked out of him, he was suddenly yanked along the ground at a fearful pace. The roan was running wildly through the timber with Sam tied to it by the long rawhide rope. And as he bounced and slid along the ground, he knew he would have to stop the horse somehow or be dragged to death. Seeing several tree trunks whiz by, he grabbed for one but missed. The horse made a circle and Sam stumbled to his feet. With all the strength he had in his body he wrapped the loose rope around the trunk of a pine. Shaking with the exertion, Sam held onto the rope with one hand and slowly began to pick at the dirt and pebbles embedded in his face and chest with the other.

Finished with removing most of the dirt from his chest, Sam glared at the roan. It stood, its head up, staring at Sam with an ugly look in its eyes.

Sticking his chin out, Sam said to the horse, "You won this one, but I'm gonna' ride you and that's that."

Gathering the rope in and untying it from the tree, he eased up to the horse again. Whispering to it, Sam again pulled himself into the saddle of the roan. Again the horse began to buck. This time, Sam clung to the saddle as if to life itself. Snorting and squealing, the horse bucked and pitched. Realizing Sam wasn't about to fall off this time, the roan stretched out and began to run. Despite its short legs and round body, Sam was surprised at its swiftness. Leaning low over the running horse he gripped the saddle with one hand and the scrawny mane with the other. Across the small valley the horse ran and into the timber on the far side. Pulling for all he was worth, Sam hauled the head of the roan around and again the horse ran across the grassy valley.

For the better part of an hour the roan ran back and forth across the valley with Sam clinging to its back. Breathing heavily, the roan began to slow, so Sam thumped its ribs with his heels and again the roan began to run. For another ten minutes Sam kept the roan at a lope around the interior of the valley. Foam dripping from its mouth and sweat covering the horse, Sam let it slow to a walk and with a firm hand guided it back to his campsite. Reaching his lean-to, Sam dropped to the ground. His legs weak from the battering ride, he held to the horse's mane for a moment. Then with the rope in one hand he untied the leather strap on the saddle and pulled it from the roan's sweat-stained back. His legs chafed and sore, Sam led the roan to the seep and let it drink. Then he staked it out on a fresh patch of grass. Dropping down near the seep, Sam bathed his chest and face with water, then glared at the roan as it cropped the grass. He mumbled, "I don't know who won that round but at least I didn't fall off."

His legs aching and stiff, his face and chest sore from being dragged, Sam limped to his shelter, put several strips of dried buffalo in his battered copper pot with some water, and nudged it close to the smoldering embers of the fire. Leaning back against a log, he picked at a loose thread on his frayed trousers. He needed some clothes or pretty soon he would be running around naked.

Smelling, Sam wondered what his mother would say if she could see him now? Then the smile faded as he wondered if his mother still lived—or Moroni, for that matter. Feeling himself sliding into despair, he fought at the tears that sprang from his eyes. No, he wasn't about to let his predicament get him down. Running a hand over his face, Sam straightened his back and got to his feet. Soon he would start for home, but first he had a lot to do: become a better shot with the bow, make some clothes and somehow gentle the hammer-headed roan. Limping to the rawhide sack containing the two leather shirts, Sam pulled them out and examined them. Yes, they would do. Sitting beside his small fire, he began to work at fashioning himself some new clothes.

CHAPTER 14

Using a crutch, Moroni made his way onto the porch of his cabin and settled on a long wooden bench made from a split log. He was still very weak. Disgusted, he rubbed at the sore spot on his chest. He had to get better, and quickly. Somewhere out there was his stepson Sam and he knew the boy would be expecting him to come for him. But as yet Moroni knew he couldn't even get on a horse, let alone ride one. Feeling the gentle rays of the early summer sun, Moroni looked out over the long meadow and watched his brother-in-law, Hugh, finish with the planting of a potato crop. In the three weeks Moroni had been laid up, the brawny, red headed man had planted nearly four acres of wheat, corn, and potatoes along with a few squash. To Moroni, Hugh seemed to have an unexhaustable supply of strength and energy. And yet Moroni was weak as a newborn calf, barely able to hobble from the cabin to the barn. A worried look on his face, he saw Sarah walk from the cabin, with Charles in her arms. Sitting beside him she smiled and touched his arm.

"Moroni, please don't brood over this," she said gently.

Heaving a sigh, he looked away, "I just feel so useless."

"I'm just glad you are alive. You could have very easily been killed."

He didn't reply but looked into her blue eyes and nodded. For several minutes they sat, not speaking, but still understanding each others' thoughts. In the short time they had been married, Moroni and Sarah somehow always knew what the other was thinking. Reaching over with his hand, Moroni pushed a corner of the blanket away so he could better look at his new son. *So peaceful*, he thought to himself, and we bring him into a world of death and violence.

"It's a miracle, isn't it?" asked Sarah's mother, Greta, as she walked out onto the porch.

"It is," replied Moroni, not taking his eyes from his son.

Her dark eyes smiling, Greta said, "You know, you two remind me of Rolf and me. We can see into each others' minds." Then with an impish grin she asked Moroni, "Has Sarah ever told you of how Rolf and I met?"

"No," replied Moroni, looking at Sarah.

"Oh, Mother," Sarah groaned, but there was a smile on her face when she protested.

Seating herself on the bench next to Moroni, Greta looked out toward the meadow. "I was born somewhere in Mexico, I think. You see, when I was about seven or eight my village was raided by Indians. Most of the men and older boys were killed and the women and children were taken captive. I can still remember the screams and the smoke from the burning buildings. They tied us all together with rawhide ropes and started us walking. It took many weeks and some of the captives died, but we arrived in California. There we were all sold as slaves."

"Mama used to tell us this story all the time when we were little," Sarah broke in.

"And somehow, I'm not sure if you believe me, after all," said Greta, a grin on her face.

"Well, it's so . . ." began Sarah.

"Like a fairy tale?" asked Greta.

Nodding, Sarah blushed.

"Yes, it does kind of sound like you and me," said Moroni, with a grin of his own.

Blushing even more, Sarah nodded and pushed playfully on his arm.

Her hands spreading the apron evenly on her lap, Greta

went on. "I was sold to a Russian fur trader by the name of Ivan. He used us as slaves. And after he had been drinking he, as well as his wife, would beat us. One day when I was about fourteen he flew into one of his drunken rages and began to beat me as well as another girl." Continuing, Greta's eyes took on a faraway look. "Terrified half out of my wits, I ran from his house and into the street. He had seen me run from the house. And when he followed me I ran down the street not caring where I went. I hadn't gone far when a burly seaman from the bay caught me in his arms."

"It was my father," whispered Sarah.

"You're spoiling the story," chided Greta.

Her eyes shining, Sarah giggled and shrugged her shoulders.

"Let's see, where was I now?" said Greta smoothing her apron again.

"You ran into my arms," came Rolf's voice from the side of the house.

Laughing, Greta shook her head. "Come on," she motioned to her husband who stood grinning through his beard. "This is as much your story as it is mine."

Chuckling and shaking his head, Rolf stepped up on the porch and squatted next to Greta. "Well, here I was just off a ship and wandering around the dusty little town when this purty little Mexican gal runs right into my arms. Little did I know what was to come."

"He nearly got himself killed by Ivan's men," said Greta.

"I'd say," Rolf said ruefully. "There were about six of them and one of me."

"What happened next?" asked Moroni, warming to the story.

"Well, to make a long story short, I dragged myself over to the well in the center of town, and after cleaning myself up, I sneaked over by this cantina and just watched things for a bit. Then when it got dark I caused a little bit of a distraction and whisked your ma away."

"A distraction?" Moroni asked, a questioning look on his face.

Laughing, Greta said, "About dark, Ivan's two warehouses full of furs and other goods caught on fire somehow."

A grin on his face, Rolf winked at Moroni and continued, "You should have seen them rascals run!"

"And then my Viking hero broke down the door and rescued me and the rest of Ivan's slaves," finished Greta.

"That does sound pretty wild, doesn't it?" said Moroni, shaking his head.

"I'll tell you what wild was," said Rolf. "Getting away. I knew Ivan would think we had gone back to my ship so we started north. As soon as Ivan found out we weren't aboard the ship he sent a bunch of his hired men after us." Pulling on his beard, Rolf finished with a faraway look on his face, "I just hope the Lord will forgive me for what I did."

"He'll forgive you," said Greta, her face beaming. "We crossed the desert with Ivan's men following us. Along the way they got some Indians to help them track us."

"I never want to be that thirsty again," broke in Rolf. "Anyway, we made it to Salt Lake and fell in with them evil Mormons."

"It didn't take you very long of listening to them evil Mormons before you decided to become one," Greta put in, smiling at her husband.

Blushing through his beard, Rolf just ducked his head. "Anyway, Moroni, I finished modifying your pistols." Then handing the Colts over to Moroni, he explained further. "They take the same cartridge as your Henry now. It's something I've been fooling with for some time. I brought up some steel cylinders and with my tools I can do a pretty fair job of it."

With his thumb, Moroni flipped open a hinged gate on the side of the revolver's frame. "You just slide the cartridge in here?"

"That's right," Rolf explained. "And use this spring-loaded rod on the bottom to push the empty case out."

His eyebrows raised, Moroni asked, "Are you sure this works?"

"Sure, Brother Browning has been doing this for a while now. In fact, he even has plans for a self-loading rifle and pistol."

"A what?" asked Moroni.

"A self loader," Rolf replied. "He figgers on using the gas from the powder charge to work the action so all you got to do is pull the trigger and the gun will just keep firing."

A grin formed on Moroni's face, as he looked skeptically at his father-in-law. "Oh, come now."

"I didn't believe it at first, but the way he has it drawn up and the way he explained it to me I really think it will work."

Shrugging his shoulders, Moroni replied, "I wish I would have had one of them self-loaders when that Sioux jumped us. But thank you for the revolvers. They will be a big improvement."

With a wave of his hand, Rolf dismissed Moroni's thanks, "Just put 'em to good use. And don't kill anybody that don't need it."

Nodding, Moroni took Sarah's hand and said, "I just feel so guilty. Here I am laid up and Hugh is doing all the planting and you are working on my pistols and . . ."

"Don't worry about it," said Rolf. "You just get well and then we'll go looking for Sam. That old mountain man, Rufus, is still looking. If he finds anything he'll let us know."

Silent, Moroni knew they were right, but still he was restless. Relaxing, he held Sarah's hand and looked farther down the meadow. There he could see Jeni and Katie keeping watch over the cattle and horses as they grazed on the lush grass. Everything was so peaceful. Yet Sam was missing; all trace of him had disappeared. Running the options of the Sioux over in his mind, he wondered where he had gone. South? Unlikely. North? That was unlikely, too, as was east. From what Sarah had told him, Gall would kill the Sioux outright if he ever caught him, and from what he had learned of Indians they didn't put up with troublemakers within their own band. West. The Sioux could have gone west. Flexing his hands around the walnut grip of his revolver he knew he had to drive himself. Soon. Soon he would be well.

CHAPTER 15

Standing in front of his log lean-to, Sam ran his hands over his new clothes. Well, not so new, but better than what he had been wearing. He had cut down the shirt made from antelope hide and it now served as a jacket of sorts. The heavier elk-hide shirt he had cut the arms from and now wore them as leggings. He had cut a long strip from the best blanket and used it as a breechcloth. And finally, with a pair of Horse Ear's spare moccasins, he was better clad than he had been in weeks.

In his latest exploration of his valley he had found some sparse clumps of chokecherry, and after cutting some of the straighter limbs he was now in the process of making arrows. Squatting on a fallen log that served as his chair as well as his work area, he picked out a limb from his pile of potential arrows, and with the old obsidian knife began to scrape the bark from it. As he worked on the arrow shaft, Sam was surprised at how much work it took just to stay alive and fed. He was now down to less than fifty pounds of dried meat and so far the only game that had wandered into his valley was a small herd of antelope. A frown on his face he remembered what had happened when he had tried to sneak up on them. The animals had spotted him at once when he stepped from the cover of the trees, and before he had crept fifty feet, the fleet-footed herd of pronghorn had vanished. For a moment he had toyed with the idea of chasing them on his horse, but even though riding the tall, wild roan was a little easier now, he knew there was no way he could hope to catch the antelope.

Finished with the arrow shaft, Sam picked out three feathers from a raven that had died or been killed some time ago. The feathers were a bit weathered but he knew he needed them on the shaft as well as a steel or obsidian point. Last summer while Moroni was building their cabin and barn with the help of a dozen of the Shoshone, Sam had watched an old wrinkled Indian as he patiently made arrows. Now he was grateful he had spent those lazy summer days watching the old arrowmaker. With his teeth he trimmed one side from each of the feathers and with a bit of wet sinew he secured them to the shaft. Then, picking out another limb, he started again.

It was late afternoon when Sam had completed a dozen arrows. As yet only four had points on them—crude obsidian points he had chipped from a large chunk of the material he had found near an old campsite on one of his forays around his valley. He now had eight good arrows: four with steel points that he was saving for hunting or self-defense and four with the flint points. Sliding the eight good arrows into the otter-skin quiver he walked the few hundred yards to an old buffalo wallow. Studying the earthen banks, Sam figured they wouldn't damage his arrows if he shot into them. On the bare dirt bank, he drew a rough circle on the soft dirt, then walking back about thirty yards he drew one of the obsidian-tipped arrows from his quiver, and put it on the bowstring. Pulling back with all his strength he aimed at the circle and let the arrow fly. With a twang the arrow flew wide of the target and left Sam hopping about, holding his left arm. Tears coming to his eyes, Sam looked at his arm. He realized then the bowstring had scraped his arm when he released the arrow.

Looking at the arrow stuck in the dirt three feet to the left of the target he mumbled, "I gotta' get a whole lot better before long, else I'll starve—or something will eat me."

Walking down to the target he pulled the arrow free from the dirt. With his hand he brushed off the point and trudged back to his camp. At his log again, he cut a piece from a leftover piece of tanned deer hide. Then with some leather string he used it to fashion an arm-guard to protect him from the bowstring.

Reaching the wallow again, Sam fit another arrow to the string, drew back and fired. This time his arrow was closer to the target. Again he shot. His arrow struck the edge of the circle he had drawn in the dirt. Feeling somewhat better about his marksmanship, Sam practiced shooting until dusk was upon him. Gathering his arrows, he whistled a tune as he returned to his camp and supper.

A week of constant practice left Sam with sore shoulders from pulling the bow, but he could now keep all the arrows inside the circle at forty yards. But how would he do from the back of the roan? On his daily rides the runty horse was easier to ride, but it seemed that the roan would watch for an opportunity to throw Sam every time. One time the roan had shied violently for no reason at all, throwing Sam to the ground and then dragging him for a hundred feet before he stopped. Sam still didn't dare ride the roan without the rawhide rope looped around his waist. And when Sam put the saddle on the beast, he would generally attempt to take a bite out of him. But today was the day. He was going to give shooting from the roan a try. The quiver full of arrows on his back and the bow looped over his shoulder, he mounted the horse and rode at a slow lope around the valley. Sam hoped that by riding the roan around for a bit he would get all the mischief out of him. Entering the thin pine timber on the far ridge, Sam made the roan scramble up the ridge. Once on top, Sam looked out over the wide plain to the east. There in the distance he saw the purple haze of far-off mountains with thunderheads building among the peaks. Sam had no way of knowing they were the beginnings of the

Black Hills or the Pa Sapa to the Sioux, their stronghold. Then closer, not more than a mile off, he spotted the shaggy forms of buffalo. Standing up in the stirrups, Sam shaded his eyes to get a better look. From what he could see there looked to be several thousand at least, with more moving out of a long draw that led away to the south. Here was meat on the hoof. But could he kill one without getting hurt or killed, himself?

Now for some unknown reason the roan started forward on its own. Its ears forward, the little horse seemed to sense that a hunt was imminent. A wild grin on his face, Sam urged the horse forward. He had plotted a course that would take him within a hundred yards or so from the buffalo before they could see him and from there he would attack the side of the herd, hopefully making a kill before they could run too far. For a moment, Sam wished he had brought his lance with him. After killing the grizzly, he had fastened the lance head to a slim pole about eight feet long. For a second, he wondered if would be easier to kill one of the huge beasts with the lance than with the bow, but shaking his head he set his course.

Tense and filled with excitement, Sam trotted the roan down the ridge and through a shallow draw that led at an angle toward where the buffalo were grazing. Riding swiftly along, Sam felt the excitement building in the roan, too. Much closer now, he could hear the grunts of the huge animals and the thud of hooves on the ground. Under him, Sam could feel the roan tensed up like a spring. Riding close to the edge of the draw, he risked a peek over the rim. The herd was no more than a hundred yards off now. From the actions of the buffalo he could tell they had no idea he was around. Pulling two arrows from his quiver, Sam held one in his hand with his bow and the other he put sideways in his mouth. Closing his eyes he whispered a silent prayer for his safety. Lifting his head, his eyes bright with excitement, Sam urged the roan up over the lip of the draw and toward the grazing buffalo.

For the first fifty yards the beasts had no idea he was near, then one of the closer bulls lifted its head and from under its shaggy brow watched the white boy galloping toward it on a runty roan pony. For several seconds the huge bull studied the approaching boy, then with a bellow, lifted its tail and began to run. At once the herd of buffalo began to stampede away from Sam, streaming toward the south. Drumming his heels against the sides of the roan, Sam gripped the rough saddle with his knees and the bow and arrow with his hands. Galloping closer to the thundering herd of buffalo, Sam choked on the dust. Then to his surprise, the roan pulled close to one of the smaller cows. Careful to stay in his seat, Sam gripped the bow and tried to fit the arrow to the string. It took him several tries to get the arrow on the string. Then as he began to draw the bow back, the roan jumped a shallow gully that cut through the grassland.

Nearly losing his seat, Sam clutched at the elk horn on the front of the saddle. Again the roan drew next to the cow and again, Sam managed to get the arrow on the string and draw back his bow. Thunk! The first arrow slammed into the side of the running cow. As he released the arrow, the roan swerved away from the running cow as if he expected her to fall.

For several seconds Sam watched the cow but he could see no sign of her weakening. Taking the arrow from his mouth he put it on the string and again the roan slid next to the running cow. Drawing the bow back, Sam released the arrow and watched as it slammed into the side of the buffalo. And again the roan slipped away from the cow. Coughing on the thick dust that filled the air, Sam wished for the cow to fall, but despite the two arrows buried to the feathers in her side she lumbered on.

Trying to peer ahead through the dust, Sam began to

wonder how far they had come and what lay ahead. Knowing he had come quite a way from his valley in chasing the buffalo, Sam realized he had to kill the cow as soon as possible. Squeezing the saddle with his knees he reached around and tried to pull an arrow from his quiver. Getting an arrow out he saw it was one of his homemade ones. With a grimace on his face, he prayed it would work as well as the two with the steel points. Then he urged the roan next to the running cow. The arrow on the string, Sam pulled back and released. Once more he slammed an arrow into the side of the cow. This time the buffalo let out a low bellow and tried to hook the roan with a horn. Dodging out of the way, Sam nearly fell. But gripping the saddle with his free hand, he watched the cow slow, then topple on its side. Pulling the horse away from the running herd, Sam watched as the rest of the buffalo stampeded by. Wiping at the sweat and dirt on his face, he peered through the billowing dust for his buffalo. Lying on its side, the three arrows sticking up, the cow looked quite dead. Feeling drained, Sam began to tremble. Walking the roan over to the buffalo, he watched for any sign of life. Satisfied the cow was dead, he dropped to the ground next to the buffalo. His knees nearly buckled from the wild chase.

When he stood again, Sam had to hold tight to the saddle on the roan to keep from falling. For once Sam thought the little roan was worn right out. Sweat and grime caked its sides and its ears drooped a little and for the first time, Sam couldn't detect any mischief in its eyes. Still not trusting the horse, however, Sam took the rawhide rope from around his waist and tied it around the horn of the buffalo. Then, setting his bow aside, he drew his knife and began the task of cutting away the meat. Beginning the cut at the buffalo's neck, he cut along the spine, then down the hind leg. Grasping the hide, he was about to pull the hide back when he heard the roan snort. Looking up from his skinning, his heart nearly stopped. There, sitting on their horses but a few yards away were three Indian warriors and behind them a half dozen women and children.

First, glancing quickly toward his bow, Sam knew, even if he could get to it, the warriors would probably kill him before he could get an arrow from the quiver. Then the words of Moroni came to him.

"Indians are different from us. Not bad, just different. If you treat them with respect, they will most times treat you the same."

Then an idea came to him. Straightening up, Sam motioned at the buffalo with one hand and said, "This is too much. You can have half."

The warriors looked at one another and back at Sam but said or did nothing.

Then with his knife, Sam made an imaginary line across the carcass of the buffalo and pointed to himself. Then, pointing to the other half, he motioned to the mounted warriors. At this, the oldest of the warriors, a man of perhaps forty slipped from his horse and walked to the buffalo. Patting the half of the buffalo Sam had indicated was his he motioned to himself and the other Indians.

"Yes," Sam replied, nodding his head. "That half is yours."

Bobbing his head once, the older man said, "Washtay." Then facing the rest of his group he shouted a few more words in his language. At once the women rushed forward and with amazing speed began to butcher the cow. Sam watched as the three women in the group cut away the hide and began to pile meat on the two pieces of hide they had laid out on the ground. As the women, chattering away, cut the meat into manageable chunks, the older man pulled the three arrows free from the carcass. Examining the obsidian-tipped arrow, his eyebrows arched up and he motioned to Sam.

Smiling tentatively, Sam nodded and replied, "Yes, I made it."

At this, the warrior said some words to the other two warriors who were engaged in devouring the raw liver. He held out the arrow. Smiles broke out on the faces of the warriors. The youngest one, a slim young man not much older than Sam with a pockmarked face, slapped him on the shoulder and said something to him in his language.

Not understanding what they were saying, Sam wondered if they were Sioux. Then he remembered how to say Gall's name in the Sioux language. But what if they weren't Sioux? What if they were Crow? Or another enemy tribe?

With nothing to lose, Sam thumped himself on the chest and said, "I am the son of Gall." Then again he pointed to himself and said again, "Pizi."

At the last word all the Indians there turned and faced him, their dark eyes without expression.

CHAPTER 16

Hiding behind a screen of thick timber, Rufus Ordoway and No Arrows watched the Flathead Indian village of about twenty lodges strung out through the winding meadow below them. In the last weeks they had ridden north looking for any sign of Sam and so far found nothing. It seemed to Rufus that the young boy and his captor had fallen off the edge of the earth. They had visited a half dozen small Indian villages inquiring about Sam or any rumors of a white boy who had been taken by any of the Indian tribes.

Below them, along the grassy stream banks, a half dozen children played and further out in the meadow nearly a hundred horses grazed. Everything to the eye looked peaceful. And as far as Rufus knew, the Flathead were peaceful.

Shifting in the saddle of his horse, Rufus looked at No Arrows and said quietly, "Should we mosey on down?"

Without replying, No Arrows nodded and urged his horse down through the timber and toward the village.

As they rode out of the timber and onto the grassy flat, the children stopped their play and watched. For several moments they stared. Then shouting, they ran for the lodges. As the children stampeded for the village, several warriors appeared with weapons in their hands.

"Have you ever had any dealings with the Flatheads?" asked Rufus quietly as half a dozen mounted warriors rode toward them.

"Some," replied the Shoshone warrior.

"I spent a winter with Antelope Man's bunch about ten years ago," said Rufus as the warriors drew up before him and No Arrows.

For a few heartbeats the Flathead warriors and Rufus and No Arrows stared at each other, then the oldest of the Flathead, a squat, powerful man wearing a red cloth shirt and a stuffed raven tied to the top of his head asked in broken English, "Howdy, me Billy Raven. You want to eat?"

Nodding, Rufus replied, "That would be right neighborly."

Then, as one, the Flathead warriors turned and started back toward the lodges. Glancing at No Arrows, Rufus urged his horse behind the Flatheads and followed.

Riding into the center of the village, Rufus could tell this band was on the prosperous side. They seemed to own a fair amount of horses and were dressed well. The women who watched as they rode into the village all seemed to have a copper kettle to cook in on a tripod in front of their lodges. Drawing up before an older lodge covered with the drawings of hunt scenes, the warriors dropped from their horses and nodded their heads at an older man who stood before the lodge, supporting himself with an ornately-carved staff. His grey hair was braided and wrapped with otter fur and he wore a blue army jacket over his once-powerful shoulders. The old man, with a faint smile on his face, watched Rufus and No Arrows.

Sliding from his horse, Rufus inclined his head toward the old man and said, "Greetings. Your warriors offered us the hospitality of your village."

In English, the old man replied, "You favor us with your visit. I thought perhaps Rufus The Horse Thief was returning the ponies he stole from this poor man many years ago."

His face white as a sheet, No Arrows looked from the old Indian to Rufus, who stood bug-eyed, staring back at the old man. Looking around at the hundred or so Flatheads gathered, he couldn't ever remember being in such a spot. For a fleeting moment, he would have gladly gone back and charged the attacking Sioux with nothing but an empty bow.

Grinning weakly at the old man, Rufus said, "I can see that Antelope Man has a long memory."

The smile on his lips growing wider, Antelope Man looked at No Arrows and said, "I can see that Rufus The Horse Thief rides with a warrior of the Snakes. You had better watch your horses or this white man will have them all."

Still not sure of what was going to happen, No Arrows blurted out, "Rufus stole some horses from me three snows ago. But I stole them back along with one extra."

"Ah," replied Antelope Man, an eyebrow rising. Then looking back to Rufus, he asked, "Have you finally met your match, Rufus The Horse Thief?"

Appearing contrite, Rufus nodded his head, "Yes, I have."

"Good, then let us eat and we will talk," said Antelope Man signaling for several women to bring some food.

Following a meal of elk, camas cakes and boiled dog, Rufus sat next to No Arrows on a buffalo robe. Reaching into a leather bag, Rufus pulled out a twist of tobacco and offered it to Antelope Man. "A present and an apology for stealing your horses."

"It is nothing," replied the old man. "I have many horses and you had none. As a young man I would have stolen even your shirt. What is done is done." Then as if he knew Rufus was here for a reason, he looked to No Arrows and Rufus. "What brings you here?"

"We are looking for a boy. A white boy that was stolen by a young Sioux a few months ago."

His brow wrinkling in a frown, Antelope Man asked, "A Sioux? Where was this boy stolen from?"

"His father is a good friend of mine and he has a house down on the west side of the great Tetons," interrupted No Arrows. "He was stolen from there."

"A Sioux that far west?" questioned Antelope Man.

"He was outcast and riding with two Big Bellies." Replied No Arrows. "My friend killed the two Big Bellies but the Sioux stole my friend's son, Sam, and got away."

Thinking for a moment, Antelope Man said nothing. Then, turning to Billy Raven, he said a few sentences in his language. Billy Raven then replied and got up and walked toward one of the lodges. After scratching at the entrance, he went in.

A few moments later he returned followed by a young man of fifteen or so. Shyly, the youth looked at the two guests, then at the chief.

Gently the old man asked the youth a few questions and after thinking for a moment, the youth replied.

Turning back to Rufus, Antelope Man said, "Falls From His Horse was hunting early this spring, just when the snow was leaving. While hunting he saw three strange warriors looking our band over but when he spotted them they rode away to the south. He says that one was dressed as a Sioux and he had a bad feeling in his heart when he saw them. He felt they were evil."

"This sounds like our boys, doesn't it?" Rufus said to No Arrows.

Without replying, No Arrows nodded.

Getting to his feet, Rufus said to Antelope Man. "Thank you for your generosity, but we have far to travel, and we need to keep looking for this lost boy."

Meeting Rufus' gaze, Antelope Man struggled to his feet. "You must have much respect for this man whose son you are looking for."

"He is my greatest friend," replied No Arrows.

"Then that is enough; may the Great Spirit guide you," said Antelope Man, holding out his hand.

A week of hard riding found Rufus and No Arrows on the banks of the Madison River. It was midsummer now and the sky overhead was a startling blue. Watering their horses, Rufus and No Arrows splashed water over their heads and upper bodies.

The water dripping from his beard, Rufus looked sideways at No Arrows and said, "We're gettin' mighty close to Crow country."

Nodding, No Arrows replied, "Yes. They claim this part of the land."

Bending down and drinking deeply again, Rufus said, "You know, we could both loose our hair going this way. After we get past the Crows, the Sioux are next."

"I know that, but I wonder if the young warrior would really go back to his people?"

"We have searched all over Flathead country and even talked to a few Blackfeet and nobody has seen anything," said Rufus.

"Don't get me wrong," said No Arrows. "I would ride alone and unarmed through all the Black Hills if I knew I could get Sam back, but I just wonder if the young Sioux renegade would try and return home?"

A questioning look on his face, Rufus asked, "You don't think he would?"

Shaking the water from his hair and face, No Arrows said simply, "I know what Washakie would do if one of his men acted that way."

"What would he do?"

"Kill him on the spot," replied No Arrows. "And from what I have heard, Gall is much more unforgiving than Washakie."

Standing and stepping into the saddle of his horse, Rufus said, "We'll ride east for another day, then cut south toward the stinking water."

Agreeing, No Arrows mounted his own horse and followed.

CHAPTER 17

It was turning to summer now. Using a cane, Moroni walked slowly toward the barn. Pausing halfway there, he pulled off his black slouch hat and wiped his forehead.

"Hot," he muttered to himself. Then pulling his hat back on he walked into the coolness of the barn. For several moments he studied the pile of hay in the loft. Even though he figured they had at least twenty tons, they would need more to outlast the winter with the added stock. Between himself and his father-in-law and Hugh, they had forty assorted cattle along with eleven horses and a team of mules. Thudding the tip of his cane into the packed dirt of the barn floor, he chafed at his lack of strength. He should be out looking for Sam or at least helping Rolf, Hugh, Sarah and the rest with cultivating the crops, cutting hay and building a cabin for Rolf and his family. But as yet, the best he could do was hobble around the yard, standing guard. That was what they called it. Whenever he would get restless, Sarah or one of the others would tell him that he was doing his part by standing guard. Thumping the tip of his cane into the ground again, he thought to himself what a lot of nonsense it was.

Making his way from the barn, he went to the corral and leaned against one of the posts. Gazing down the long meadow, he could see the gold of the wheat and the different greens of the potatoes, corn and other crops, and beyond that, his sister-in-law sitting on one of the horses keeping watch over the cattle and other horses. It was an everyday job for the seventeen-year-old girl to herd the livestock out into the lush grass of the surrounding valley. Even though it had been a somewhat dry year so far, the grass in most places was knee-high and the stock fattened rapidly.

Hearing voices from inside the new log cabin belonging to Rolf, Moroni looked over at the home. Rolf and Hugh had built the three-room cabin in just under a month and now they were busy moving their belongings inside. When Rolf began to build, he surprised Moroni by wanting to build his cabin so that with Moroni's cabin facing the barn, his new one would be at the top, forming a horseshoe pattern of sorts—Moroni's cabin and the log barn forming the sides and Rolf's cabin the bottom. When Hugh built his, the four buildings would form a square.

"Better for defense," Rolf had claimed, and Moroni had readily agreed.

During his convalescence, Moroni had made himself a wide belt with thirty loops sewn in for cartridges and now he wore this belt with one of his remodeled revolvers in a crossdraw holster at all times. When it came down to it, none of them were very far from a gun at any time. Living where they did, it was necessary. One day when Melissa had commented on the necessity of everyone packing a rifle or a pistol, Jeni had replied, "I don't care what they would say in the Salt Lake Valley. It's different up here."

Catching his breath, Moroni realized that what Jeni had said was right. The people in the Salt Lake Valley would surely look down on a woman carrying a rifle, but here one didn't dare go without one.

Without realizing it, Moroni's hand went to the spot on his chest where he had been hit with the arrow. Taking a deep breath, he coughed a bit, then stretched his arms above his head. It just seemed that he couldn't get enough air at times although he felt like he was getting better. A grim expression on his face, he watched as Sarah walked from the doorway of the new home. He was at times surprised how well Sarah was doing despite all that had happened. But there were also times at night when he would wake to find her looking from their single bedroom window toward the north, her lips moving in silent prayer.

Waving, she began to walk toward him carrying baby Charlie. A smile came to his face when he thought of his new son, who was already forming a personality unique to himself. And Katie was growing, too. Every night and morning at prayer she would ask for Sam's safe return.

At his side now, Sarah took his arm and asked, "A penny for your thoughts?"

"Just the same old thing," replied Moroni. "Just wondering about Sam and trying to get well."

"One thing at a time," Sarah replied, tugging on his arm. "First you get well, then we worry about Sam. Besides, Rufus and No Arrows are still looking."

"I worry about them, too," Moroni said. "I just hope nothing has happened to them."

"They will be fine. Those two have lived out . . ."

Sarah's voice trailed away as she looked down the meadow toward where Jeni was. Following Sarah's gaze, Moroni could see the girl moving the stock toward the cabins at a rapid rate. Glancing at the sun, Moroni knew something must be wrong. It was at least two hours before Jeni was supposed to bring the cattle and horses in.

"Get to your pa," Moroni said brusquely. "And find Hugh."

Holding the growing fear inside her in check, Sarah began to run for the new cabin. Switching his cane to his left hand, Moroni looked to make sure the gate to the large corral was open. For several seconds he watched as the slim girl continued to move the livestock at a rapid gait toward the cabins.

"Something must be wrong," he muttered under his breath as he watched the girl urge even the slower cattle into a run.

Using the cane, he broke into a slow run toward his own cabin and his rifle. Climbing the three steps up on the porch, he reached inside the open door and picked up the Henry. Opening the action he checked to make sure it was loaded, and, breathing heavily, he hobbled back to the yard.

As Jeni ran the herd of cattle and horses into the corral, Moroni could see that she pointed behind her and said something to her father who was closing the gate.

Looking down the long meadow to where it opened out into the valley he could see nothing. But if his sister-in-law was worried, then something was wrong.

His cane in one hand and rifle in the other, Moroni hobbled over to where everyone had gathered, with the exception of Hugh.

Drawing near, Melissa, with a worried note in her voice, asked, "Have you seen Hugh?"

Her blonde hair waving from side to side, Jeni said, "No, I haven't, but there is a bunch of Indians coming up the valley."

"Just men, or are there women and children, too?" asked Rolf of his daughter.

"From what I could see it looked like women, too, but there was a bunch of warriors out in front that were armed and painted."

His lips pursed, Rolf glanced at Moroni. "What do you think?"

"We can't let them know how few we are. Sarah and Jeni can watch from inside my place and you, Melissa and Greta, can watch from yours."

"What about the barn?" asked Rolf.

"We can't spare anyone to put there," replied Moroni. "Besides, If they try to get any stock out of the corral they will have to burn the poles or else take them through the gate and I'll have a clear shot at them if they do that."

His eyebrows raised, Rolf looked like he might disagree.

But then he nodded his head. "All right, but watch yourself."

Handing his rifle to Sarah, Moroni motioned toward the cabin. "Get my other pistol and you take this. And make sure one of you has a rifle poking out from the firing slits."

Her eyes large with fear, Sarah nodded, then brushed her lips against Moroni's. "You be careful." Then she was gone toward the cabin.

His other Colt tucked in his waistband, Moroni waited for several minutes before the first of the Indians appeared. Like Jeni had said, there were about twenty warriors riding in front of the procession, painted for war. They wore feathers in their hair, and vermillion streaked their faces. With bells jingling from the bridles and other tack on the horses, the warriors made quite a show, especially with their weapons in their hands. Most were armed with bows or lances but there were two muzzle-loading rifles in evidence also.

His back to the barn, Moroni faced the warriors as they rode their horses into the center of the yard. Then as one, they drew up about twenty yards in front of him. For several heart-beats nothing was said. Only the stamp of a horse hoof or the jingle of a bell could be heard in the yard.

Then the one who appeared to be the leader, a man of about forty, wearing a white cloth shirt and a badger fur for a cap shouted at Moroni, "What you do here? This my land!"

From inside the cabin, Sarah poked Moroni's rifle through one of the firing slits that he had cut in the window shutters. The cross-shaped slits were cut into the heavy wood shutters to give the defender a good field of fire. Now Sarah eased back the hammer on the Henry and aimed at the warrior who was shouting at Moroni.

In a calm voice, Moroni replied, "I live here. This is my home."

"Bah!" shouted the Indian. "You lie! This my home! Now you leave!"

His hand resting on the butt of one of his revolvers, Moroni smiled and shook his head, "No."

His eyes nearly bulging from their sockets, the warrior jerked the head of his pony around and grabbed a war axe from his saddle. "Then I kill!"

As the warrior brandished the axe, he started to urge his horse toward Moroni, but was brought up short. He was now staring into the barrel of Moroni's revolver.

His eyes bugging out even farther, the warrior growled, "I kill you."

The smile still on his face, Moroni answered, "My friend, you had better back on out of here and we can try and get acquainted again, because if you take another step, I'll blow you right out of the saddle."

"You all alone," the warrior sneered. "We kill!"

Grinning even wider, Moroni said, "Now it's we, is it? Well my friend, I'm not alone." Then in a louder voice he called out. "Okay men, let's let them count rifles."

At this Sarah and Jeni poked their rifles from the firing slits even further, as did Rolf, Greta and Melissa.

Then, to Moroni's relief, came the deep voice of his brother-in-law from the loft of the barn. "I'll be killin' a dozen me ownself so dinna' be gettin' too greedy, me brother."

Smiling from ear to ear, Moroni uncocked the pistol and thrust it back in his waistband, "Now, my friend, don't you think it's time you repented of your sins?"

The fire mostly gone from his eyes, the warrior grated out, "I no friend."

"I'm sorry to hear that," replied Moroni. "My name is Moroni Stewart and I have always been a friend to the Indian.

In fact one of my best friends is No Arrows of the Shoshone."

With a sour look on his face under the badger hat, the warrior sniffed and said, "I am Three Hands. I am Shoshone, but I do not know this person, No Arrows."

"I'm sorry to hear that. But we can be friends if you wish."

His eyes assessing the dwellings and the barn, Three Hands growled. "I no white man's friend." Then twisting his horse's head around, he glared back at Moroni, "We stay here, too."

Then kicking his horse into a gallop he led the warriors out of the yard and back down the meadow.

Heaving a sigh and wiping at the sweat that began to run down his face, Moroni reached down for his cane he had dropped. Watching the band of over seventy Indians and two hundred horses travel back down the meadow, he felt Sarah at his side.

"I'm glad that's over," she said, gripping his arm.

Moroni was about to reply when to his horror the Indians stopped at where the long meadow entered the narrow valley and began to set up camp.

"It's not over," he said dryly as he watched the Indians pitching their lodges not over a half mile away.

"Oh no," moaned Sarah as she, too, realized what was happening.

"What are those savages doing?" asked Hugh, walking up beside Moroni and Sarah.

"Looks like they mean to stay a while," replied Rolf, as he, too, joined the group.

"What are we going to do?" asked Sarah, a slight tremble in her voice.

His own feelings in a turmoil, Moroni replied, "There is nothing we can do except wait them out."

CHAPTER 18

Furious, Moroni tossed his cane aside and walked to where his appaloosa stood, saddled, and waiting. Once again the Indians had driven their pony herd into the standing wheat and oats that were just beginning to ripen. In the week since the band of Shoshone had moved into the entrance of the small valley it had been a constant battle to preserve not only peace but the meager crops Hugh and the rest of them had cultivated over the summer.

Stepping into the stirrup, Moroni hauled himself up into the saddle. Wincing with a twinge of pain, he paused for a moment, then urged the big stallion into a run toward the lower meadow where the crops were.

Galloping into the middle of the pony herd, Moroni lashed out with his rawhide lariat, driving the Indian horses out of the ripe wheat. Gripping the saddle with his left hand to steady himself against the pain, he managed to drive all but two of the horses from the grain when he heard the thunder of hooves coming up behind him. Turning in the saddle, he caught the sight of a rope loop shooting out toward him. Ducking his head he drew his revolver and whirled the stallion. There behind him, three Indians were attempting to box him in and pull him from the appaloosa. Not having any of that, Moroni slapped the nearest Indian on the side of the head with his Colt, and as he slumped from his pony, Moroni covered the other two with his pistol.

His voice shaking with rage, Moroni stared at the remaining two Shoshone and said, "I've had enough! Now move your horses away from here!"

Either not understanding or choosing not to, the remaining two warriors glared sullenly at Moroni. For several seconds Moroni and the two warriors stared at each other. Then, with hate in their eyes, the two Indians dropped from their horses next to their companion who had sat up and was rubbing his skull where Moroni had whacked him. Propping the groggy man up in his crude saddle, the two warriors slowly rode their horses back down the valley toward the hide lodges that were positioned at the end of the wide meadow.

Catching his breath, Moroni watched them go and wondered what would happen now. Holstering his revolver, he looked at the trampled grain. It was the third time in a week the Shoshone had driven their horses into the crops. It was done on purpose, too, and Moroni and everyone else knew it. It wasn't just a few horses that wandered into the crops; it was always the whole herd. So far all that had happened were a few shouted threats from Three Hands when the horses were driven out, but now that he had hit one of them, Moroni wondered what would happen?

Hearing horses coming from behind him, he twisted in the saddle and watched as Hugh, along with Sarah and Jeni, rode up.

"What's happened?" asked Sarah, her eyes going to the lodges.

Feeling relieved, Moroni replied, "Three of the warriors were driving the horse herd into the crops, and when I tried to stop them one of them tried to rope me."

"And?" asked Sarah.

"And I slugged one of them with my pistol."

"Well, this is about to come apart," Hugh said dryly as he motioned toward where a dozen mounted Indians started from the lodges.

Seeing the armed Indians approaching, Moroni said,

"Sarah, you and Jeni go on back. This could get real ugly."

Smiling nervously, Sarah replied, "Not on your life. Four guns are better than two. And besides, when have I ever run out on you?"

Unable to make a reply that would persuade Sarah to go back, Moroni watched as the Indians rode closer. Knowing he couldn't handle the rifle and stallion both, he drew one of his pistols and held it down next to his leg out of sight from the approaching warriors. From behind him he heard the *click, click* of Sarah cocking her rifle.

For a moment, Moroni wondered if Three Hands and his men would try to run right over them. But at the last moment they stopped just short of Moroni.

Hate glittering in his eyes, Three Hands shouted, "What have you done? My man maybe die!"

"Your warrior tried to run your horses into my crops. When I stopped him he tried to rope me. I will not have that." Moroni said evenly.

With a shouted curse, Three Hands pushed his horse next to Moroni and with a war axe in his right hand looked as if he might try a swing, when suddenly he was thrown from the saddle. Hugh, his temper snapping, had dropped from his horse and with a mighty heave unhorsed the furious Three Hands. His beard and hair bristling with rage, the Scot advanced toward the disoriented Indian.

Reaching down, Hugh picked the warrior up by his shirt and held him up.

Then with his face no more than an inch away from Three Hands he gritted out, "Listen to me mon. I'll ha' no more o' this! You either quit behavin' like a savage or I'll be beatin' ye half to death!"

Growling another curse, Three Hands spit in Hugh's face.

For a moment time stood still. Then shouting a wild highland cry, Hugh threw the Indian chief over his shoulder. Then as if he were pouring out his frustrations all at once, he began to pound Three Hands with his fists. Only once did the Indian manage to try a blow of his own and it went over the Scot's shoulder. Finally, Moroni knew he had to stop it or Hugh would kill the man. Pushing the appaloosa close he reached down and grabbed Hugh by the collar.

"Hugh! Stop it. You'll kill him!"

Backing up, Hugh let the beaten man fall to the ground like a sack of grain. Then, wiping at his face, he glared at the rest of the warriors who sat their horses looking on glumly as their leader lay in a heap before them.

His chest heaving and his hair and beard wild, Hugh fixed the warriors with his glare and roared, "All right, who be next?"

Nervously the warriors cast glances at each other but wouldn't meet Hugh's glare. Then the bravest of the warriors, a tall man dressed in nothing but deer-hide leggings dropped from his horse and advanced on Hugh, an evil-looking knife clutched in his fist. Crouching, the warrior held the knife before him and slid a few steps toward Hugh, who focused his eyes on the knife, and watched and waited. Quick as a striking rattler, the warrior thrust at Hugh's midsection. Twisting aside, Hugh was only scratched by the tip of the blade. Then again the warrior swung the blade at the Scot. This time Hugh was waiting. Slapping the knife away from his body, he grabbed the warrior by the knife arm and his hair, and threw him to the ground. The knife spun from the warrior's grip as he struggled to rise. But the Scot grabbed the warrior by a leg and began to spin him around. His massive neck bulging from the effort, Hugh spun the Indian around several times, then let him fly into the gaping warriors who were still mounted. With howls and shouts, two of the warriors were knocked from their horses. And the man who was thrown shrieked a cry of pain as he was stepped on by a stampeding horse. His pistol ready, Moroni was worried that one of the warriors would try his luck with a bow or other weapon, but now they were thoroughly cowed. Shouting howls and cries of dismay, the warriors picked up their injured companions and rode pell-mell for their lodges.

Glancing around at Sarah and Jeni, Hugh took several more deep breaths. A crooked grin crept onto his face, "I'm sorry for me outburst."

Chuckling despite the close call, Moroni said, "No problem." Then returning his Colt to his holster, he pulled off his black slouch hat and wiped at the sweat.

"I wonder what will happen now?" asked Jeni, uncocking the shotgun she had been carrying.

"No telling," Moroni replied, keeping a wary eye on the lodges and now hearing the wailing of several women. "They might pull out and leave us alone, but Three Hands is a good hater so he just might wait 'til he's feeling better and try something again."

"It might not be Three Hands that gets revenge," Sarah said. "Look over there."

Following his wife's gaze Moroni was chilled to the bone. Over the north ridge he could see at least several hundred Indians riding over the crest toward the cabins and the barn. Without speaking, Moroni led off at a run toward home.

Riding into the yard, Moroni noticed Rolf as well as his wife and Melissa standing by with rifles. Climbing down from the appaloosa, Moroni bent to catch his breath again. After pulling out the Henry, he shooed the stallion into the corral. With Rolf at his elbow, he watched the band of Indians ride slowly toward the homestead.

"Looks like quite a bunch," commented Rolf.

Without replying, Moroni nodded his head then looked at where Sarah and the other women stood on the porch of his cabin.

Then Katie jumped up and down and shouted, "Papa, No Arrows is coming."

Shading his eyes, Moroni wondered if his adopted daughter could be right.

At his side, tugging on his hand, she shouted, "Papa, it is! Look at one of the leaders. The one on the black horse."

"At least it's not a raiding party," said Rolf. "They have their women along."

"It is No Arrows," called Sarah from the porch where she stood holding baby Charlie now. Then awkwardly putting Moroni's prized field glasses to her eyes with one hand, she added, "Rufus is with him, but I don't see Sam."

Now Moroni could see the white man as well as no Arrows clearly. But who were the Indians?

Then Rolf said softly, "That's Washakie's bunch. See that big man out in front riding the buckskin and wearing the plaid shirt?"

"Yes," Moroni replied simply.

"That's Washakie himself. He's got his women and children along so they are probably just moving camp."

Most of the traveling Indians were swinging wide of the homestead now and continuing toward the Shoshone village at the end of the valley, but four figures detached themselves from the procession and rode into the yard.

Looking weather-beaten and tired, Rufus and No Arrows dropped to the ground and nodded to Moroni.

Rufus spoke up. "Sorry, but we ain't seen no sign of your boy."

"But do not lose all hope," added No Arrows. "It is a big

country out there and there are still places to search."

Wiping at the dirt and grime that caked his face, Rufus said, "We talked with a bunch of Flatheads up north. One 'o them was an old friend and a hunter from the village who said he saw the young Sioux early in the spring. But no one else we talked to, red or white, seen hide nor hair of the Sioux or Sam."

Indicating Washakie with a nod of his head, No Arrows added, "We traveled south through the country of the stinking waters. And after we crossed the divide we came across Washakie's band. They are traveling north toward the buffalo country."

Nodding, all Moroni could muster was, "Thank you."

Meeting the level gaze of the tall, square-shouldered Shoshone chief, Moroni walked to him and held out his hand, "It's a pleasure to meet you."

Dropping to the ground beside his pony, Washakie took Moroni's hand with a firm grip and shook it once. "No Arrows speaks well of you."

Not sure of how to respond, Moroni said, "I have heard many good things of you, also." Then with a hand he indicated Rolf, Hugh, Sarah and made introductions.

Washakie acknowledged the group, then narrowed his eyes. "There has been trouble?"

"It was an accident," Moroni said, unsure of how to go on.

Gazing at Hugh, who still bore the look of a fight, Washakie asked, "What has happened?"

His face losing its color, Hugh replied, "The chief, Three Hands, and his warriors have been causing a bit of trouble in the last week. Just this morning, they drove their horses into me grain field and when they were told to get them out, they refused. And well, I used me fists on them."

For a moment nothing further was said, then Washakie said to No Arrows, "We will look." Mounting his horse, he rode at a gallop down the meadow toward the crops.

His gaze following Washakie and No Arrows as they rode away, Moroni said to Rolf, "They say Washakie is a fair man, but what will happen when he sees what Hugh did to those men?"

"He might kill 'em," spoke up Rufus. "That man rules with an iron hand, but as far as I know he is a friend of the whites."

Startled, Moroni glanced at the mountain man. "What do you mean 'kill them'?"

"Washakie is a fair man but he don't put up with no nonsense either. Story goes is one 'o his men was a beatin' his woman and Washakie told him to quit. Well, the feller kept it up and the old boy got his rifle and shot the man who was a-beatin' his woman. Kilt him dead. Mostly the Shoshone does what he says and mostly he is purty fair about it."

"The mon doesn't need to be killed," spoke up Hugh, mopping his face with a damp cloth that Melissa had brought him. "I just want him to keep his beasts from me crops."

Using the field glasses Sarah had handed him, Moroni watched as Washakie and No Arrows looked the trampled crops over, then continued toward the small village at the end of the meadow.

Washakie and No Arrows had been gone for nearly a half hour when Rolf pointed and said, "Look, here they come."

Coming at a trot up the meadow, rode Washakie as well as No Arrows with two other warriors leading a half dozen ponies.

Entering the yard, Washakie slipped from his buckskin and walked to Moroni. "I have spoke with the man called Three Hands. He will not bother you anymore and he sends these ponies as payment for the damage he has allowed to happen. Is this fair with you?"

"Well, yes," Moroni stammered. "But please, no payment is

necessary. If Three Hands will just keep his horses from our fields, we can get along fine."

"The horses are necessary," Washakie said evenly. "Three Hands has done wrong and must pay. Just as if you had done wrong, you must pay."

Moroni said graciously, "Thank you. We don't want any trouble."

Standing tall and looking at Moroni, Washakie replied, "We must learn to live together, the whites and the Shoshone. Three Hands is sometimes a bad person and sometimes not. But I have spoken with him and he will be gone in the morning. He knows what will happen if he bothers you anymore."

"I'm just grateful you came by," Sarah said, trying to show gratitude.

His dark eyes on Sarah, Washakie answered, "My people are going to the buffalo country and a day ago a voice inside my head said to come here." Then shrugging, he added, "A leader must listen to things like that."

Noticing Katie, Washakie rested his gaze on her. "She is of my people?"

"Yes," replied Sarah. "We found her after the fight on the Bear River. Her father and mother were killed."

Washakie said nothing for a few moments. Then he asked Katie, "You are happy with the soldier who cannot be killed and his wife, the woman who knows no fear?"

Gravely, Katie nodded her head and replied, "They are my new father and mother. I am loved here."

His gaze going back to Moroni and Sarah, the Shoshone chief nodded once, then shook Moroni's hand again. "If she is loved, that is enough."

Then without another word he mounted his horse and with the two warriors following, he rode down the trail his people had taken.

Watching the Shoshone Chief ride away, Moroni eyed No

Arrows who had stayed. "The soldier who cannot be killed?"

A faint smile on his face, No Arrows shrugged, "You are well known to Washakie. And Sarah also."

"I don't know about 'not being afraid'," said Sarah dryly.

"But it is what you have done when you were afraid is what counts," said No Arrows, his grin spreading wider.

"What will happen now?" asked Moroni.

"Three Hands and his band will move. Perhaps they will go with Washakie to the buffalo country," replied No Arrows.

"I'm just glad Washakie showed up when he did. Things could have been ugly in a hurry," commented Rolf.

Speaking up, Greta said, "Come on, let's get Rufus and No Arrows something to eat and they can tell us what they have seen and where to look for Sam next."

Scratching his stomach, Rufus nodded, "That sounds like a right fine idea."

Chuckling at the old mountain man, Moroni put his arm around his buckskin-clad shoulders and led him toward the cabin.

CHAPTER 19

"My horse is a good horse," Sam said in the Sioux language. He then looked to Bear Man, the young Sioux warrior with the pockmarked face to see if he had said the words right.

"Yes, that is right," answered Bear Man, poking Sam playfully in the chest with his finger. "But I am not sure if that is true. Your roan is the ugliest horse I have ever seen."

Giving his new companion a wry grin, Sam nodded, "That is true, my friend, and he has a bad temper, too."

In the month he had been with the family group of Killed His Horse, the older man of nearly fifty, Sam had not only rapidly learned much of the language, but had become fast friends with all of the Sioux, and especially with Bear Man. In sharing the buffalo he had killed, Sam had unknowingly performed one of the acts that would have proven himself a worthy Sioux warrior: he had shared a kill with those less fortunate than he. It was while feasting on the freshly-killed meat that he watched as a half dozen more Sioux had come out of hiding in a shallow, brush-choked ravine a little way off. And it was obvious from these latest additions that this small group had seen a fight and been the losers. With only seven horses in the group, the three remaining warriors, one of which was Bear Man, were the only ones mounted. At thirteen he could barely be called a warrior, but he was strong enough to pull a bow and so he was called upon by necessity to defend his family. The other four horses pulled travois with the wounded. Later on, after learning a bit of the language, Sam had been told their story:

A week before Sam had met them, they had been traveling to meet another family group when they had been attacked by a raiding party of Crow. At the onset, four warriors, three women and a small child had been killed along with the horses stolen. Retreating into a narrow canyon, Killed His Horse had recovered all of the wounded and led a fighting withdrawal. Several times the stronger party of Crow had nearly overrun the Sioux, but time and time again the older warrior and Bear Man had shot arrows into the lead Crow warriors. Finally tiring of seeing their best men being killed or wounded by the Sioux, the Crow had set fire to the brush that filled the narrow canyon. At first, Bear Man had told Sam they figured they were all going to be rubbed out. But then the wind had shifted and blown back and the fire had died out. When night had fallen, Killed His Horse had crept from the draw and stolen seven horses, then run off the others. "Then came the best part," said Bear Man. Killed His Horse had mounted the best of the horses and after painting himself and singing his war song, he had ridden down to meet the Crow single-handed. After their horses had been stolen and far too many of their best warriors killed or wounded—when they saw the painted and chanting warrior bearing down on them, the Crow had broken and fled.

But in the fight most of the Sioux possessions had been stolen or destroyed. Hungry, with only a few horses and five badly-wounded members, they had seen a rough time until they met Sam.

During the time it took for the wounded to recover, they had taken refuge in Sam's small valley. In the beginning, Sam had been a little nervous. But as he began to learn the language he found the Sioux to be easy to get along with. At first he wondered if they had understood when he had told them he was Gall's adoptive son. And on learning more of their language he was surprised that they had grasped what he told them. Later he told them the story of when he and his mother had first met the warrior known as Gall and the later attack of Horse Ears and his abduction. After hearing his story and seeing the bear claw necklace, the Sioux held him in a different light and he had really become part of their family. He had always thought that many of the Indians were humorless, but the more he got to know Killed His Horse, he found the older man to have a great sense of humor. It seemed as if he was always playing jokes on Bear Man, his son, or one of his two wives, Yellow Woman or Mother Bird.

"How far is it you are going?" asked Sam in Sioux as he worked patiently making more arrows with Bear Man.

"We journey further to where the sun rises. There we will meet others of our band." Softening some sinew with his teeth, Bear Man paused for a moment, then went on. "We were going to the big summer gathering, but the Crow attacked us so now we will be late."

"Won't your friends be worried about you and come looking?"

Eyeing Sam thoughtfully for a moment, Bear Man shook his head, "No."

"But Gall went looking for his sister," Sam said once again trying to understand these people.

Pulling the thin strip of sinew tight on the steel arrow point, Bear Man nodded his head. "Yes, that is true."

Still not satisfied with the answer he had been given, Sam wanted to say more but didn't want to strain the friendship needlessly. Hearing movement, Sam looked up to see Killed His Horse walking next to where Bear Man and he sat working in the shade.

Tall and erect, the older Sioux warrior wore his hair in two braids wrapped in otter fur. A streak of vermillion was painted through the part in his hair and the ever-present grin was formed on the lips as always.

"Ho! The Wolf Chaser and my son work on arrows." This came as a statement and at once, Sam wondered what the warrior was up to.

Seated on a rock, the older warrior pulled out his pipe and filled it. Expertly, Kills His Horse lit the pipe with a flint and steel, and taking a few puffs of the vile mixture, cast an eye at Sam. "I want to ask the Wolf Chaser if he is not worried about his white parents?"

Nodding, Sam replied, "Yes, but I'm not sure where they are or if they are still alive." The image of his mother lying on the ground with blood all around made him nearly choke with emotion, but steeling himself, he went on.

"When Horse Ears attacked, all I saw was Ma laying on the ground and Moroni shooting. I really didn't see much of what happened. I know Moroni killed one of the others but . . ." Shrugging his shoulders Sam trailed off.

His eyes sad and the smile fading from his face, Killed His Horse drew on his pipe then said, "It is a hard thing to lose ones' parents." Then knocking the ashes from his pipe on a rock, he glanced at Bear Man and continued:

"When I was but a young man my father and mother as well as my younger sisters were killed by Pawnee. I was away at the time and when I found out what had happened I went wild in the head. For most of that summer I hunted the Pawnee. I killed many of them. I tell you, Wolf Chaser, it was not a good thing. A black demon lived in my heart and I lived for nothing but to kill Pawnee. Then one night I had a dream, a dream that saved my life as well as my spirit. You see, when a person becomes as I was, they are nearly dead in the spirit and we believe that even when a person's body dies, their spirit lives on. But my spirit was almost dead."

Cleaning the bowl of his pipe with a piece of bone, Killed His Horse shrugged his shoulders, "I will not talk any more of this for it makes my heart sick, but I tell you—do not ever let revenge take over your life."

Looking closely at the older warrior, Sam had never seen this side of Killed His Horse. Not knowing how to reply, he and Bear Man worked in silence for a few minutes, then Sam looked up, "I'm not even sure of how to get home. I know we lived over the Tetons. On the west side, I mean."

His eyes hopeful, Bear Man looked at his father and said, "You can live with us. I have never had a white friend before."

Having heard the horror stories of how fierce and warlike the Sioux were, Sam wasn't sure of how to reply, but Killed His Horse shrugged his shoulders and the old familiar grin came to his face again.

"That is fine with me. I don't know what others will say but Mother Bird says you are already like a son to her, so I guess no one will bother you much."

Sam took Kills His Horse's meaning. Mother Bird, his second and youngest wife, was childless, and besides taking a special liking to Sam, was, in no other words, huge. Standing over six feet tall and with a powerful build, the woman was easily one of the strongest people Sam had ever been around. Unsure of her age, Sam guessed she was about thirty, but she was still graceful. And most of the time, she put up with her husband's jokes and tricks.

Slipping another finished arrow into his quiver, Sam nodded, "I would like living with your people. It would be an honor."

A smile spread all over Killed His Horse's face. He said, "That is good. Tomorrow we will begin traveling again. We are too far west now and I worry that perhaps the Crow will come back."

Smiling back at Killed His Horse, Sam said, "I would be happy to be a part of your family."

Touching Sam on the shoulder lightly, Bear Man said with a smile, "Then you will be as my brother?"

"I guess that will be so," Sam replied.

His eyes brightening, Bear Man said, "I have never had a brother before. We will have great fun. And maybe we can go steal some horses from the Crow!"

Laughing, Killed His Horse shook his head, "Perhaps you both could grow a few more summers. You are only thirteen, now. I would think you could wait a little while." Then seeing the dejected look on his son's face, Killed His Horse added, "We'll see what is provided."

Getting up and shaking his legs, the older warrior said, "We will leave at first light."

Watching his father walk away, Bear Man leaned close to Sam and said, "You'll see. We will have great fun."

Smiling back, Sam hoped so. *But what about Mother and Moroni? Wouldn't they come looking?*

CHAPTER 20

The aspen leaves on the ridge above the cabin were tinted with gold in the predawn light as Moroni, No Arrows and Rufus finished packing their horses. Things had been peaceful since the departure of Three Hands and his band. They had, as Washakie said, left the next morning and hadn't been seen or heard from since. The crops were harvested and the barn was full of cut grass. There should still be at least several months of good weather to search for Sam. Checking the packs on the two packhorses they were taking, Moroni felt a presence behind him. Turning, he saw Sarah standing next to him.

Reaching out, he touched her cheek with his hand. Saying nothing, he looked into her blue eyes and felt a longing. He had to look for Sam before winter set in and sometimes he wondered if Sarah really approved of his going. She kept saying he was still too weak from his wound.

"I have to go, Sarah," he finally whispered.

"I know, but it doesn't make it any easier."

Reaching out, he pulled her close and buried his face in her hair. Breathing in, he closed his eyes and held the picture of her in his mind. Then pulling himself away he brushed at a tear that had started its course down her cheek.

"If I promise to be careful will it make any difference?"

Smiling through the tears that were flowing, Sarah shook her head, "Not really, but don't take any unnecessary risks. Sam is safe where he is. I know it *here*." Saying the last, she touched herself over her heart.

Seeing that No Arrows and Rufus were mounted and waiting, Moroni leaned in and gave Sarah a kiss, "I'll be back."

Then stepping into the saddle of the appaloosa, he urged the horse forward. For several minutes he rode along behind the Shoshone warrior and Rufus. As they began to climb the ridge, he turned and looked back. For a moment he couldn't see her, then his eyes caught her standing next to the pole corral. Standing in the stirrups, he waved and saw her wave back in reply. For several seconds he looked down on his new home and at the woman he so loved. Then, turning, he followed his companions.

* * *

With a start Sarah woke from her dreams. A quick look outside told her from the position of the moon that it was after midnight. Hearing the soft breathing of Charlie in his crib she sat up on her bed and wondered at what she had just seen in her dreams. Or was it a dream? Moroni had been gone for over two weeks now and during that time she had found it hard to sleep. But what of this dream? Going to the window in her bare feet, she looked out at the night sky. The moon shone brightly, casting a silver glow over the yard. All looked so peaceful now. Shivering slightly, she wrapped her arms around herself and thought of her dream. She had seen Sam living with some Indians. It seemed as though she had watched his every move for a whole day. But she could only remember bits and pieces of what happened. And the odd thing was, he seemed happy. How could her son be happy as a captive in an Indian village? Or was he a captive? Her thoughts running away with her, she went back to her bed and wrapped herself in the blankets and quilts. Closing her eyes, she whispered a quiet prayer. Then, as if a light came from the darkness she knew without a doubt she had seen Sam.

Her tears flowing, she whispered aloud, "Thank you, Father."

Wiping at her eyes, she smiled through the tears. She knew now that Sam was all right. With a huge burden lifted from her heart, she closed her eyes and fell into a deep sleep.

* * *

Pausing in the skinning of the elk he had shot, Moroni looked to where his two companions sat on their horses watching for any sign of danger. Shivering in the cold wind, Moroni blew on his hands to get the circulation going and bent to his task again. Placing the hide hair down on the frozen grass, he began cutting large chunks of meat from the carcass and putting them on the hide. The fresh meat would be a welcome addition to their diet. It seemed to Moroni that in the three weeks since they had left his cabin, the three of them had lived on jerked meat, water and nothing else. Even the horses were worn out. It would be good to rest for a few days in what Rufus called *the Bilin's*. Moroni had heard of the Yellowstone country and all of the wonders that were supposed to be here and now he knew they weren't just tall tales. For the better part of the day they had traveled through a strange world of belching geysers, mud pots and hot springs. In the air was the heavy smell of sulfur.

"Injuns won't come here much," Rufus had said. "They think all kinda' evil spirits live here." And now they were going to lay up here for a few days of much needed rest.

Riding his tired horse next to Moroni, No Arrows pointed toward a thick belt of lodgepole pine that separated what he assumed was the Fire Hole River and some cliffs and said, "I am going to find some shelter in there. Rufus is going to look around a bit, then join us."

Without replying, Moroni nodded his head and continued cutting away meat from the elk carcass.

Pulling up the collar of his buffalo-hide coat, Moroni wished he had fur hats like No Arrows and Rufus. The wind was making a cold day bitter and soon it would be night. Weary, he thought of all the traveling they had done, and for

---

what? He guessed it was like Rufus had said: at least they knew where Sam *wasn't*.

Gathering the four corners of the hide, Moroni tied it securely with a piece of rawhide and heaved it up onto the saddle of the stallion. *At least sixty pounds of meat*, Moroni thought. *And after I take this back I'll come get the two hindquarters. That should be enough for a while.* Breathing deeply to catch his breath, Moroni held the hide containing the meat on the saddle for moment. Then with a rope he lashed it down.

Leading the appaloosa into the lodgepole thicket, Moroni smelled wood smoke. A few yards further into the tangle of thin trees. he saw a nest of huge boulders that looked as if a giant had piled them in the center of the belt of timber. It was there that No Arrows had begun to build a shelter. Using dead standing poles, the Shoshone had propped half a dozen of them against a large crack in between two of the boulders. He was now covering the poles with the pack covers and a spare sheet of canvas they had carried with them, creating a snug covering.

Tying the appaloosa next to the shelter, Moroni took the elk meat from the saddle and put it just inside. After pulling the saddle from the tired stallion, Moroni carried his gear inside and plopped down next to the fire. Holding his hands out to the crackling blaze, he looked at No Arrows and tried a tired smile.

"You are tired, my friend," No Arrows said.

Without replying, Moroni nodded. It felt good just to sit here where it was warm and out of the wind. The traveling they had done had taken its toll on him more than the others. Sometimes he still found himself short of breath and at times like this he would become exhausted. Getting to his feet, he went to the packs, and pulled out the battered pot and frying pan to prepare a meal—a real meal with hot biscuits and elk steak. When the thick steaks began sizzling in the pan, Moroni's mouth began to water at the aroma. Feeling a bit better he went on with his preparations as No Arrows brought more dry wood in for the fire.

"Did Rufus say how far he was going to go?" asked Moroni.

Shaking his head, No Arrows replied, "He just said he was going to look around."

"Well, if he doesn't get back here, I'm going to eat all this by myself," said Moroni dryly.

Chuckling, No Arrows slid closer, "It smells good. I had forgotten how good something besides dried meat and pemmican tasted."

Hearing a horse coming through the timber, Moroni peered from the shelter to see Rufus riding into their small campsite. Bundled in his bear-hide coat and a strange-shaped fur hat with a white weasel tail as a tassel, the old mountain man looked cold.

When he saw Moroni and No Arrows at the shelter he said, "Ain't nuthin' out thar but a few critters and they be nigh froze to death. What you got cookin', some o' that elk?"

Unable to keep from laughing, Moroni nodded, "Put your horse up and we'll eat."

Finished with their first real food in days, Moroni and Rufus sat against their saddles in the snug shelter and listened to the wind as it whined around the boulders and rushed through the tops of the pines. No Arrows had insisted on going back for the rest of the elk and had taken the packhorse.

For several moments both were lost in their thoughts. Then Rufus spoke up, "Tell me about your boy. Tell me what he is really like."

Looking at Rufus huddled on a buffalo robe staring into the fire, Moroni asked, "What do you mean?"

Gazing at Moroni, Rufus said, "Nobody has really told me

what the boy is like."

"First, I would like to ask a question," Moroni said. "Why are you helping me?"

Poking another stick into the fire, Rufus answered, "I got my reasons."

Staring at the old mountain man, Moroni prodded, "May I ask why?"

Returning his gaze to the fire, Rufus was quiet for a moment, then said, "When I was about six my folks lived down Texas way. My pa and his brother and their families took land down there. I can't remember much, but one day the Comanche came. Pa and them fought 'em for a while but they were all killed—everybody but me, that is. Well, I was hidin' in what passed for the barn and this big ol' Comanche found me. I figgered I was dead for sure, but he throws me on a horse and away we went." Pausing for a moment, Rufus picked up his coffee cup and refilled it. "I was raised to the age of about fourteen by the Comanche when some rangers hit the village I was in. For all that time I kept hoping someone would come for me ,but all of my family was dead. But I still kept hoping. Well, I see the rangers ridin' in and I went a runnin' toward them and nearly got myself kilt. See, I was brown as any injun and dressed like one, too, and when I see this ol' ranger throwing down on me with his pistol I figgered I was a goner. But I threw up my hands and hollered out, 'I'm Rufus, I'm Rufus.' Well, them rangers was amazed to find me. But they took me back with them. Took me a while tryin to be a white person again but I guess after a few years I had my belly full of the east so I took off. And now here I am. Nothing to show for my efforts, but at least I'm free."

"That's amazing," Moroni said. "Tell me, did the Comanche treat you bad?"

"Nope, that was the odd thing of it. They treated me purty

good. Old Snake Finder—that was the Comanche what took me—was a purty good pa. I went back after a few years looking for him but he had gone under."

"So that is why you are helping me?" asked Moroni.

"That about sums it up," replied Rufus. "I figger I can lend a hand, and believe me, I know what that boy of yours is going through."

"Thank you," said Moroni. " Sarah and I appreciate your help."

Shrugging, Rufus said, "Ain't nuthin'. I got nowhere else to go at the moment."

Hearing the approach of a horse, Moroni looked out to see No Arrows leading the pack horse laden with meat and another figure following him. It was Hawk!

After the packhorse was unloaded and the fire built up, Moroni put several more steaks in the pan and looked across the fire at the strange Indian—if he was in fact an Indian. For as long as Moroni had known the man he never could make up his mind if he was white or Indian. Or was he something else?

Smiling at Moroni and No Arrows, Hawk shivered slightly. "It is cold. I fear winter is coming."

Staring intently at Hawk, Rufus ignored the comment and asked, "Don't I know you?"

Turning his smile to Rufus, Hawk said, "No, I don't believe so."

Showing discomfort, Rufus wiggled around on his robe for a moment, then fell silent.

Moroni was about to ask Hawk if he had seen any sign of Sam when the strange man held up his hand, "I have seen no sign of Samuel, but he is in no danger. You are."

Surprised, Moroni asked, "What do you mean?"

"Here, in this place you are very high up, and a blizzard will come in a very few days. If you don't leave now, you may be trapped."

"But it isn't even October yet . . ." Moroni began.

"You must leave now," Hawk said. "I will lead you."

Moroni was about to comment again when No Arrows cut him off, "The Holy One is right. The elk and the buffalo are leaving this high place. Even the wolves have gone. I think we should leave."

Saying nothing for a few moments, Moroni looked into the eyes of No Arrows. "You are sure?"

Without replying, the Shoshone nodded.

Looking back at Hawk, Moroni asked, "Are you sure about Sam?"

"I feel it is so," Hawk replied.

Weary to the bone, Moroni didn't want to leave this place, but he knew better than to go against the advice of Hawk.

Getting to his feet, Moroni said, "Then I believe we should leave. Now."

CHAPTER 21

The snow was nearly a foot deep now. Looking out into the yard, Sarah couldn't help but worry about Moroni, Sam and all the rest of them. Opening the door of the cabin, she glanced back at Katie sitting near Charlie's crib. A smile on her face, Sarah watched her adopted daughter play with Charlie. It never ceased to amaze Sarah how Katie could capture Charlie's attention. Since his birth they had become attached to each other in a way words could never explain. Walking out onto the porch, Sarah shivered and clutched her coat about her. It would be dark in an hour. Her mind full of fears for her husband and son, she looked to the far ridge and wished for them to come riding down it.

It was barely into October and the storm had hit two days ago. At first it had just been rain here in the valley, but on the mountains, and especially the Tetons, there had been snow. What if Moroni was caught on the other side of the divide? It might be spring before he could get through. Her lower lip held in her teeth, Sarah walked down the length of the wood porch and looked again toward the ridge.

The snow was falling faster now and she couldn't even make out the scattering of aspen at the foot of the ridge, let alone the slope itself. Noticing movement in the barn she could make out the forms of her father and Hugh putting the horses away. Earlier in the day they had ridden out in search of a deer or elk and, Sarah told herself, any sign of Moroni. But they had returned an hour earlier with no game or any word of her husband.

Going down the few steps, Sarah picked up an armful of

split pine and carried it into the house. She had already spent one winter here and she knew that following the snow would come the cold. Bitter cold.

Stacking the wood inside the door, she returned for another armful when she met her father coming in with his arms loaded down with the fragrant pine.

"Why don't you and Katie and Charlie spend the night with us?" asked Rolf, his beard white with snow.

Closing the door behind him, Sarah shook her head, "That's all right, Papa, we'll be fine here."

Nodding, Rolf knew Sarah would never leave her cabin. He knew she would stay up half the night waiting to hear the thump of boots on the board porch—for Moroni to come in.

Heaving a sigh, he asked, "Will you come over for supper?"

Her eyes filled with worry, Sarah replied, "We'll be fine. Don't worry." Then with a crooked smile she added, "Papa, Moroni will be home soon. I know it."

His eyes lowering, Rolf knew better than to argue with his eldest daughter. "If you need anything, just holler."

"I will, Papa." Then leaning forward she kissed him on the cheek and followed him to the door.

When her father was gone, Sarah put on a heavy pair of gloves to protect her from the heat, put several of the chunks of pine in the stove, and began fixing the evening meal for herself and the children. It didn't take much with just the three of them, but tonight she began to prepare much more than usual. Going once more to the small window, she looked out. A real blizzard was underway now. The wind had begun to pile the powdery snow up against the porch. With a pang of fear, she realized the snow could very well be several feet deep on the level by morning.

The evening meal finished, Sarah looked at the extra food and wondered why she had prepared so much. Brushing back her hair, she looked at Charlie asleep in his crib and then over at Katie. Sitting next to the heavy iron stove the little girl was playing quietly with her rag doll. For several moments, Sarah watched Katie as she played.

Katie lifted her head and looked at Sarah, "Mama, I think Papa will come home tonight."

Looking into the dark, serious eyes, Sarah couldn't help but feel that her daughter knew without doubt that Moroni would come back.

"How do you know that?" asked Sarah, going to Katie.

Returning her attention to her doll, Katie replied, "I don't know. I just do."

Running her hands over her daughter's dark tresses, Sarah whispered, "Let's sit for a while."

Getting up, Katie followed Sarah to the rocker. Crawling up on Sarah's lap, Katie pulled a thick quilt up over them.

Gazing at Sarah, the little girl put her hand on Sarah's face and whispered softly, "Mama, I love you."

Hugging Katie close, Sarah replied, "And I love you too."

Wiggling a bit to get herself comfortable, Katie wondered, "Do you think Jesus knows where Sam is tonight?"

"I'm sure he does," replied Sarah, catching her breath.

Sighing deeply, Katie was silent for a moment, then said, "Mama, tell me a story of Jesus."

"All right, which one would you like to hear?"

"The one when he was borned."

A smile on her face, Sarah replied, "That sounds like a good one." Then rocking ever so slightly, she began: "A long time ago in the days of Caesar Augustus . . ."

* * *

Shielding his eyes from the biting snow, Sam followed Bear Man from the shelter of the cottonwoods and toward the village of buffalo-hide lodges that meandered for at least a mile down the shallow river. He and Bear Man had gone exploring early that morning for want of something better to do and were just now returning to the Sioux winter camp. Blinking his eyes at the driving snow, Sam marveled at how far he had come in the last month. Since meeting Bear Man, Killed His Horse, and his family group, he had traveled east with them in search of more of their own people. And during that time, Sam mused, he had become a horse thief. At times he wondered if he had done wrong or if it was just survival. A week after they left his sheltered valley, they had stopped for the night in a low-lying clump of trees that sheltered a small spring. Just before dark, Killed His Horse had gone hunting, hoping to find an elk, buffalo or any other kind of fresh meat. Just as darkness set in, he had returned. The normal huge grin on his face gone, the older warrior had carefully covered the one cooking fire the women had kindled and in a soft voice informed them there just happened to be a camp of about a hundred Crow not over a half mile away. On hearing this, the women began making preparations to leave.

A sly gleam in his eye, Killed His Horse said, "Are we not the greatest of warriors? Are we to sneak away in the night?" Leaning forward, he added, "I think we should sneak in and take some of those fine horses."

At this, Yellow Woman and some of the other women cast doubtful glances at Killed His Horse, but Mother Bird spoke up, "I think that would be a good thing. I am tired of walking and I would like a nice pony to ride even if it is an old runty horse that belonged to a Crow."

The old familiar grin returning to his face, he hastened the women on their way with all of the horses packing their few belongings. Unsure of what course to take, Sam had hesitated. Then Mother Bird had taken the rawhide lead rope of his roan. "I will take care of your buffalo runner until you come back with many more horses." Bending down and taking hold of Sam's shoulder she had added, "Make your mother proud, but be careful."

Following the lead of Killed His Horse, Sam and Bear Man, along with the other two young men of the band, crept near the sleeping village of Indians and made off with nearly every horse in the herd. The only ones they couldn't get to were the war horses tied at the owners' lodges.

When Sam questioned Killed His Horse on this, he had replied with, "They are the best horses in the camp. Their owners do not want them stolen."

Without asking, Sam knew without a doubt the Crow would be after them as soon as they discovered the missing horses. And with a certain amount of dread he knew they would be mounted on the best horses in the village.

Half-filled with the fear of being caught and the other half of him elated with the prank, Sam galloped through the night herding the nearly two hundred horses toward the rendezvous with the women and children. When they met the women, everyone changed to a fresh horse, then pushed on. And on. For two days straight they rode at a lope in an easterly direction hoping to outdistance their pursuers or run into a larger camp of Sioux.

It was on the third day when Bear Man, riding at the front of the galloping herd of horses, circled back and began to whoop and call out. From his spot at the rear of the herd, Sam spotted at least fifty mounted warriors riding toward them at a gallop. His stomach feeling queasy, he pulled his bow from its case and hoped he could at least help hold off the attacking horde, when Killed His Horse rode out to meet the advancing warriors. What was the older warrior going to do? Drive off more than fifty of the enemy all by himself? Then to his astonishment, Killed His Horse began to shake hands and talk with the strangers.

"It is our people!" Shouted Bear Man, riding his jaded horse next to where Sam was staring open-mouthed at the reunion.

Once at the Sioux village, Sam was again surprised. On entering the huge circle of lodges, Bear Man, Killed His Horse, and the other two warriors began shouting out their version of the Great Horse Steal, as they called it. Accompanied by the trilling of the women, the warriors rode around the camp shouting out their songs of bravery. At first, Sam was too astonished to do anything but watch. Then Mother Bird shoved him toward where Killed His Horse and the others were.

"Go with them," she hissed. "You are a great one, too!"

A bashful look on his face, Sam trotted his pony over next to Bear Man, who, upon seeing Sam, shouted out at the top of his lungs, "This is Wolf Chaser. He has stolen war horses of the Crow, too! He fears nothing!"

Still unsure of how to act or what to do, Sam just sat on his pony and stared around with amazement.

Killed His Horse, as the leader, was the one who divided up the horses. To Sam's amazement, Killed His Horse gave him twenty—an equal warrior's share.

Pulling Bear Man aside, Sam asked, "What do I do with twenty horses?"

A wild grin on his face, Bear Man replied, "Anything you want. You are a rich man now."

That had just been the beginning. Sam spent the rest of the fall hunting and learning from his adopted family. He learned more of the language and customs of the Sioux. And he met up with Gall again. On hearing of the big horse steal and the possible retaliatory raid by the Crow, nearly three hundred Sioux warriors from surrounding villages had assembled. Riding out in search of the Crow they found nothing, but curiosity got the best of Gall and several of his companions.

Hearing that a white boy with the name of Wolf Chaser was one of the thieves, they had ridden to the village. There he found Sam along with Bear Man engaged in breaking several of the horses they had taken. Following a tooth-rattling ride on a half-wild paint, Sam pulled his saddle from the horse and turned it back to the huge Sioux herd. Massaging his back, he saw Gall sitting on his war horse grinning at him.

"We meet again!" said Gall in broken English, sliding from his horse and walking to Sam.

In Sioux, Sam replied with, "It is good to see you again, my father."

An eyebrow arched, Gall asked in his language, "How have you come to my people?"

It took all afternoon to bring Gall up to date on what had happened since their last meeting. Shaking his head, Gall expressed amazement, "You are a strong one, Wolf Chaser. You will be a driving force among your people one day."

Sam felt his heart fill with gratitude toward the young warrior, and gave two of his horses to Gall. "You gave much to my real mother and me. I hope these horses will show my thanks."

Before riding the short distance back to his own village, Gall had said, "We will talk again this winter."

What followed was as close to a carefree existence as Sam had ever known. He was free to do whatever he wanted, when he wanted. He and Bear Man hunted, practiced with their bows, raced their horses, and in general had the time of their lives. But in the quiet times at night, he would think of his mother at home. Was she still alive? Did she still think of him or did she believe him dead?

* * *

With a start, Sarah awoke. The fire had died down in the

stove and a chill had come to the room. A soft hiss from the snow outside was the only sound she could hear—with the exception of a pop now and again from the stove. Then she heard it—a thump from outside. The hair on her neck standing up, she quickly stood and clutched Katie to her chest. Then hurriedly, she put her sleeping daughter down on the low bed in the corner and picked up her rifle from the rack. Again she heard a sound from outside near the barn, then a low voice. Was someone stealing the stock? In this storm? Going to a window, she peeked through a firing slit. Nothing . . . nothing but blackness. Then she heard a soft footfall on the wooden porch. Pulling back, she cocked her rifle and stood ready.

A knock sounded on the barred door and a voice called, "Sarah? It's me, Moroni."

Running to the door, Sarah yanked it open. It was her husband! Snow-covered, with dark circles under his eyes and a heavy growth of beard, he tried to smile, "Sorry I'm so late."

The sobs building up in her, Sarah dropped her rifle and threw herself into his arms.

CHAPTER 22

Sliding back his chair, General Connor rose from his desk and walked to peer from the tiny window of his office. Again he would be leading the army against hostile Indians, but this time he would have a much larger force. The war in the east was about through and this would free up troops for his use. From the dispatches he had received, Sherman was cutting a swath through Georgia, and Grant had Lee nearly penned-up in Virginia. It was now only a matter of time and the War Department had, in its wisdom, decided that the depredations on the overland trails to California, Oregon, and other points west by the Indians—the Cheyenne, Sioux and Arapaho in particular—had to stop. It was winter now and he would not again attempt a winter campaign. One reason was that he couldn't gather the necessary forces until summer, and the other was that he had few, if any, guides that knew the area well. Planning the summer's campaign out in his mind he knew the forces he had would be enough. Colonel Nelson Cole would start with his column from Nebraska, and Colonel Samuel Walker would begin at Fort Laramie, as would another force of cavalry led by himself. Counting all three columns, there would be nearly three thousand men. Never had such a force been assembled to go into hostile territory. Surely he would be able to accomplish the task with little or no trouble. After all, he had successfully destroyed a hostile camp of Shoshone on the Bear River not quite two years ago. Rubbing at the frost that had built up on the window pane, Brigadier General Patrick Edward Connor looked out on the parade ground of the post and looked forward to the summer—to summer and the campaign.

* * *

Making his way from the barn to the cabin, Moroni flexed his fingers inside his gloves and worried. He worried about the condition of the livestock as he had only enough grass to feed them half of what they needed. He had hoped to be able to pasture the cattle and horses until at least November. He had not expected winter to come so soon. He, as well as Rufus, No Arrows, and Hawk, had barely made it back over the pass from the Jackson Hole country when the snows began. They had emerged from the canyon of the Snake River in a blinding snowstorm, and for four days the blizzard had not let up. Then it had taken them another five days of brutal travel to make it to his homestead. Arriving home in the middle of the night, they had been nearly dead from exhaustion. Staggering up on the porch he had lifted a hand and knocked on the door. When it opened, there stood Sarah, and in his mind no one had ever looked more like an angel.

For over two months now, his family as well as Rolf's and Hugh's had been holed up in their little valley with the snow piling up and the temperatures bitter cold.

Following his beaten path around the side of the cabin, he filled his arms with cut pine and walked up on the porch. Pausing, he glanced over to his father-in-law's cabin and noticed Hugh was swinging an axe, splitting wood for kindling. Kicking the snow from his boots, Moroni mused to himself that it seemed it was a constant round of work to keep the horses and cattle fed, along with wood cut for the fires, and once in a while, fresh meat for the table. Bumping into the door of the cabin, Moroni pushed the door open and walked into the warmth.

"You look frozen," commented Sarah. She was standing next to the iron stove, heating water for Charlie's bath.

"I feel frozen," replied Moroni, dropping the wood into the box next to the stove. Stamping his boots, he wished for some of the heavy buffalo-hide moccasins that No Arrows and Rufus wore. Absently he wondered how those two were faring. A week after they had returned from the Yellowstone, the old mountain man and No Arrows had gone south toward the main fork of the Snake River with a promise to return in the spring.

Taking off his heavy coat and gloves and hanging them up, Moroni peered over Sarah's shoulder as she bathed Charlie. Kicking and babbling, his son loved bath time. Splashing water all over that part of the room, Charlie howled with delight.

"You!" Sarah growled, wiping at the water that covered her face. Plucking Charlie from the tin tub she began to dry him with a clean towel, much to her young son's disgust.

"He likes the water but doesn't much care for the drying off," Moroni observed with a grin.

"He's a heathen is what he is," Sarah replied.

"He's my brother," said Katie as she came into the room from her snug loft. Pushing her face next to Charlie's as he peeked through the heavy towel, she began to tease him.

Standing back, Moroni marveled at his family, and with a sudden pang remembered there was so much missing. Sam.

Seeing the haunted look come onto her husband's face, Sarah put her arm around him. "It's all right. Remember the dream I told you I had? And what Hawk has told us?"

His eyes still bearing the pain, Moroni nodded, "I know, but I just can't help it." Giving Sarah a gentle squeeze he asked, "Where is Hawk?"

"Gone over to see if he could help Melissa."

And there was another mystery. Since returning from the search for Sam, the strange man had accepted the invitation to stay with Moroni and Sarah for the winter. Moroni had asked Hawk to stay, feeling that he wouldn't, but to everyone's surprise he had accepted. Even though Hawk had been with them for better than two months, Moroni still hadn't been able to really get to know the man. Hawk seemed always gentle and always willing to teach, but he never really answered a direct question.

"So that was why Hugh was out cutting wood like a madman," Moroni said, knowing his brother-in-law was attempting to blow off some steam he was building up over the impending arrival of his first child.

Agreeing, Sarah said, "She is due at any time now, and mother isn't sure about things."

A frown creasing his forehead, Moroni asked, "What do you mean?"

"She just isn't sure things are right. And with the pains Melissa has had, I guess she is pretty worried."

"Perhaps we should go over," Moroni offered.

Thinking for a moment, Sarah finally assented, "Let me get my coat."

Just then a furious pounding sounded at the door.

Hurrying to the door, Moroni opened it to behold Hugh standing on the porch his eyes wild and his beard and hair standing on end. His mouth worked for a few moments before he finally managed, "I'm a father."

Grinning, Moroni slapped him on the back and announced, "Congratulations are in order, then."

"Twice, me thinks," croaked out Hugh.

"Twice?" asked Sarah her voice rising in pitch.

"Aye," managed Hugh. "'Tis a lad and a lass."

Overjoyed with the news, Moroni threw back his head and began to laugh.

* * *

Leaning against the willow backrest inside the buffalo-hide lodge, Sam looked intently at the old Sioux warrior as he told another of the stories for which he was famous. When the weather was bad like it was today there was nothing Sam and Bear Man liked better than to go to the lodge of *Zuya*—Going To War. It seemed when there was nothing to do but hole up in the lodges to wait out yet another winter storm, the lodge of Going To War would be nearly full of young boys wanting to hear a new story from the old man about the spider or another trickster and something good to eat from Going To War's wife. Never had the boys been disappointed. It seemed like the aged warrior always had several new and exciting stories and there was always something good to eat while the story was told.

Letting his mind wander, Sam thought back about what had happened to him over the last few months. It was nothing short of a miracle, really, and at times it felt like a dream. After meeting up with Killed His Horse and then traveling to the larger Sioux and Northern Cheyenne winter camps, he had seemed to slide into the life as if he were born to it. With both Gall and Killed His Horse as adoptive fathers it seemed as if the people of the Sioux and Cheyenne accepted him as just another of them. With one exception, that is, Sam thought with a crooked grin on his face.

It had happened just a week after they had moved into the larger of the winter camps and he and Bear Man along with several other young Sioux boys were racing horses on the flat above the river when three larger boys broke into the races and began to taunt and lash out at Sam with their quirts. Enraged by the teasing, Sam pulled a war club he had fashioned from a stout stick and the lower jaw of the grizzly he had killed and thumped the biggest of the bullies on the skull. Unconscious and blood flowing freely from a cut on the side of his head, the boy named White On The Chin slumped from his pony. The other two boys, howling with fear, fled for the winter camp.

140

"Is he killed?" asked one of the boys, his eyes large with wonder.

Sliding from the back of his horse, Bear Man examined the unconscious boy. "No, he lives."

"His father is an important man," said another of the boys nervously. "Maybe we should leave."

At this, all the boys but Bear Man took off in a cloud of dust racing their ponies for the safety of their own lodges.

Gazing at Bear Man, Sam asked, "What should we do?"

Bear Man pulled at his lower lip with his teeth and replied with some of his father's wit, "Perhaps you should take his scalp."

Glaring at his friend, Sam shook his head, "That would not be good. I think we should go see your father."

His face becoming grave as the wounded White On The Chin began to revive, Bear Man agreed, "Yes, I think that would be good."

Reaching their lodge, the two youths found only Mother Bird. Her eyes narrowed when she heard the tale. She shook her head, "The boy is a bully and his father is worse. There will be trouble." Then, thinking for a moment, she said to Bear Man, "Go find your father."

Seeing the concern come over his best friend and Mother Bird, Sam knew at once he was in danger. Ducking into the lodge, he emerged armed with his bow and lance.

"What are you going to do?" asked Mother Bird, her eyes going to the weapons.

"I'm not going to let anybody punish me for defending myself," replied Sam.

Just then he saw a crowd coming toward the lodge, led by a barrel-chested warrior with a steel belt axe in his hand. Following the warrior with the axe were two other warriors leading a pony with the still-stunned White On His Chin slumped in the saddle.

"You!" shouted the warrior with the axe. "You have attacked my son!"

His chin jutting out, Sam replied, "He attacked me first. I only defended myself."

"You lie!" howled the warrior. "Now you will pay, you little white devil."

Advancing at a menacing walk, the warrior brought himself up short as Sam drew an arrow on his bow.

"Put that down or I will spank you with it!" growled the warrior.

"One more step and I'll put an arrow right through you," gritted Sam trying not to show how afraid he was.

"And if he doesn't, I will," came a voice from off to the side.

Sparing a glance, Sam was relieved to see Gall, along with several members of the *akicita*—or what passed as the camp guards.

Speaking in a calm voice, Gall went on. "Your son is a bully and got what he deserves. You are a bully and will get what you deserve if you don't leave."

His face paling a bit, the warrior looked at Gall and the others. Muttering darkly he grabbed the lead rope of the pony his son was mounted on, and with the others of his party, turned and left.

The next morning White On His Chin's family was gone from the winter camp. When Sam asked why, Killed His Horse just replied, "They were troublemakers. It is best they are gone from here."

Since then, Sam had lived the life of a young man of the Sioux. But he still wondered about his mother. Was she all right? And was the new baby alive and well? And what about Moroni? Was he still searching for him?

CHAPTER 23

Spring at last! Breathing in the fresh prairie air, Sam trotted one of his horses across the greening prairie. The last patches of snow were receding from the slopes of the hills and the first of the spring flowers were beginning to poke their heads through the warm earth. Above him, huge flocks of ducks and geese winged their way overhead with a symphony of sound. The warmth of the spring sun on his bare shoulders felt good and he was eagerly looking forward to warmer weather after the long, dark winter.

Pausing their horses, he and Bear Man looked over the great sweep of the land before them. Sam had learned much and grown immeasurably in the long winter. His normally blond hair was sun-bleached now, and his skin nearly as brown as his companion. Broader in the shoulders, he was able to pull the much more powerful bow Killed His Horse had given him. He was gaining in strength every day.

As hard as that first winter had been with his mother and Moroni, he didn't want to spend another here with the Sioux. The old men of the village agreed that winter had been one of the worst in memory. He had seen hunger and cold, and many of the weaker horses had died. During the long winter nights it had been necessary at times to keep a guard of men and boys over the horse herd to keep the wolves away. One time when he, as well as Bear Man, had been standing guard on a bitterly cold day, a pack of nearly fifty of the hulking grey beasts had attacked the herd. Firing arrows as fast as he could, Sam had killed or maimed a wolf with every shot, but it didn't seem to matter to the survivors. In a matter of a few moments, the wolves had pulled down several horses and only the arrival of a dozen warriors had stopped more horses from being killed. With an involuntary shudder, Sam had heard that a young girl of only five had been killed and eaten right in front of her terrified mother in a Cheyenne village only a day's ride away. What if that had been Katie? A wistful look on his face, Sam thought of his sister and wondered how she was.

"What is it you think about?" asked Bear Man, noticing the far-away look in Sam's eyes.

"My white family," replied Sam.

"You miss them?"

Without replying, Sam nodded.

"Have we not been like a family to you?" asked Bear Man, hoping to cheer Sam up.

A quick smile coming to his face, Sam replied, "Yes, you have, and you are like a brother to me. Killed His Horse is like a father and Mother Bird and Yellow Woman are like my mothers. But I do miss my own mother, father, and sister, and the brother or sister I do not know yet."

For a moment the two sat on their ponies in silence. Then Bear Man said, "I would be sad to see you go."

"And I would feel bad to leave," said Sam. "But I need to find my parents and see if they are all right."

Agreeing with Sam, Bear Man replied, "What you say is right and that is the honorable thing to do." Then puffing out his chest, Bear Man added, "I will ride with you if you wish it."

"That would be kind, but there will be many dangers."

"We have seen danger," said Bear Man proudly. "Have we not stolen horses from the Crow? Have we not killed many wolves when they attacked our horses?" Then getting the same grin his father usually wore on his face, he went on, "Have you not killed one of the great yellow bears? We have nothing to fear."

A faint smile came to Sam's face. He shook his head, "I

don't know about not being afraid. I was plenty scared when that bear came for me, and I know you were scared when we stole all those horses from the Crow."

Grinning bashfully, Bear Man replied, "But it was what we did when we were scared."

"That's what my white father always told me," Sam said, staring off into the west.

"Your father sounds like a wise man."

"Yes," Sam replied. "He is a good man. I guess I never realized it until I began to miss him. He taught me a lot, and Killed His Horse has also taught me many things."

"That is the way of fathers," said Bear Man simply.

Just then one of the young men who had been a friend of Sam and Bear Man came galloping up on his pony. Out of breath, his eyes shone with excitement, "There is war talk. A rider from the Cheyenne to the south has come. He says that there is an army of blue coats coming to fight us."

Staring at each other, Sam and Bear Man turned their horses and galloped them back to the village.

Inside the vast circle of buffalo-hide lodges, life to Sam seemed no different. An exception was the gathering of warriors at the red-topped lodge of Half Moon, where an older man passed as the nominal leader of this band. In the time Sam had lived with the Sioux, he had found out just how simple life with the Indians could—or just how complex.

Just a week after he and his adopted family had rejoined the band, he had asked Killed His Horse who the main chief was.

The older warrior had just shrugged his shoulders and replied that there was no such thing. A person of the Sioux was free to follow whatever man or group of men he wanted, and no one man had the right to tell another what to do or where to go. In the following days, Killed His Horse, with the help of Mother

Bird and Bear Man, had gently taught him in the ways and traditions of the Sioux. Sam found that a man was well thought of if he gave freely of his horses, goods and meat from the hunt. He remembered with some embarrassment that after he had seen Killed His Horse and the others give away most of the horses they had captured, he had decided to do the same. After all, what was he going to do with that many horses? He had given two of the best to Gall, one each to Yellow Woman and Mother Bird, and then, feeling magnanimous, he had given six others to prominent men around the village.

Because of his generosity, Sam's stature within the camp had been elevated, and he had been offered a young girl for a wife. He had noticed that one particular warrior who always seemed to have bad luck was without a good horse. So one day, in generosity and ignorance, he secretly tied two of his horses to this particular warrior's lodge. The next morning the warrior approached Sam and Killed His Horse, wanting to know which of his daughters Sam wanted for a wife. Sam's face turned crimson. Though he had been unable to answer, Killed His Horse explained to the warrior that Sam was just trying to be kind.

At first Sam had been afraid the warrior would be offended that he didn't want either of the girls, but the warrior, whose name was Goose, was a distant relative of Killed His Horse. He laughed and said he had thought Sam was just a little young to be wanting a wife. Then with a good-natured smile on his face, Goose had left, followed by his daughters. But as far as Sam was concerned, the damage was done. The youngest, a slim, dark-eyed girl, a year younger than Sam named Sits In A Row seemed to pay a lot of attention to him after that—so much, in fact, that the boys began to tease him about it. After all, how was he to know that tying horses to a warrior's lodge meant that you wanted one of his daughters for a wife?

146

Stopping their ponies at the lodge, Sam and Bear Man watched the gathering for a moment. Dismounting, they were about to walk over to see what the fuss was about, when Killed His Horse was seen walking back.

Waiting until his father grew closer, Bear Man asked, "What is happening? Are blue coats coming?"

Chuckling and shaking his head, the older warrior replied, "Some of the Hang Around The Forts have come to tell us that a new soldier chief is bringing many soldiers into our country this summer."

Knowing that Killed His Horse was referring to the Sioux who hung around Fort Laramie, Sam wondered why there would be soldiers coming into what he now knew as the Shifting Sands River Place, or what was known to the whites as the Powder River country.

"Did they say why the soldiers are coming?" asked Sam.

"The whites to the south are angry because some of the Cheyenne have been raiding and killing down there. The Hang Around The Forts say that in two or three moons a new soldier chief is coming here to make us all go live near the agencies and the reservations."

Standing on one foot with excitement, Bear Man asked, "What are we going to do, Father?"

"Nothing. The soldiers may come and they may not. The Hang Around the Forts are just wanting favors and trying to create trouble."

Still hoping for some future excitement, Bear Man asked, "If they come, will we fight them?"

His eyes taking on a wise look, Killed His Horse walked to the shady side of his lodge and sat down against a backrest made from woven willows. "Sit, my sons," he said in a low voice.

Knowing another teaching session was about to begin, Sam and Bear Man hurried to sit beside their father.

Moving around to get himself comfortable against the backrest, Killed His Horse motioned to the gathering of Indians. "Why do you think the Hang Around The Forts have come to tell us this news?"

"To warn us," Bear Man replied.

"Why should they warn us?" asked Killed His Horse.

"So we can fight the blue coats when they come into our country," answered Bear Man righteously.

The familiar grin coming back to his face, Killed His Horse said, "My son, those Indians that come from the trader's fort at Laramie only want one thing: they want the white man's goods. They drink the firewater that makes a person crazy. No, my son, they only want us to come and live near the fort so the traders will give them presents." Leaning forward, he looked sideways at Sam, then directly at his son. "The soldiers are white men. Your brother here, Wolf Chaser, is a white man, too. If the white men come to this country and you fight them, are you going to fight Wolf Chaser, also?"

Embarrassed, Bear Man ducked his head. "I am sorry, my father, and I am sorry if I have offended you, too, my brother."

Pushing lightly on Bear Man's shoulder, Sam offered, "It's all right. Let's not worry about it."

His eyes lighting up, Bear Man suggested, "Let's go for a ride."

Bouncing to their feet, the two boys, pushing the possibility of conflict from their minds, gathered bows and quivers of arrows, and headed for their ponies.

CHAPTER 24

Breathing in the warm air and the heavy smell of the freshly-turned earth, Moroni followed the team of mules along as they pulled the harrows over the last of the planted wheat.

It was nearly time . . . time for the search for Sam to begin. Winter was over now and they had more than six acres of fertile bottom land planted to wheat, corn, potatoes, and other foods as well as other grains needed for yet another brutal winter. Wiping at the sheen of perspiration that had formed on his face, Moroni looked over the ground that he, Hugh, and Rolf as well as the women had tilled and planted. It was good. And it was time.

Driving the team of mules into the yard, Moroni noticed Sarah coming from the house. He knew what she wanted—she wanted to come with him on the search. It was odd. Part of him wanted her along, but the rest of him didn't. He didn't want her to have to endure the long hours in the saddle, the weather extremes, the danger and the thousand other things that could and probably would happen; but his heart wanted her along.

Hanging the heavy leather harness in the barn, he heard her soft footstep behind him. Looping the long check lines over the peg in the wall, he waited for her to say something. For several moments he ran his hands over the smooth leather of the harness. Then he turned and looked into her blue eyes, and fell right in.

"I can't take you with me," he mumbled, unable to put his heart into what he was saying.

With the beginning of a smile on her face, she asked, "How can you not?"

His eyes still staring at the dirt floor, Moroni didn't dare look into the blue eyes of his wife again, knowing if he did, he would give into her desire to come with him.

"Moroni, look at me."

Biting at his lower lip, Moroni gazed again into Sarah's eyes. In the depths he saw again the strength that had attracted him to her the first time he laid eyes on her. Reaching out he brushed at her blonde hair that hung loose over her shoulder.

"You're going to make me give in, aren't you?" Moroni asked in a whisper.

Without replying, Sarah nodded.

Again falling into the depths of her blue eyes, Moroni knew there was no way on earth he could leave her again. Pulling her close, Moroni kissed her hair and closed his eyes and let himself go for a moment.

Then pulling back, he held her at arm's length and said, "Sarah it will be hard, and we may not even find him. And what about Charlie? How can you leave him?"

Her eyes large, Sarah replied, "I know we may not find him. But I know he is still alive. Mother has already agreed to take care of Charlie."

Pulling her close again, Moroni said softly, "Are you sure about this?

In response, Sarah pressed her head against his shoulder.

Letting out a sigh, Moroni whispered, "We'll leave in two days.

* * *

Checking the feet of the three horses he planned to use as packhorses, Moroni looked carefully for any sign of weakness. Satisfied that all the horses had sound feet, he straightened and began putting the pack saddles in place. Shivering slightly from the predawn chill, he began to pack the horses with all the supplies they would need for what Moroni felt would be an all-summer search. Rufus and No Arrows had returned the day before and had insisted they go along on the planned trip. Welcoming the addition of two strong men, Moroni had readily agreed, but on further consideration, he had wondered about taking the Shoshone warrior along. They were heading right into the heart of Sioux and Cheyenne country and he wondered if taking the Shoshone along might provoke a fight, as the Shoshone and the Sioux were enemies.

Hearing a soft footfall behind him, Moroni turned expecting to see Sarah, but it was No Arrows.

Noticing the odd expression on his face, Moroni asked, "What is wrong?"

For a moment, his friend stood staring into Moroni's eyes, then said in a low voice, "My friend, I have a feeling."

"What is it?" asked Moroni.

"I fear that you will think I am not your friend and I am a coward."

Taken aback by No Arrows' comment, Moroni asked, "What is wrong, my friend? Don't you know we have come too far together for me to ever think you a coward?"

His face showing a far-off expression, No Arrows said, "I have had a dream, a bad dream that says you will fail in your journey if I go along."

Moroni took his friend by the shoulder. "My friend, I would never doubt your courage or your dreams. The truth is, I have been having bad thoughts about you going along. I, too, wonder if it would be wise for you to accompany us."

"But who would take my place? You will need a strong party to go into Sioux country or the Black Hills."

"I will go."

Turning, Moroni and No Arrows saw Sarah's father, Rolf,

standing in the doorway of the barn.

Beginning to smile, Rolf added, "No Arrows can take my place here and I'll go along. That will keep two strong fighting men here to protect the ranch and three of us plus Sarah to go looking for Sam."

"What about me?" Now Hawk was standing beside Rolf.

What about him, thought Moroni? The unusual man had stayed with them all winter long helping out wherever he could and always teaching, but Moroni hadn't thought of Hawk as an addition to the search party.

His eyes smiling, Hawk asked again, "What about me? I would like to accompany you. Perhaps I could be of some help."

For a moment, Moroni considered questioning Hawks' decision to come. He had never seen the Indian—if that was what he was—carry a weapon of any kind with the exception of the odd knife he always wore. What would happen if there were a fight? Feeling a pang of shame he remembered the long two days and nights he had spent in the winter camp of the Shoshone just before Connor's California troops had very nearly wiped it out. Never in his life had he seen anyone act so calmly under fire the way Hawk had acted.

"You would be most welcome," Moroni said with a smile.

* * *

It was past midday now and Moroni looked back over the small party of people who accompanied him. Right behind him rode Rolf and Rufus. Two of a kind yet so different. His father-in-law was just as wise in the ways of the wilderness as the old mountain man, yet in Rolf there was a deep belief in God that Rufus seemed to be lacking—or was there? At times Rufus would act so hardened as to make a person wonder. Then in the next sentence he would offer something so profound it would make one believe he had studied at the feet of a prophet. Behind them rode Sarah on her paint gelding. Dressed in a divided buckskin skirt and a dark blue shirt she rode as well as any man he had known. Catching her eye, he raised an eyebrow. Flashing him her smile, she gave a slight nod of her head. No, Moroni thought, he would not have to wait on Sarah. She had become nearly as trail-wise as he had. Following the three packhorses laden with food, supplies and trade goods came Hawk. Once he might have doubted the strange man but now Moroni had even more questions. Packing for the journey, he had produced from somewhere an odd-looking bow and a quiver of arrows as well as a short sword made from some of the finest steel Rolf said he had ever seen. Moroni had asked no questions when seeing Hawk armed as he was, but in reply to the unasked questions they all had, Hawk had stated, "I will see this journey through."

Night found Moroni and his group twenty miles north of his homestead. When the stock had been taken care of, he walked back to the secluded campsite Rufus had found nestled back against a sheer cliff. From the camp, looking through the thin screen of pines, he watched the horses cropping at the thick spring grass. Squatting near the small, smokeless fire Sarah had built, he watched as she prepared the evening meal.

At first he had offered to help, but Sarah refused it. "You need to help with the horses and other things. I'll take care of preparing the food."

Watching as Sarah, with practiced motions, quickly prepared food, he was amazed at how she managed to ride as far as they had come today and still have the energy to fix supper.

"Where are Rufus and Father?" she asked without looking up.

"Scouting the trail ahead. Rufus thought there might be a closer pass that may be free of snow."

"Hawk?" she asked.

"Fishing. Would you believe that?" Moroni said, a grin on his face.

"That sounds like what Sam would be doing," Sarah replied.

"It does," agreed Moroni.

For a moment Moroni and Sarah sat in awkward silence, then Moroni said, "We can only do what we can and then put our trust in God."

A tear formed at the corner of her eye and she nodded.

Letting his gaze go to the meadow where the horses grazed, Moroni saw the heads come up on several of them. With rifle in hand, he slipped to the edge of the trees. For several moments he watched the stallion in particular. Then he saw Rufus and his father-in-law ride into the meadow. Casting a glance back to Sarah, he motioned with his hand that all was well, and he walked forward to see what the two had learned.

Resting against his saddle, Moroni pulled his coat more closely around him. There was still a chill in the air, even though it was early summer. Making room for Sarah as she sat next to him and snuggled close, he looked across the flickering fire at Rufus and Rolf.

"If the pass is still snowed in, what is the quickest way over the divide?" asked Moroni.

"We'll have to go a couple of days further north," replied Rufus. "A couple of days' hard ride and we can head east into the Stinking Water country. From there it's straight east for ten days 'fore we git to the Powder. I figger that be where the Sioux should be. Most of them, anyway."

Putting his arm around Sarah, Moroni asked, "Have you ever had anything to do with the Sioux?"

"Yup," replied Rufus.

154

Moroni waited a moment for more, but when nothing came, he asked, "Good or bad?"

"Ain't nuthin' but bad comes from them varmints," Rufus grunted.

Raising an eye at Rolf and Hawk, Moroni decided not to pursue the issue. Instead he asked Hawk, "Do you speak Sioux?"

Nodding, Hawk replied, "Yes, I can get along."

Relieved, Moroni was about to reply when Rufus spoke up, "Heard some news down to Fort Hall. Might concern us."

Noticing the faraway look in Rufus' eyes, Moroni said, "Go on."

"That whole country we be goin' into is going to be hotter than a fry pan. Traders at Fort Hall say some idiot army colonel named Chivington kilt a whole village of Cheyenne down to Sand Crick, and the Cheyenne, Sioux, and Arapaho are out for blood. Some feller says the Cheyenne burnt Julesburg and kilt everybody there."

"This doesn't sound good," replied Rolf, speaking quietly.

"That ain't all," Rufus said. "They also said they made old Pat Connor a general and he's got five thousand troops. And he's goin' into the Powder River country this summer with one thing in mind."

Unable to help himself, Moroni asked, "What might that be?"

"To kill every Indian male over the age of twelve."

With a sharp intake of breath, Sarah asked, "You can't be serious?"

"That be the talk at Fort Hall. Do I believe it? Some of it I reckon is true, but whatever the case we better be a watchin' our scalps or we'll go under for sure."

Staring into the fire, Moroni said quietly but with steel in his voice, "It doesn't matter. I'm still going on." Then looking up at Hawk, he added, "I have to. I'll trust in God and press on."

Holding tightly to his hand, Sarah added, "I'll trust him, too."

After a glance at his wife, Moroni said to the others, "I don't blame any of you if you want to turn back."

"I'll stay," said Rolf with a hard edge to his voice.

"And I," added Hawk.

Gazing from Moroni to Sarah, Rufus bobbed his head, "You ain't leavin' me. Count me in."

"Maybe we should swing down to the army fort at Laramie," said Rolf. "Might be we will hear something useful."

"That's a right likely idea," offered Rufus. "I'm for that."

His eyes moist with tears, Moroni nodded his head, "Thank you. Thank you with all my heart."

Pulling his blanket up over his shoulders, Rufus grunted, "I be turnin' in then. We won't be gitten' much sleep for some time with where we are goin'."

CHAPTER 25

It never ceased to amaze Sam just how quickly the fifty or so lodges of the band of Sioux he lived with could be pulled down and packed for travel. One moment the lodges were standing, and in twenty minutes they were packed on travois or packhorses along with all the other household goods belonging to the families who stood milling about ready for the leaders of the band to start out.

Mounted on a pinto he had kept from the stolen horses of the Crow, Sam waited for some of the other youths to join him and Bear Man. They waited on the fringe of the huge mass of horses, women, children, and dogs who were ready to start out. It was what Sam figured was sometime in July now and throughout the summer, Killed His Horses' band had constantly moved east, away from the Bighorn mountain range. A series of raids by the Crow had cost the Sioux at least a hundred ponies, three warriors and one woman who had apparently been in the wrong place at the wrong time. And now the band was moving even further east. The move was causing discontent among some of the young men who believed that the older men, the leaders, were acting in a cowardly fashion. Several times in the last month bands of warriors had gone in search of camps belonging to the Crow, but none had been successful with the exception of one small band of warriors numbering only ten who had yet to return. Now rumors flew around camp that the small group of warriors had been wiped out, never to return.

Staring west, Sam wondered about his family. Were his mother and Moroni still alive? If they were, why hadn't they

SHOSHONE TRAIL II: HANS' PASS

come for him? Putting away the thoughts of doubt, he shook his head and absently wondered about what had happened to the soldiers who were supposed to be coming. Perhaps Moroni would be coming with them. After all, he had been a soldier in the war in the east, and he did know the general who was leading the soldiers. The Hang Around The Forts seemed to show up every so often to keep the Sioux updated on the progress of the new soldier chief—or the seemingly lack of progress. The last news they had heard was that many of the soldiers didn't want to come into the Powder River country. They wanted to go home now that the war in the east was done. It was just as well. The Sioux were more concerned with fighting the Crow than white soldiers.

Suddenly Sam's thoughts were interrupted by Bear Man. "Do you think some of the warriors will go after the Crow?"

"I don't know," replied Sam, coming back to the present. "Maybe Gall or some of the others will."

"Father says that many of the people are angry. They say we should make a strong war party and go work the Crows over."

Smiling faintly, Sam nodded. He, too, had seen some of the shouting matches of the younger warriors and the older men. At first he had believed the Sioux generally respected their elders, but now with the raids and depredations going unanswered, some of the people in the village were becoming angry.

Not getting a response from Sam, Bear Man went on. "Perhaps we should get a war party up. I know we could get at least twenty of the warriors our age to go."

It took all of Sam's concentration not to laugh at that. *Warriors their age.* They were young boys—what chance would they stand in a real fight with a strong Crow warrior?

"Star Face would be our leader," added Bear Man.

So that was it, Sam thought to himself. Just a week ago a handful of Cheyenne had joined the camp and among them were several warriors and boys who had raided the whites down south along the Platte, and one of the older boys had picked up an old worn-out musket. From somewhere he had found a little powder and ball for it and now he fancied himself a big warrior; when in truth, even as poor a shot as Sam was with a bow, he could shoot much farther and better than someone using the old trade musket could—that is if it didn't blow up.

"What do you think?" asked Sam, letting the excitement of a chance to go on a raid overpower his good sense.

"I think we had better not let Father find out."

"I think so, too. When does Star Face want to leave?"

"Tomorrow night. Each warrior must have a good weapon and extra horse. We will leave as soon as the moon goes down."

So, it was settled, Sam thought. Suppressing a wild grin he wondered faintly if his mother would approve—Sarah or Mother Bird.

* * *

A lump of excitement building in his chest, Sam held the lead ropes of the pinto and the roan as he waited near the clump of pine Star Face had designated as the meeting place for the war party of youths that were going to ride against the Crow. Several times Sam had held doubts about going on this war party, but the fear of being called a coward overcame the fear of getting killed or hurt. Shivering slightly in the chill night air, he looked into the darkness for other members of the raiding party to show up. Around him were grouped at least twenty-five young men, the oldest not yet fifteen.

Just a few feet away, he could hear Star Face, the Cheyenne youth, boasting of his encounter with the whites. "It was easy. The three white men just stood there begging for their lives while we killed them with our clubs."

"Did you kill one of them?" asked an unseen youth, his voice filled with excitement.

Fumbling with his words, Sam heard Star Face answer, "No, but I touched one of them as he was dying and I have his fine rifle."

In the darkness, Sam was able to hide the smile that played around his mouth. He absentmindedly wondered what would happen if the Cheyenne boy were to come face to face with a soldier armed with a good gun or a full-grown Crow warrior looking for another scalp for his collection. Then with a sudden clarity of mind Sam knew what was going to happen. He had seen in his mind a vision of some of these young men lying dead. Shaking his head as if to clear the vision, Sam did his best to sweep the horrible scene from his mind. Mounting the roan, he, along with Bear Man, followed the lead youths into the darkness and toward the west.

CHAPTER 26

Standing erect, his face turning crimson, Brigadier General Patrick E. Connor nearly let loose his temper. He was faced with yet another setback in the expedition that should have begun more than a month ago. First it was rain, rain, and more rain that slowed the supply wagons. Then it was no supplies, then it was poor or nonexistent horses for the cavalry, and now mutiny. Several of the regiments raised for service in the Civil War were refusing to march from Fort Leavenworth. In anger he had telegraphed the commander of the district to use "grape and canister" to get the troops under control. Turning from his desk, he popped a fist into his palm and wondered what else could go wrong. In the spring the paper strength of his combined three columns would have exceeded five thousand men. Now his force alone would be less than a thousand, and that included a large force of Omaha and Pawnee scouts. Gritting his teeth, Connor exited his office and strode briskly out onto the packed dirt of the Fort Laramie parade ground.

On seeing his commander come from the headquarters building, Lieutenant Oscar Jewitt saluted and asked, "What may I help you with, sir?"

Pondering his young aide's question for a moment, General Connor cast an eye to the north and asked, "Has there been any word from Colonel Cole in Nebraska?"

"No sir," replied Jewitt. "Ah, sir we believe the telegraph lines are down again."

Turning to eye his young aide, Connor considered this for a moment. The telegraph lines were one of the main reasons he had the number of troops he did. And detailing them out in small groups was becoming counterproductive. Too many times the lines had been cut. And everytime a repair party had been sent out, they not only found the section of downed line, but they found the troops who were supposed to be guarding that section of line slaughtered. Dealing with Brigham and the Mormons was childs' play compared with the mess he was looking at here, Connor mused. Looking out over the wide plain next to the buildings of the fort, he could see the white tents of his command waiting to leave on the expedition. But not all were ready. Just then he saw a dusty group of horsemen ride onto the parade ground and toward the store. For a moment he thought he recognized the lone woman of the group. With her long, blonde hair tied back with a leather thong, and her divided buckskin skirt, she reminded him of a woman he had met several winters ago. A very strong woman, who for some reason had touched him deeply. Shaking his head, he turned back to his quarters. No, it couldn't be.

* * *

Gripping the saddle of her horse, Sarah looked at the log building that passed for a general store at Laramie. Massaging the small of her back, she wondered absently if there were a place she could take a bath. But then, staring at the groups of idle soldiers standing about, she put that thought from her mind. Hot and tired, she wondered if they could possibly hear anything from some of the army scouts that would do them any good. On the ride east they had stopped at several Indian villages and asked for news of a white boy, but none of the Shoshone or the single band of Sioux they had talked to could tell them anything. Looking over at Moroni, she swung down from her horse and swiped at the dust layering her skirt.

Motioning at the long log building that housed the post trader and store, Moroni asked Sarah, "Is there anything you need from here?"

A grimace on her face, Sarah replied, "I can't imagine what. See what kind of information you can scrape up, and we can be gone."

Moroni knew how she felt. During their travels east they had been constantly warned about going into Sioux and Cheyenne country, and the Powder River country in particular. The Indians were seething since the massacre of over a hundred Cheyenne women and children last winter. And now, from what he could tell, the army was going after the Indians in force. Rows and rows of white canvas tents covered the flat next to the post. Long lines of picketed horses and mules and at least a hundred supply wagons were assembled. With a practiced eye, Moroni figured there were at least fifteen hundred soldiers. But would it be enough? And would the Sioux stand and fight?

"I wonder if that bunch o' half-wits can find the Powder let alone a camp of Sioux?" was Moroni's next question asked out loud by Rufus as he whipped at the trail dust with his beat-up hat.

"I figger I can find the Powder," came a voice from the shade of the store awning.

Squinting, Rufus grunted and said, "Wal', if it ain't Blanket Bridger. What you doin' here, guidin' for the sojer boys?"

"That's right," replied the legendary mountain man.

"Wal' that do count," said Rufus. "At least they won't git lost with you along."

"I'll take that as a compliment, Rufus Ordoway," Bridger commented. He got up from his chair and walked over to Rufus with his hand out.

Taking Bridger's hand, Rufus nodded at Moroni, Sarah and Rolf, "These be my friends. Son 'o theirs was took by a young Sioux a year ago. Heard any word of a youngn' about twelve with blond hair livin' with the Sioux?"

His eyes narrowing, Bridger asked, "You ain't goin' up into

the Powder River country, are you?"

"We are," answered Sarah.

Taking Sarah in with his eyes, the tall, gaunt Bridger rubbed a finger and thumb over the rough fabric of his cloth jacket. Looking back to Rufus, he asked, "Rufus, are you tired of livin'?"

A faint grin on his face, Rufus replied, "I didn't think I was."

"Remember what happened the last time you crossed the Bighorns? You nigh unto lost your hair. You go up into that country right now and you'll go under for certain. The Cheyenne be out for blood and the Sioux be just as mad right now. Why, I'd sooner go after a grizzly with a willer than . . ."

"You be gittin' mighty windy," Rufus interrupted. "Now can you tell me if you heerd of any white youngens?"

Pursing his lips, Bridger eyed Sarah for a moment. "The boy yours?"

"Yes," she replied, with a flat expression on her face.

"Tell you what," Bridger began. "I'll go see a couple of the Laramie Loafers I know. They just got back from the Black Hills. I'll see what they have to say."

"Laramie Loafers?" asked Moroni, a puzzled look on his face.

Chuckling a bit, Bridger answered the question. "They's the tame Sioux. The ones that hang around the fort here. The wild Sioux call 'em the Hang Around The Forts. They go back and forth tradin' information, goods, and most likely, guns and powder."

Nodding, Moroni watched the mountain man walk off toward where he had seen several dozen tepees pitched.

"What now?" asked Sarah.

"Let's rest a mite and wait 'til Bridger gits back," said Rufus.

"Sounds good to me," said Rolf, speaking for the first time.

Putting his arm around Sarah, Moroni guided her to the shade of the awning. "Come on, we can wait here."

Trying to smile, she nodded, "I guess we can wait just a bit more."

* * *

The sun was slipping below the horizon when Bridger returned with a short Indian man with a hideous scar where his left eye used to be. Sitting on the log porch, Bridger nodded at Rufus, "This here is Sinks, he might have some news for you."

His good eye staring deadpan at Moroni, he held out his hand.

"I figger the son wants a present," said Rufus softly.

Going to one of the pack horses, Moroni pulled out two skinning knives and a packet of brightly-colored beads. Handing them to the Indian, he said to Bridger, "Tell him that if his information pleases me, I'll give him more."

Nodding to Moroni, Bridger spoke several sentences to the warrior.

Cocking his head to one side for a moment, Sinks talked rapidly back to Bridger, then looked with his one good eye at Moroni.

"You people be all tired of livin," grumped Bridger.

"What did he say?" asked Sarah.

When his gray eyes turned to Sarah, Bridger shook his head. "Missy, this here feller says he's seen a white boy all right. About the right age too."

"Where?"

"Up on the Tongue River camped with a feller named Killed His Horse." Then, wiping at his forehead and looking glum he added, "You go up there and you'll lose your scalps."

"We'll go, but I don't know about losing our scalps," said Moroni, handing the Sioux a red blanket. "Killed His Horse, you said?"

"'At's right," said Bridger mournfully. "Why can't you just wait until Connor gets his troops together and go along with us?"

Swinging aboard the appaloosa, Moroni replied, "I'd just as soon go it alone. Last time I ended up in a battle between Indians and soldiers I nearly got killed."

As the others mounted their tired horses, Bridger noticed the strange-looking Indian. *Well, at least they got a guide with them,* he thought to himself. Then looking toward the post headquarters he had a sudden thought: *If Connor gets his men together they just might get started before the snow comes.* Digging the toe of his boot into the ground he had another ugly thought: *We don't want to be riding around on those northern plains in winter. Connor had better get his act together and quick.*

CHAPTER 27

To Sam, this adventure was looking more like a bad dream. For the first few days of the journey with the war party—if it could be called that—things went smoothly and as planned. But now the group of young warriors was experiencing difficulty. In an effort to outdistance the group of older warriors sure to be following them with the intent of bringing them back home, the young warriors had pushed their horses at breakneck speed. Now the grueling pace was beginning to tell on both the horses and the boys. All of the boys had been instructed to bring two horses along so they might switch horses when one became tired. But many of the youngsters had not chosen their mounts with as much care as necessary. Half of them were down to one horse. And two of the boys had just become horseless as their remaining horse had become lame.

Fuming, Star Face looked around at the dejected-looking group of young warriors. "How is it many of you are without a war horse?"

Standing in the shade of a squat pine, Bear Man glanced at Sam. "He is angry with us, but look at his horse. The one he is riding is about done in. And his other was left behind last night."

Without replying, Sam nodded and wondered what was going to happen next. He had fared better than most of the other boys, as his roan—even though it was in all probability the ugliest horse along—had suffered far less than any of the others. The pinto, even though a little foot-sore from the pace, was still able to keep up.

"If you had been fighting the white soldiers, as I have, with the horses you have brought, we would all have been killed by now," added the Cheyenne youth.

Now one of the Sioux boys spoke up. "Your horses are no better than ours. I think all of your talk of fighting white soldiers is hot wind."

His face darkening, Star Face glowered at the one who had spoken up.

Hoping to diffuse the situation, Bear Man offered, "Let us rest until night. Then we can push on. A short rest will help our horses."

"If we rest, our fathers will catch us and give us a whipping," said Star Face.

"If we don't, and try to fight a bunch of Crows on tired horses, we will be dead," Sam said. "We can live through a whipping from our fathers but you can't survive getting killed."

Sam's comment caused snickers and giggles through the small band of boys clustered in the grove of pines.

His face turning crimson, Star Face made as if to make a comment, but then ducked his head when one of his Cheyenne friends supported Sam's comment. "The white one is right. We need to rest."

Stifling a curse, Star Face glared at his friend, then said, "We will rest until dark."

* * *

Pushing on in the moonlight, Sam began to have a sick feeling in his stomach once more. Riding the tough little roan, he kept pace alongside Bear Man and wondered what was to come. Was he turning into a wild Sioux warrior? He was a horse thief, that was for sure. And from the stories he'd been told, he knew the whites hanged horse thieves. But here among the Sioux, being a good horse thief was to be respected—that, along with being a good hunter and a fierce warrior. Well, he was a fair hunter and now here he was riding along through the night intending on raiding some sleeping Crow village with the full intent of killing and scalping another human being. He knew Moroni had killed other men in the war, and afterward in defense of himself and his mother. And his mother had even killed that ugly old mountain man that had bought Gall's sister. But that was different. It was in defense of one's life or the lives of others. Now he was the one riding into the night with the intent of causing other people harm. These and a hundred other questions ran through his mind as he rode along with the group into the darkness.

* * *

Sarah woke with a start and threw the blanket from her. Sitting up, she wrapped her arms around her knees and began to shake.

Feeling Sarah sit up, Moroni wiped at his eyes, leaned up, and put his hand on her shoulder. Whispering, he asked, "Is everything all right?"

Staring around the dark campsite nestled in a juniper-choked draw, Sarah whispered back, "It's Sam."

Coming fully awake, Moroni pulled Sarah close to his chest and asked, "What is it?"

"He's in danger."

Knowing that Sarah possessed a strong intuition for what her son was doing, Moroni didn't question her dreams or her knowledge of what might be happening to Sam.

Holding Sarah tight, Moroni remained silent and let his own thoughts run. It had been a week since they had left Laramie, and during that time they had lived on the edge. Riding into the country claimed by the Sioux, they hadn't dared to build a fire to cook with. And instead of traveling along the trails, they had instead ridden slowly and carefully through the roughest country, hoping to avoid all contact with the roving war parties that were said to be coming down from the north.

A silver sliver of moonlight streamed down through the trees, lighting the campsite. There Moroni could see the sleeping forms of Rolf and Rufus along with the picketed horses. Staring at the empty blankets belonging to Hawk, he wondered for a moment where the man was, then spotted him standing next to the horses. Running his hands over the animals' faces and necks, he seemed to be talking to them. Turning, he saw that Sarah and Moroni were awake. On cat feet he walked to them and sat down.

"You are troubled." Hawk's words came more as a statement than a question.

Nodding, Sarah whispered, "Sam is in danger."

"A mother's intuition is very strong," Hawk agreed. Then a faint smile flickering on his own face, he added, "My own mother always seemed to know when I was about to get into trouble. It seemed she would always know what I was going to do before I did it."

Her eyes lighting up, Sarah replied, "I know what you mean."

"And now you know how *your* mother felt," Hawk said.

A smile coming, Sarah nodded, "Yes, I suppose so."

"We fathers are not blessed with this gift," Hawk said in response.

His curiosity aroused, Moroni asked, "You have never talked about your family. If you don't mind me asking, where are they?"

At his question, Moroni and Sarah saw a soft, faraway look come into the strange man's blue eyes. Brushing at a smudge of dirt on his buckskin trousers, Hawk sighed. "I have a wonderful family."

Unable to control her own curiosity, Sarah asked, "Where are they? I would like to meet them."

A gentle smile coming over his face, Hawk said, "You will

get to meet them, Sarah, but it will be some time, I am afraid. For now they are far from us."

"But why?" Sarah asked, leaning forward. "Surely you miss them. Why don't you bring them to our homestead? There is land enough for all."

A sad smile came to Hawk's face. He replied, "Sarah, my daughter, my family has left this mortal life. My wife, sons and daughters have been gone for many years."

Taken aback, Sarah felt sorry for her pressing questions. "I am sorry, I had no idea . . ."

"It is all right," Hawk interrupted. "Remember what Christ has promised, and what he died for. Remember, Sarah, if we live righteously we will have eternal life and spend the eternities with our loved ones."

For several minutes they sat in the clear night air in silence. Then Moroni, unable to restrain his questions any longer, asked, "Hawk, who are you really?"

"Who am I?" Hawk began. "I am but a man, and in my poor way I do my best to smooth the way for others as my brethren have done."

More mystified by Hawk's answer than before, Moroni arched an eyebrow at the man, but said nothing.

Seeing that Moroni and Sarah were still curious, Hawk smiled gently and asked, "Would it make any difference if I told you my real name?"

Surprised by Hawk's question, Moroni paused, "I don't know. But it might answer some of my questions."

"Would it make it any easier for you to follow any advice I may give?"

"What do you mean?" asked Moroni.

"The children of men are given the word of God, not only the scriptures, but from living prophets. And even then, God's word is ignored, or worse, corrupted. Would it make any difference if you knew my real identity?"

Holding Sarah close, Moroni shook his head, "No, I suppose not. I guess my curiosity just gets the best of me at times."

"Everything will turn out for the best if you but choose the right," Hawk said gently.

"I am sorry if we have hurt your feelings," Sarah offered. Then, taking Moroni's hand, she went on. "Moroni, I'm sorry for waking you and upsetting you."

Smiling at his wife, Moroni shook his head, "Hawk is right. We just have to have faith."

Seeing the love in the eyes of both Moroni and Sarah, Hawk was prompted to add more, "Know this, brother Moroni: I was once much like you are. Once I was called to defend my people against tyranny and evil, and as much as I hated it, I was compelled to kill in defense of freedom." Then, his eyes burning with an intensity that neither Sarah nor Moroni had seen before, he added, "Always remember this: Never seek revenge or strike out at your enemy first, but fight with the fury of righteousness when your God, religion and freedom or your wives and children are threatened."

His eyes filled with understanding, Moroni nodded and replied, "Yes, I understand now."

"It is enough," Hawk said. "Now we must rest. There is still much to do and a long way to travel."

CHAPTER 28

Progress at last! Riding at the head and to the upwind side of the long column of cavalry, infantry, supply wagons and artillery, Brigadier Patrick Edward Connor stared into the distance. There on the horizon he could just make out the blue and purple peaks belonging to the Bighorn range. Still chafing from the delays and now his inability to stay in contact with the other two columns that would form the jaws of his trap to sweep all of the Indians out of the wide expanse of country between the Black Hills and the Bighorns, Connor resisted the urge to lash out at his subordinates. Spurring his horse up to the crest of a low ridge, his eyes swept the layout of the country before him.

Turning to the group of men beside him, Connor looked them over. He had, besides the soldiers in his command, a group of Pawnee scouts commanded by Captain Luther North, and a small company of Omaha and Winnebago Indians under a Captain Nash. These he sincerely hoped would be of great value to his plan. The Pawnee scouts were recommended highly by other army commanders who had used them before. And he knew the Pawnee and the Cheyennes well—as the Sioux were the bitterest of enemies. This bit of information would work to his advantage when it came to the fighting.

Motioning to Captain North, he asked, "Where, in your opinion, are the hostiles at this time?"

Riding closer to Connor, North, a tall, spare man with dark hair and mustache, waved in the general direction of the Powder, "Somewhere up there, General."

"When we find them, we will punish them," stated Connor.

"Yes sir," replied North, shifting uncomfortably on his horse.

Looking off into the distance, Connor said nothing.

"You gotta' find them first," said North, hoping to educate the general. "My Pawnee figger they might not want a fight with this big a bunch of soldiers. The Sioux and Cheyenne might just disappear."

"And if they don't?"

"Then you got a fight on your hands."

"Which we will win, of course," stated Connor with conviction.

"Yes sir."

His eyes going to North, Connor said, "You don't believe we can whip the hostiles?"

"It depends on if you find a small camp or if they are in one of their big summer camps."

Staring incredulously at Captain North, Connor asked, "Surely you can't doubt that this column alone isn't capable of defeating the whole of the Sioux nation?"

Nervously looking at Captain Nash and the other scouts, North said carefully, "General, my boys have been fighting the Sioux and the Cheyenne for a lot of years. My boys are telling me there might be upwards of three or four thousand warriors up there along the Powder and the Tongue Rivers."

His eyes widening, Connor shook his head, "That's impossible. There aren't that many Indians left in the whole country."

Meeting Connor's level gaze once more, North shrugged his shoulders, "Suit yourself, General, my Pawnee scouts will trail along and do their part whatever comes."

Still feeling stung by the comments of Captain North, General Connor looked once more toward the north. *Now*, he thought to himself, *where are the hostiles?*

* * *

Hidden in a dry, brush-choked wash not half a mile from a large camp of Crow Indians, Sam and his companions stared at each other and did their best not to show their fear. They had ridden into the draw in the middle of the night and at daylight the group had discovered the camp of at least a hundred lodges on the flat below the hiding place. Now they were trapped. Due to the lay of the land there was no way for the group of young warriors to move without being seen by someone in the village. That is, if they were not discovered first. All morning, part of the herd of several hundred horses had began grazing closer and closer to where the draw emptied out onto the plain where the village lay. And with the horses were several dozen boys whose job was to watch the horses throughout the day. Watching the horses grow closer and closer, Sam wondered if the best thing to do was to try and make a break for it, taking along as many of the horses as possible. But scattered around the village were the war horses of the warriors tied at their owners' lodges. Squinting his eyes at the memory, Sam remembered what had happened the last time they had raided a camp of the Crow.

Leaning close to Sam, Bear Man whispered, "I think our leader is going to make a try for the horse herd."

Agreeing, Sam responded, "I think so, too. But remember what happened last time?"

Bear Man remembered well what had happened. They had slipped away in the darkness with plenty of time to switch to fresh horses. Now, if they stampeded the horses right in plain view of the camp, the Crow warriors would be right behind them offering no chance for the boys to switch to a fresh horse.

Feeling sick to his stomach, Sam watched as Star Face began to talk quietly to some of the young warriors around him. Gesturing toward the vast herd of grazing horses, the young Cheyenne was probably telling the rest of the boys how easy it was going to be to wait until the horses were just a little closer. Then with a whoop they could stampede them off and over the ridge. What he wasn't telling them was that the warriors from the village would be right after them with one thing in mind: vengeance.

It was later in the afternoon now, and Sam wiped at the sweat forming on his back and neck. Star Face had made it known not an hour before, that as soon as the Crow's horse herd had grazed next to the white rock at the mouth of the draw he was going to sweep down and gather as many horses as he could and make a run for it. Swallowing against his thirst, Sam knew he had tried some crazy stunts in his short life, but nothing like what they were about to attempt in the next few minutes. Watching Star Face as he stared down toward the white outcropping of rock, Sam wondered if he would die in the next several hours. A glance at the sun told him that darkness was still at least four hours off. Could they stay ahead of the Crow that long? In the darkness could they lose their pursuers? A gray mare had just walked next to the white rock and was staring intently up into the draw. Had she seen or smelled the horses belonging to the raiding party? Sam knew in his heart that their hiding place would be discovered any time now. Swallowing against the fear that began to build, he glanced at Bear Man. In his friend's eyes he saw fear there also.

"We have to stick together," Sam whispered.

Bear Man began to reply but was cut off by the wild whoop of Star Face. Then, as one, the raiding party swept down toward the horse herd and the few Crow youths who were still standing watch.

Whacking the roan with his strung bow, Sam watched as the huge herd of horses lunged into a run up the wide valley.

Shouting a wild cry of his own, he saw several of the Crow boys standing open-mouthed as they watched their horses go thundering away. Hearing a thump, Sam saw smoke drift away from Star Face. The youth had tried a shot at one of the fleeing boys. Now his gun was empty. Did the Cheyenne know how to reload from the back of a running horse? Just then, one of the young horse guards popped up out of the grass beside Sam and began to run for safety. Gripping his bow, Sam thought for a fleeting instant about trying a shot, but then he swerved the roan and brought him up behind the running, terrified youth. Whooping, Sam slapped the boy on the crown of his head with his hand as he went by. That would suffice, he thought to himself, as he joined Bear Man in the wild ride behind the thundering herd of stolen horses.

Running their horses hard for the first few miles, Sam dropped toward the rear of the herd, where once out of the dust he could glance back. Pausing the roan just for a second, his heart fell. There, not more than a mile back, he spotted a clump of horsemen following—the warriors from the Crow camp! Whipping the roan around he rode hard next to where Bear Man was riding.

Beside his friend he shouted, "The Crow are following."

His teeth bared in a grimace, Bear Man nodded, then shouted back. "We have lost some of the horses, and some of ours are growing weak."

With a look of disgust, Sam could see that most of the young men were whipping the last of the strength from their worn-out mounts. Then a horse went down, spilling its youthful rider. Scrambling to his feet, the young warrior reached for one of the horses galloping by, but missed. Trying again, the boy managed a hold onto the mane of one of the last horses. Pulling himself up on the back of the running horse,

Sam knew the boy had lost his bow and was now armed with only a knife. Shaking his head in disgust, Sam knew that no matter how the boys were armed it would be a short fight against the older, more experienced Crow warriors.

Sweat streaked the sides of the roan now, and Sam wondered how much more the horse had to give. But so far the runty animal was still running smoothly. Many of the horses in the stolen herd began to tire and drop out, and Sam watched in disgust as several of the youths tried to push the flagging animals back into the running herd. Didn't they realize there were at least a hundred Crow warriors behind them bent on revenge? Shouting at Bear Man to follow, Sam urged the roan forward, next to where Star Face was riding.

Drawing near to the Cheyenne youth, Sam leaned over and shouted above the thunder of the horse hooves, "The Crow, they are following!"

Glaring at Sam, Star Face made no comment for a moment. Then shouting back at Sam he replied, "We can fight them!"

A look of amazement on his face, Sam made no reply. Did Star Face really think they could fight better than a hundred of the best warriors of the Crow?

Yelling back, Sam tried to talk some sense into the boy, "There are more than a hundred!"

In reply, Star Face threw Sam a look of disgust and pulled his pony to a stop. As he flew past the Cheyenne, Sam saw he was attempting to load his old musket.

Looking over at Bear Man, Sam shouted, "What should we do?"

"Run!" shouted his friend back. "The Crow are right behind us!"

Then as if to punctuate his remark, a high scream was heard from the rear of the thundering horse herd.

His eyes wide, Sam didn't need Bear Man to tell him what

had happened. One of their companions had been killed by the pursuing Crow. With a sick feeling in his stomach, he knew it was a matter of time before they were all brought down. What could he do? What would Moroni do? Once, Moroni told him of the fight at Shilo and how many of the men had panicked and ran, but that several of the regiments had stood fast and fought until they nearly ran out of ammunition. Then slowly they had fallen back thus giving the reinforcements time to arrive. The only thing was, there would be no help coming. No blue columns of cavalry, no flags waving. Nothing. And right now, Sam would have settled for a mob of howling Sioux to stream over the far pine-topped ridge still several miles distant. Then in his mind he knew what had to be. His teeth gritted, Sam knew it had to be done or none would survive.

Pulling the roan around he shouted at Bear Man, "Gather as many as you can! We will shoot at the Crow and try and keep them back."

In the whirling dust and the running horses, Sam and Bear Man were finally able to collect half a dozen of the boys from the raiding party. Sparing a glance behind them, Sam could see that the Crow were about to overtake another of the boys who had fallen behind. Shouting, Sam told them what he wanted them to do: "Stay just ahead of the Crow and when they draw near, shoot at them and try and hold them off from the rest. And above all, stay together and don't get split up." Fear clouding their eyes, but with a set to their jaws, the young warriors dropped back to the trailing end of the horse herd. Along the way they had picked up several more young men. And now all that stood between the galloping herd and the weaker of the boys were ten boys determined to hold off the Crow for as long as possible.

Looking over at the Cheyenne youth who was Star Face's friend, Sam called, "Where is Star Face?"

A look of horror and dismay on his face, the youth pointed with his bow at a crowd of Crow warriors several hundred yards to the rear, swarming over a body on the ground. Averting his eyes for a moment, Sam pulled himself together and wondered if in the next few moments they would all meet the same fate.

Shaking the scene off, Sam motioned to the other young warriors. And bringing their horses to a slow lope, they watched for the Crow to begin their charge again.

His bow held in his left hand, Sam watched as the mass of enemy warriors started for them. Shouting to the Sioux boys to stay in a rough line, he motioned for the boys to keep themselves between the fleeing horse herd and the rest of the youths. Closer the Crow came. Hearing the shouts and war cries, Sam's blood nearly turned to ice. But steeling himself, he prepared his bow and quiver of arrows.

A thud and a blossom of smoke shot out from the war party of Crows. They had a gun. From what he could tell, the Crow were mostly armed with clubs and axes. *Had they, in their haste, picked up whatever weapons were handy? Or were they so confident as warriors that they figured bows and guns weren't needed to wipe out this band of boys? Was it the old gun that Star Face had owned?*

Just then two more shots came from the Crow. A grimace on his face, Sam looked to see if any of the boys had been hit. Luckily, none had. Shouting a war cry, Bear Man waved his lance, taunting the Crow. The enemy warriors pushed toward the young Sioux warriors. An arrow ready on his bow, Sam watched for his chance. Closer a Crow warrior came, then just as Sam pulled his arrow back the older warrior dropped to the opposite side of his horse. For a moment Sam held his fire, but then Moroni's words came to him: "Best way to stop a cavalry charge is to shoot the horses. They are a lot easier to hit than a man and it does the job." Pulling the arrow back he fired the arrow and watched as it sailed into the horse's shoulder. Stumbling, the horse spilled head-over-heels, throwing the rider. A grim look of satisfaction on his face, Sam shot another arrow into the horse of another charging enemy warrior. Again the horse went down in a cloud of dust, crushing the howling warrior. Now the other boys, seeing what Sam was doing, began to shoot the horses of the charging Crow warriors. A dozen horses were down before the Crow warriors, shouting in anger, drew back a bit. Following the fleeing herd of horses and the few weaker Sioux boys, Sam counted the arrows left in his quiver. Ten. Sparing a glance at the sun, he wondered how much longer the fight would last. *Would the Crow leave?* No, here they came again.

Calling to Bear Man, Sam said, "Here they come! How many arrows do you have left?"

"Not enough!" shouted Bear Man.

Then the friend of the now-dead Star Face rode next to him. "We shouldn't be shooting their horses," he complained.

His mouth agape with astonishment, Sam managed to reply, "Would you rather be dead? This is not a fight for glory, we are fighting for our lives!"

The young Cheyenne knew Sam was right, but it went against his pride to kill the horses and without fighting for glory and honor.

Sam wanted to explain himself further, but the Crow were upon them again. Shooting two more horses with four arrows, the Crow again drew back, but not as far this time. Now Sam knew they would wait for darkness and then they would finish it. Closer now to the pine-covered ridge, Sam wondered what lay over it. *Would there be a place to hide? Or was there just more open country? Perhaps that was what the Crow were doing now, just biding their time.*

CHAPTER 29

From their hiding spot in a brush and pine-choked draw they watched the activity of the sprawled out Indian camp below them. As far as Moroni could see, on both sides of the small river there were circles of buffalo-hide lodges. He had stopped counting at two hundred.

"They be Sioux," whispered Rufus, lying on his stomach next to him.

"What do you think?" asked Moroni.

"I think we'll lose our hair if we go down there."

Glancing over at Sarah, Moroni raised an eyebrow.

"I think it's worth a try," she said softly.

A grim expression on his face, Rufus said in a low voice, "Look Sarah, that feller Gall probably ain't down there and these Sioux don't care one whit if Gall figgers you are a Sacred Woman. I already seen one blue coat what was probably took off some dead soldier boy, and see that lodge there? The one with the red buffler painted on it? That be the scalp of a white woman hanging from the shield in front of the lodge."

Her blue eyes pleading with Moroni, Sarah said, "I feel we can do it."

Pursing his lips and blowing, Rufus muttered, "It's your scalp."

Riding their horses from the cover of the draw, Moroni knew by the actions of the Indians in the village that their party had been spotted immediately. At least a dozen mounted warriors armed with bows, clubs and lances galloped their horses toward them. Women rushed about, herding their smaller children into the safety of the lodges, while older men and boys watched with curious eyes.

Drawing up in front of Moroni, Sarah, and the others, the warriors stared at them with dark, expressionless faces.

For a moment no one said anything then Moroni held out his hand and said, "We come as friends."

The foremost of the warriors, a broad shouldered man with a white scar across his nose stared hard at Moroni. Then looking closer at Hawk he said in broken English, "You ghost man. Why you come here?"

Speaking in Sioux, Hawk answered, "We come as friends. My sister the Sacred Woman seeks her son who was stolen one year ago."

The scar-faced warrior narrowed his eyes, "Why do you come with a soldier chief and other warriors? Do you bring us bad luck?"

"I do not bring anything bad. We only search for a lost one."

A scowl on his face, the scar-faced warrior sighed and said, "Come, you will speak with the Big Bellies."

Leading off, the warrior and the others grouped themselves around Moroni, Sarah and the rest. For a moment, Moroni wondered if it was an honor guard, until Rufus leaned close, "That scar-faced feller ain't too happy with us. He's takin' us to talk with the Big Bellies. They are sorta' like the camp chiefs."

"I didn't know you spoke Sioux," Moroni said in a quiet voice.

A strained expression on his face, Rufus swallowed hard and muttered, "I speak it all right."

Studying Rufus, Moroni wondered why he was acting so oddly. Was something in his past haunting him? Pushing the questions from his mind, Moroni looked ahead to where the warriors were taking them. Riding their horses across the shallow river, the armed warriors guided Moroni and his companions toward an awning made from brush. There, sitting on blankets and buffalo robes, were several older men.

Drawing near, the scar-faced warrior slipped from the back of his horse, strutted to the awning, and spoke several sentences to the group of older warriors. One of the men glanced at Moroni and his party for a moment, then said something to the scar-faced one. Stiffening slightly the warrior cast a glance at the older man. Then he walked back to Hawk.

The scar-faced warrior's eyes glanced toward each one in the party, in a rough voice he said, "Big Elk and the others will speak to you."

"Well, that be something," muttered Rufus under his breath as he dropped to the ground beside his horse.

Stealing a glance at the scar-faced warrior, Moroni waited for a reaction, but the warrior stood stone-faced next to his own horse.

Seeing several young Indian boys who looked to be about Sam's age, Moroni had a sudden spark of inspiration. Going to one of the packhorses, he opened a pannier and pulled out several steel skinning knives. Approaching the four boys he held them out. "You are strong young boys who look like they could use a good knife. Please accept them as gifts. All I ask in return is that you watch our horses while we speak with your chiefs."

Puzzled, the boys stood staring at Moroni until Rufus translated Moroni's word into Sioux.

Surprise showed on the faces of the boys as they gravely took the knives from Moroni. Then with solemn looks they gathered the lead ropes of the horses and stood quietly.

Turning back to where the others stood, Moroni took Sarah's hand and ducked under the brush awning.

"You shore know how to work 'em boy," commented Rufus as he stood at Moroni's elbow.

Glancing at the mountain man, Moroni offered no reply. But Rufus went on.

"Them horses are safe now. You got them young'ns honor-bound to help you and their pride demands they guard them horses with their lives."

Saying nothing, Moroni faced the five older warriors who had stood from their seats as Moroni and the others walked under the awning. Old and wrinkled, the men looked to be in their sixties, at least. All of them bore scars of some sort or another and their long braids that fell over their chests were mostly gray. But in their eyes sparkled life and wisdom. Then one called out to the scar-faced warrior in Sioux.

Looking carefully out of the corner of his eye at Rufus, Moroni saw him blanch and hold his breath. Then the mountain man whispered a translation. "The old warrior there, Big Elk is his name, just cussed old Scar-face there for not gettin' us some robes to sit on. Asked him if he war a slinkin' Pawnee to treat guests the way he was treatin' us."

Soon several robes were brought and placed on the ground under the awning. Once Moroni, Sarah and the others were seated, Big Elk motioned with one hand at Hawk and spoke several sentences in Sioux.

Translating, Rufus spoke softly to Moroni. "Big Elk wants to know what we are doing coming into their country with an army of white soldiers not far behind us. He also wants to know why we bring a woman with hair of gold along."

Now Hawk was speaking back to the old chief. Once again translating, Rufus went on. "Hawk says we don't want anything to do with the soldiers. We are only looking for the Sacred Woman's son who was stolen last year, and that the Sacred Woman is a friend of Gall as is her son and husband."

At the last, several of the older warriors murmured to each other. Once again Big Elk began speaking to Hawk. Rufus translated to Moroni and Sarah. "The old feller says he can see that Sarah be a Holy Woman and he feels she will be the mother of a great people someday. But he has not heard of a white boy among his people. He also says that Gall's bunch is further north along the Tongue or the Rosebud Rivers."

Gripping Sarah's hand, Moroni whispered, "Don't worry, there is still hope."

Now Hawk was speaking again with Rufus whispering the translation. "Hawk says many thanks for helping us. He says he hopes the Sioux prosper and that they find many buffalo this year." Pausing for a moment, Rufus began to translate Big Elk's reply, "He says he hopes we have a safe journey and we find the lost boy. But he can't answer for what other bands of the Sioux and Cheyenne might do. They are very angry about the big massacre down at Sand Creek last winter."

Leaning over, Moroni whispered to Rolf, who had sat in silence during the talk, "Will you get some goods from the packs? I don't think it would hurt."

Nodding, Rolf got up and walked to one of the pack horses, then took out an armload of gifts. There was brightly colored ribbon, beads and brass tacks along with several more knives and some heavy needles. Passing these items out between the older men and some of the other Sioux warriors, women and older children, he was rewarded with smiles and looks of pleasure. Stopping last at the scar-faced warrior who had brought them into the village, Rolf offered him a skinning knife. Taking it, the scar-faced warrior dropped it in the dirt, then turning on his heel, stalked away.

"Oh, that be bad medicine, it surely is," said Rufus softly.

"What do you mean?" asked Sarah.

"That scar-faced old son refused Rolf's gift and now he ain't bound to abide by any agreement the older warriors made."

"In other words," Moroni said. "As soon as we leave here, he will come after us."

186

"Yup," observed Rufus sourly.

Moroni's gaze returning to Big Elk and the other older warriors, he was aware they were pleased with the gifts. And with cordial nods they walked with Moroni and the others to their horses.

As Sarah took the lead rope from the Sioux youth who had been watching her horse, the slim dark-eyed boy put his hand on her arm and said something softly in Sioux. Looking at Hawk, she asked with questioning eyes.

A warm look on his face, Hawk said to Sarah, "The boy says he has heard of a white boy that lives with a warrior called Killed His Horse. He also says that the white boy has the same color of hair as the Holy Woman. That is all he has heard."

Her eyes filling with tears, Sarah put her hand on the boy's slender shoulder, "Thank you so much."

Seeming embarrassed, the boy turned and left with his companions.

Casting a glance at the sun, Rufus said, "We can be twenty miles away by dark if we push."

Knowing the mountain man wanted to be as far away as possible from the scar-faced warrior, Moroni agreed, "Let's ride."

Once out of the Sioux village, Moroni kept watch for any sign that they were being followed. Nothing yet . . . but then riding at a run out of the village came at least fifty horsemen. Reaching for his rifle, Moroni was stopped by Hawk. "Wait, let us see who it is."

As the riders came closer he could make out their features. It was the young men who had watched their horses while they talked with the old warriors, and it looked like they had brought along a bunch of their companions. Riding closer, they formed a rough circle around Moroni and his party.

"What are they doing?" asked Sarah, catching Hawk's eye.

A faint smile came to his face as he spoke to the youth who had givin Sarah the scanty information about the white boy. Looking directly at Sarah, the boy replied in Sioux.

Also looking at Sarah, his smile growing, Hawk replied, "Curly Buffalo says he and his friends will ride along with us to protect us—for a while, that is."

Getting the meaning, Sarah smiled at the youth and wondered how much the scar-faced one would dislike being put down by the older warriors as well as the boys. The corners of her mouth turning down she was afraid they all just might find out.

CHAPTER 30

Sam could sense the roan beginning to weaken under him now. It had been a long, hot day and soon it would be finished. *In more ways than one*, Sam thought to himself. Unless there was a miracle waiting to happen, the Crow were going to kill him and the rest of his friends within the next few moments. Taking a quick count of the arrows he had left, he saw four remaining. A glance at the other boys showed they were in the same shape with the exception of one who had none, and there were also three boys fewer than at the start of the running battle. They had fallen to arrows or bullets.

Slapping the roan with his bow, Sam tried to coax more from the horse. But it was useless. The little animal was about played out and would soon be running on heart alone. Feeling the ground beginning to slope upward, Sam wished they could make it to the cover of the pines, but again the Crow urged their horses forward. A grim expression on his face, Sam was thankful that at least the Crow were even shorter of arrows and rifle ammunition than the boys were. The enemy warriors had fired their bows and muskets at first but due to their haste in trying to overtake the stolen horses, they had apparently left their village without collecting most of their weapons. In fact, during the long chase, he had seen several dozen of the Crow warriors with nothing more than a knife or a war club.

Feeling the roan stumble, Sam pulled the horse's head up and put an arrow to his bow. Drawing the feathered end to his ear he released and watched the arrow thud into the chest of a howling warrior who was about to club down one youth whose horse had fallen with exhaustion. Seeing the dying warrior clutch at the feathered end of the arrow and roll from his horse, Sam bit at his lip. First a horse thief, and now he was a murderer. His stomach rolled. He wondered if he deserved to die.

Turning the roan to go and try to rescue the running boy who was vainly trying to outdistance the nearest Crow, Sam was relieved to see Bear Man swerve down to the youth. Holding an arm out, Bear Man intended for the boy to grab onto him and thus he would pick the boy up and put him behind on his pony. Lunging for Bear Man's arm, the boy grasped his hand, but the pony was either too tired, or it lost its footing, for it went down under the added weight. His heart in his throat, Sam knew there was no one else close enough to help, so he urged the roan down the slope toward his friend. Throwing himself from the roan, he grabbed Bear Man's shoulder and pulled him to his feet.

Stark terror in his eyes, the other boy gawked at the charging enemy warriors and began his death wail.

Roughly shaking the boy, Sam shouted in his face, "Courage! We must not just lie down and die!"

But the boy continued to wail. His mouth dry, Sam pulled the last three arrows from his quiver and prepared to defend himself when Bear Man shouted, "My bow is broken!"

His stomach tight with fear, Sam aimed at the nearest of the Crow and loosed an arrow. Wobbling slightly, the shaft sunk into the thigh of the screaming warrior, causing a howl of a different tenor. Then to Sam's astonishment the rest of the enemy warriors whirled their horses around and began a hasty retreat. Hearing the thundering sound of hooves, Sam stared wide-eyed. At least a hundred painted and well-armed Sioux warriors streamed behind him through the pines and over the hill, charging directly at the fleeing Crow. Feeling faint, his knees gave out and he plopped to the ground. Hearing Bear

Man howl with delight, Sam could only shake his head.

Regaining his feet, Sam heard his name called. It was Gall!

Galloping his painted war horse next to Sam, Gall grinned through the vermillion on his face, "You were badly outnumbered, my friend!"

Unable to voice a reply, Sam only nodded and watched as Gall galloped off in pursuit of the Crow.

Feeling a hand on his arm, Sam looked around to see several more of the young warriors of his party staring at him. Smiles began to appear on their faces.

"You are a strong leader," said one.

Another pointed to Sam and stated, "The Wolf Chaser is our war leader now. Star Face made bad choices and is dead."

At this, the surviving Sioux boys began a war chant.

Looking around at his friend Bear Man, Sam grimaced and eyed him. All he got in response was a grin.

Riding alongside Gall on the way back to the Sioux villages, Sam's mind was in turmoil. *Was he a murderer now?* He knew the man he had shot with the arrow probably didn't survive. And from the fresh scalps the returning warriors bore, he knew there would be wailing in many of the Crow lodges tonight. Gall and the other warriors had killed at least twenty of the Crow and were now congratulating themselves on a good fight where none of them had been killed and only two slightly wounded. And the horse herd! The boys had managed to keep nearly three hundred horses together and with the scalps and horses the expedition was deemed a success. But there were seven fewer boys to make the ride home. *Was it worth it?* Sam didn't think so. He had had enough of the raiding life. He wanted nothing more than to find out if his mother was still alive.

"We will call this the fight where the boys killed the enemy's horses," said Gall, a fierce grin on his face.

Glumly, Sam said nothing, but stared straight ahead, still thinking about what had happened. *What was happening to him? What would happen to him?*

"Wolf Chaser," said Bear Man riding next to him. "Do you think our fathers will be proud?"

Heaving a sigh, Sam shrugged his shoulders, "It is possible. But what about the fathers of those who have fallen?"

Noticing the sadness in Sam's eyes, Bear Man replied, "We will sing of their bravery and they will know their sons died gloriously."

Seeing Sam was deep in thought, Bear Man fell quiet. But Gall, feeling what Sam was going through, spoke up. "My son, you feel sadness for the loss of many friends. I know how you feel, for I, too, have lost companions in battle and in accidents. It is the way of life and we cannot do anything about it. You were led by and followed a young warrior who was not wise. He did not make sure you were well-prepared for the raid and did not have two horses that would stand up to the trail. And he made unwise decisions and did not have scouts out to find the village of the Crow." Taking a deep breath, Gall went on. "But you have learned much. You have learned from your mistakes." His dark eyes penetrated to Sam's core as he finished with, "You have also learned the most important lesson of all: sacrifice. You were preparing to give your life so that your friend Bear Man and the others could escape. That, my son, is the most important lesson of all. How to give of yourself. That is what makes a boy into a man."

For several moments they rode on in silence. His mind in a whirl, Sam knew what Gall had said was true. But still, how could he explain away the theft of the horses and the certain death of the man he had shot? These questions and a hundred others were suddenly thrust from his mind by a shout from near the head of the group of warriors.

Looking ahead, Sam sighted two warriors running their horses toward the returning mounted warriors.

"Something has happened," Gall muttered, urging his horse into a run to meet the warriors. Galloping along with Gall, Sam could hear and see the looks and sounds of concern between them. Halting at the front of the group, Gall waited for the two to ride up. Reining up in a cloud of dust, the first of the two scouts threw out a hand to Gall in greeting and announced, "There has been trouble. A camp of the Arapaho have been attacked by the blue coats. It was the camp of Black Bear on the Tongue. There are many killed, at least fifty, and most of the horses are stolen."

His eyes narrowing, Gall cast a glance back. "We will ride."

CHAPTER 31

He had the Indians on the run again, but this time there would be no complete victory as there had been at Bear River. Standing in the stirrups of his saddle, General Connor looked at the progress his cavalry and the detachment of Pawnee scouts had made through the Arapaho village. His men had taken over the village and now were driving the fleeing Indians up Wolf Creek through the scattered timber and brush. Looking around the captured village, Connor viewed the crumpled forms of warriors as well as women and a few children. A grimace on his face, he had again wished for none of the children to be harmed as well as the women, but he knew what had happened. In the heat of the battle his men couldn't or wouldn't separate the warriors from the women and children. Just ahead the rifle fire was again picking up. It was time to press on.

"Looks like Black Bear and his boys are making a stand, General."

Turning to the speaker, Connor eyed Jim Bridger, the legendary mountain man.

"How do you know it's Black Bear?"

Working his jaws around the ever-present chew of tobacco, Bridger spit and replied, "I know 'cuz I recognized his lodge."

Wondering if Bridger really knew what he was talking about, Connor studied several of the Arapaho dead. Seeing they had been scalped, he turned to a nearby officer, "I gave the order that none of this was to take place."

His face turning red, the officer began to answer, but Bridger interrupted, "General, the Pawnee did it."

Grinding his teeth together, Connor knew that word of the

scalping of Arapaho dead would get out and he didn't want the eastern press to crucify him the way they had Colonel Chivington after the Sand Creek massacre. But it served the idiot right. One did not make war in the manner Chivington had, and there would be no mutilation of the dead if he could help it. True, he had given the order that if any male Indian over the age of twelve resisted they were to be killed—but certainly not cut up like a side of meat.

"Jewitt!" Connor called out his aide's name.

"Yes sir," said the lieutenant weakly.

Staring at the young soldier sitting slumped in the saddle, Connor couldn't believe his eyes, "You're wounded!"

The man looked pale as death under the sunburn.

"See the surgeon!" said Connor. Then, turning to Bridger, he said with the voice of command, "Find Captain North. Tell him there will be no more mutilation of the dead. I'll push ahead with the cavalry and we'll see if we can perhaps corner this Black Bear."

Watching Connor ride off, Jim Bridger, known to the Indians as Blanket, watched in amazement. Then, shaking his head, he turned his horse toward the last spot he had seen the commander of the Pawnee.

* * *

The Arapaho known as Black Bear watched as the blue-coated soldiers prepared once more to chase his warriors, who formed the rear guard for the fleeing women and children. Calling out to a knot of warriors armed with bows and mounted on good horses, the Arapaho chief suddenly felt a knot of sorrow well up in his chest. Sitting slumped on a horse being led up out of the creek bottoms, he recognized the form of his oldest son. Racing his horse down to the three warriors who were helping the young warrior stay in the crude saddle, he hoped the wound was not serious.

"Is it bad?" He asked the older of the warriors.

The warrior didn't reply in words but with the stricken look on his face.

Gently Black Bear helped his son to the ground, and there he could see the frothy blood bubble from his chest. A wail of anguish escaped the chief's lips as he watched the life ebb from his son's body.

After a few moments of grief, Black Bear stood and smeared some of the blood on his face. With his rifle in his hand, he looked to the gathered warriors. "Come, we must defend the weak ones."

Rallying the warriors, the Arapaho chief had them race toward the blue coats and sting them with their arrows, then race away on their faster ponies. For now he didn't have to worry about the Pawnee. They were content to make off with more than half of the horses belonging to the Arapaho. In disgust, Black Bear knew his warriors could drive off or kill the Pawnee if not for the presence of the soldiers. It seemed they had become the mercenary of the white man, and what bothered him even more was that the sworn friend of the Arapaho and most of the other Indian tribes, Blanket Bridger was fighting for the blue coats.

Taking a deep breath and putting the grief and fear aside, Black Bear looked to task at hand, which was to somehow save his people from disaster.

* * *

Arriving back at the Sioux village, Sam sensed there was a change. When seeing him on the raiding parties' triumphant return, several of the people he knew and recognized turned away from him.

"What has happened?" He asked Gall, feeling somehow hurt.

For a few paces, Gall said nothing. Then he stopped his horse and pulled Sam off to the side. Looking into Sam's face, he said, "We need to talk, my son."

Nodding, Sam followed Gall away from the beginnings of

the celebration. With Bear Man, they rode quickly to the lodge of Killed His Horse. Slipping from the horses, they ducked inside. Somehow knowing the talk was going to be of a serious nature, Mother Bird and Yellow Woman left the lodge. Once seated against his favorite willow backrest, Killed His Horse sighed and looked at Gall. "It has begun?"

Nodding sadly, Gall replied, "It has. What have you heard from the village of Black Bear?"

"The white soldiers along with some Pawnee attacked them three days ago. Many lives were lost."

Nervous, Sam asked, "What does this have to do with me?"

The normal smile gone from his lips, Killed His Horse leaned close to Sam and held out his arm, "What do you see, my son?"

Not sure what he was getting at, Sam shrugged and replied, "Your arm."

"Is my arm any different from yours?"

Shrugging again, Sam answered, "Just bigger."

With a smile returning to Killed His Horse's face, he looked at Gall, "If we could only look at things that way." Then to Sam he said, "My son, you do not see it but there is a difference. There is a difference in color, and some people, white and red, try to tell others what to do. The whites have told us we must live on a certain piece of ground. That is not the way we live. So the whites come to make war on us. Now that it has happened, some of my people will look on you as the enemy."

"But I have done nothing to harm you or the people," Sam protested.

"What you say is true," Gall said. "Let me ask you a hard question. When your first father was killed by the Blackfoot, did you not hate and fear all Indians?"

"But that was different," Sam replied. "That was before I knew you. Now I know that there are good people everywhere."

Seeing the direction the conversation was going, Bear Man

asked with emotion in his voice, "Are there people in this village saying bad things about my brother, Wolf Chaser?"

His eyes resting on his son, who sat with his fists balled in anger, Killed His Horse said, "There have been a few who have made comments."

"Tell me who and I will speak with them!" Bear Man said hotly.

"My son," Killed His Horse began. "You know how it is. There are some people in this band who gossip like a bunch of old women. And now they point their tongues at Wolf Chaser because he has white skin."

"It's not fair!" said Bear Man, nearly coming to his feet.

Realizing what was happening, Sam bowed his head, "I am afraid it is time for me to leave."

"It is for your safety," Killed His Horse said gently. "We are afraid that some hothead might try a shot at you while your back is turned."

"I would kill them!" Howled Bear Man, his voice choked with emotion.

"But Wolf Chaser would still be dead," Gall replied evenly.

"I will leave in the morning," Sam said quietly.

"I will go with you," announced Bear Man, emotion choking his voice.

Feeling emotions of his own welling up inside of him, Sam shook his head, "Bear Man, you are like a brother to me. But your place is here with your family."

Now Gall spoke, "I will ride with Wolf Chaser as will some of my men. We will travel further south and hope we don't meet up with the Crow or Shoshone."

With a questioning look on his face, Killed His Horse asked, "I thought you were going to lead your men against the white soldiers?"

A flicker of a smile on his face, Gall replied, "There are some things more important than fighting. I will see Wolf Chaser home."

CHAPTER 32

Thunder rumbled off to the east among the western peaks of the Black Hills as Moroni slipped from his perch among some rocks and walked quietly down through the grass to check on the horses. Yawning, he walked softly among the tethered animals and tried to keep awake and alert. It had been over a week since they had left the Sioux camp of Big Elk. And during that time he had felt more like a hunted animal than anything else. Gradually they had made their way in a northern direction hoping for a way to find the camp where the warrior known as Killed His Horse lived or, even better, Gall. But the countryside they had passed through was filled with roving parties of Sioux and Cheyenne warriors and hunters. And Rufus was worried they were getting too far to the west.

Shivering in the cold night air, Moroni wondered at the weather changes, too. The past few days had been almost unseasonably cold. And to the east there had been some severe-looking storms. Moving quietly through the night, Moroni glanced at the protected campsite Rolf had found among some boulders. There he could see the sleeping forms of Sarah and the rest. All was quiet so far, but in the last few days they hadn't been able to make a fire for fear of attracting unwanted attention.

Yawning again, Moroni wiggled his way into his lookout once more and placed a sharp rock under him. The rock would serve to keep him awake, an old trick he had learned from old Sergeant O'Toole. A faint smile on his lips, Moroni wondered how the old veteran was. In all probability still kicking up a fuss, teaching another young officer how to stay alive.

His rifle in his hands, Moroni let his eyes and ears do the searching, and his nose as well. Once again he became part of the night.

* * *

A day after leaving the Sioux village, Sam, Gall and the four warriors riding with them met up with a large band of Sioux warriors.

Stopping to talk, Gall asked the leader of the band what had happened with the fighting so far.

The leader of the band, an especially fierce-looking warrior wearing a splendid-looking eagle feather bonnet replied, "The blue coats are working their way down the Powder now. Some warriors led by Stands Looking Back, Red Leaf and others, had stolen some of the soldiers' horses and killed a few of the soldiers and now they were moving south. The blue coats are afraid, added the leader, and Red Leaf says that the soldier horses are worn out and not much good, but it was great fun harassing the blue coats. With excitement in his eyes the warrior wanted to know if Gall would join up with them and attack the soldiers.

"No," replied Gall. "We are looking for some Pawnee scouts that are with the soldiers."

A look of concern on his face, the warrior said, "Yes, there were some Pawnee with the blue coats that attacked the Arapaho, but Stands Looking Back didn't say anything about Pawnee being with the soldiers he was having fun with."

"Then there are more groups of soldiers in the country than we thought," mused Gall.

"We should be looking out for the Pawnee," replied the warrior with the eagle-feather bonnet.

"You are right," answered Gall. Pulling his horse around, he waved at the leader, "We wish you luck."

"And to you," replied the warrior as he led his men off in search of the soldiers.

After riding for a few minutes, Sam asked, "That is not good, is it?"

"What is that?" replied Gall.

"The Pawnee."

"No," answered Gall. "It would seem the Pawnee have sold themselves to the white men, and now they are brave enough to come into our country with the blue coats."

For a few moments they rode in silence. Finally Gall added, "I should have told you sooner, but some of the Pawnee attacked a small group of Cheyenne earlier this summer and killed them all. Even the mother of Charlie Bent."

Sam knew who Gall was talking about. Charlie was the son of a Cheyenne woman and William Bent and had always tried to keep peace between the Cheyenne and the whites. But now it was said that Charlie had taken up the war club. Now he knew why.

"We should look for shelter," commented one of the warriors, interrupting Sam's thoughts. Looking toward where the warrior was pointing, Sam as well as the others could see the black clouds building over the northern horizon.

Gall wanted to keep traveling, to get away from the white men and their Pawnee scouts. But one look at the storm coming, and he knew they had better find cover and fast.

An hour after they had found shelter in a low cave hidden by a thick grove of aspen, the wind came. Ducking inside the cave, Gall dropped an armload of firewood near the small blaze and squatted near Sam.

"It will be an ice storm," Gall said over the howling of the wind.

One glance outside and Sam believed his mentor without a doubt. He could see white crystals being driven by the wind already stripping leaves from the aspen.

"Will the horses be safe?" Sam asked, concern in his voice.

A shrug of his shoulders and Gall replied, "Safer than out in the open. But I have seen hail and ice storms kill horses and other animals." Then noticing the concern on Sam's face, he patted him on the shoulder. "Do not worry, we are safe here and we have a warm fire. There may be others out there who are not as lucky."

* * *

What Gall had said was true. The morning after the ice and sleet storm they found the two missing columns of soldiers under Colonels Cole and Walker in dire straights. Their two columns had come together not more than two weeks before, and since that time they had been constantly harassed by the Sioux and Cheyenne. And now there had been an early sleet storm. They had lost some horses and mules to the Indians. And due to the shortage of feed for the horses, many had become weak and nearly useless. Some of the soldiers couldn't even get them to move. And now, looking at the ice-covered beasts, Colonel Nelson Cole knew he was in trouble. Less than a quarter of his men still had a mount to carry them, and the mules used for pulling the nearly-empty supply wagons were in no better shape. Throughout the camp he heard the sharp bark of pistol shots as the men killed the animals that were unable to ride.

His hands clasped behind his back, he peered out from under the canvas awning and asked Colonel Walker, who was sipping the last of the coffee from a tin cup, "Sam, do you have any idea where we are? And where in blazes Connor is?"

"I've no idea to the last question but my scouts tell me we are still on the lower Powder River," replied Colonel Walker.

"Your scouts are no more familiar with this country than mine are," Cole said acidly. "I'm afraid Connor is the only one who has reliable scouts."

"And reliable men," added Walker.

"Do you blame them?" asked Colonel Cole facing the other colonel. "They have been on half rations for two weeks and from what the quartermaster tells me, there isn't much left in the wagons."

His ugly mood turning even more so, Colonel Walker threw the last of the weak coffee on the ground and said, "We need to find Connor. We need to find him soon or mutiny will be the least of our worries. The men will be starving and the hostiles will finish us."

Agreeing, Colonel Cole called to the bugler standing nearby, "Blow officers' call. We need to get moving away from this accursed place."

* * *

Believing he was at the appointed meeting spot, Brigadier General Connor had waited in what shelter he could find with his troops and scouts for more than a week. However, during that time he had been able to find neither the hostiles nor Colonels Cole and Walker. Even the scouting parties of Pawnee had been able to find nothing more than old pony tracks and abandoned campsites. Since his men had razed the Arapaho camp, they had seen nothing but a few hostile scouts who fled when pursued. *And what about the two other columns that would form the three prongs of the trap? Where were they? Could they have found the main camps of the hostiles?* Calling out to his aide, Lieutenant Jewitt, General Connor decided to send out more scouts. He had to make contact with the columns under Walker and Cole.

Receiving Captain North in his tent outside of the new fort he was having his men build, Connor put his plan out to the commander of the scouts. "I need you to take your Pawnee and cover the country to the east and north. We need to find not only the main camps of the hostiles, but the columns under Colonels Cole and Walker."

"Yes sir," replied Captain North.

"Do you need further instructions?" asked Connor.

"What should I do if we find the Sioux?"

"Send a man back with the news while the bulk of your scouts keeps the Sioux pinned in place," replied Connor.

A strained look on his face, North nodded, "Yes sir."

"Is there a problem?" asked a now-impatient General Connor.

Deciding not to voice his concerns to the general, Captain North shook his head, "No sir. We'll do our best."

"Fine then, draw rations. And hopefully I will see you again in a few days with good news."

"Yes sir," replied North, turning away and wondering how he was going to do the job given and still keep his scalp.

CHAPTER 33

Pausing in the shade of some pine timber, Moroni studied the area closely. For two days following the winter-like storms that had swept through the area, they had traveled almost at a snail's pace along the eastern foothills of the Bighorns. During those two days they had seen no fresh sign of any other people, Indian or otherwise. Acting as a scout, Moroni had left the party an hour before, looking for a safe trail to the north and east, but as yet he had been unable to find anything but rough country along the foothills. Urging the stallion forward, Moroni's eyes swept ahead of him looking for any sign of a way to traverse the rough country without being seen from the well-traveled trail on the flat below. Frowning, Moroni began to worry about being exposed to eyes that might not be friendly, so following the stallion's lead he let the appaloosa wind its way down into a narrow canyon that seemed to be choked with brush, stunted trees and boulders. Fearing he was getting into an impossible place, he almost reined the stallion around when to his amazement a narrow way opened up between a twisted pine and a rock the size of a house. His curiosity aroused, Moroni let the stallion walk through the opening and onto a narrow path that seemed to be carved from the side of the steep hillside.

Traveling along the trail for a quarter of a mile, Moroni was amazed at how it followed the contour of the ridge. From several vantage points one could watch the trail down in the valley below without being seen. In fact, from the condition of the trail he doubted that anyone even knew of its existence. Pulling his field glasses from his saddle bags, Moroni studied the country for better than half an hour. Seeing nothing that sparked his curiosity or caused alarm, he turned the stallion and started back to find Sarah and the rest of the party.

Riding back into the sheltered draw where the rest had waited, Moroni dismounted and let the appaloosa catch his breath. Feeling Hawk's eyes on him, Moroni looked toward him, expecting questions. But all he received was a knowing smile and a slight nod of the head.

"I have found a way," Moroni announced, not sure what Hawk might be thinking. He was still amazed at how he had found the trail and that it even existed.

"Does it go where we need to go?" asked Sarah, getting to her feet.

"I believe so," replied Moroni. "I followed it for quite a way and it looked parallel to the main trail down on the flat."

"Does it look traveled?" asked Rolf as he prepared to mount his horse.

Shaking his head, Moroni replied, "It doesn't look like it. I didn't see any tracks or sign of travelers."

"Let's go, then," said Sarah as she swung into the saddle of her mount. Impatient to be on with the search, she led off.

Following the faint trail for better than four miles, Moroni and Sarah, with the others, came into a sheltered glade among the trees. In one corner a tiny trickle of water issued from the hillside. And nearby Moroni discovered the remains of a fire. Or several fires. Swinging down from the stallion, he let the horse drink. Then after pulling the saddle free, he turned him out on the lush grass that grew on the far side of the glade.

"The fires are old," commented Rolf as he examined the weather-worn fire pit.

"You said you've been in this country," said Moroni looking

at Rufus. "Have you ever seen the like?"

Shaking his head, the old mountain man replied, his face paling under the tan. "Never."

Sensing something was bothering Rufus, Moroni began to question him, but he felt a hand on his arm.

"He will tell when the time is right," whispered Hawk, standing next to Moroni. Nodding, Moroni watched as Rufus wandered over to the spot where one could look down on the rolling plain below. The man took a seat on a flat rock.

Watching Rufus for several moments, Moroni wondered at what was bothering the normally-jovial old mountain man. Then, with Rolf's help, he picketed the horses where they could get at the almost knee-high grass.

Building a tiny fire in the blackened cleft where there had been many a fire before, Sarah began to prepare a frugal meal. It would be the first hot meal they had enjoyed in quite a few days.

As the shadows began to fall over the sheltered glade, Moroni sifted dirt on the remains of the fire. For the first time in a long time he felt somewhat filled and secure. While he didn't think anyone from down on the plain would be able to see the orange wink of the fire in the darkness, he didn't want to take any chances. Squatting near Sarah where she sat putting the cooking utensils away, he looked at Rufus. The entire time the rest of them had eaten, Rufus had continued to sit on the rock and watch the valley spread out before him. Sarah had taken him a plate of food, but the mountain man hardly touched it.

Glancing at Sarah, Moroni said softly, "What do you think?"

In return he received a shrug, "I don't know. Something is really bothering him, but I'm not sure what we can do about it."

Nodding in reply, Moroni knew Sarah was right, yet he yearned to help the man who had given so much to him and his family. Moving as if he were part of the night, Rufus left his spot and came to where Moroni and the others were sitting.

Placing the tin plate with the half-eaten food on the ground, Rufus cleared his throat and looked at Hawk, then Moroni. "I figger you got a right to know."

For a moment, Moroni wasn't sure what to say, so he waited for Rufus to continue on.

"I been haunted by the past for the last two weeks now. I reckon you can tell something be a-botherin' old Rufus. And, well, you're right. I came through this country for the first time a long time back. I had me a partner back then. Hans was his name. A hard-headed Dutchman he was, and we was nigh inseparable. But that summer—I guess it was the summer of thirty-eight—I fell in love." A slow tear trickled down the gray, bearded cheek of Rufus as he continued the story.

"Me and old Hans had come west together with a bunch of other fellers. But after a few years we became free trappers and struck out on our own. Well, we did all right for a few years 'til we was a visitin' this Sioux village over in the Black Hills and I seen this purty little gal. And well, I just fell right in love. I asked old Hans what he thought I should do about it and he just grins and says for me to ask her pappy for her to be my wife. Well, I got the cold chills a thinkin' about havin' me a wife, but I got all sick inside when I thought about lettin' her go. So I got all shined up and I picked out some presents from my trade goods and two of my best horses and I asked her pappy for that girl to be my wife."

Drawn into the story, Sarah asked in a soft voice, "What was her name?"

"Her name? Well, she was called White Spring, and she was a beauty. Anyway, I asked her pa and do you know what he said? He asked why I wanted White Spring for a wife. Well, at that I got all choked up and I told her pa I loved her. Shucks, I was in love. Well her pa, he grins all over and takes the presents and the horses and put White Spring's little hand in mine and, well, I was the happiest man alive. Her pa, he decides to throw this big feast and we had us a right nice weddin' party. And there was my old pard Hans a grinnin' though it all."

Wiping at the moisture on his cheeks, Rufus continued, "We had us a grand old time for about a week there in the camp. Then this old son from another village shows up. Now this injun was about the meanest-lookin' feller I ever did see. And from what I found out he had been wantin' White Spring for a fifth or sixth wife for some time. Well, when this old boy found out I had hitched up with her, he got mighty mean. And when he threatened White Spring's pa I had had enough. I thumped the mangy cuss over the head and then me, Hans and White Spring took off.

"Never in my wildest dreams did I figger that old son would foller us, but he did. Him and about thirty of his warriors caught us just about a day's ride north of here. See, we was a riding hard across the flatlands over there to the east and we kept a follerin' this same ridge we are follerin' now. I knowed that old cuss was a follerin' us but I didn't see no way across this here ridge. I thought we were goin' under for sure when outa' nowhere comes this old injun." Looking sharply at Hawk, he went on, "This old injun takes one look at us and says, foller me, and, well, we was so desperate, we did. We follered him right up into this same pass that lies just up head. I never would have thought there was a pass through this here ridge, but sure enough this old injun took us right to it and then he just disappears. Odd. That injun was odd. He had sky blue eyes and looked like he was about a hundred years old. But he stayed ahead of us all the way."

Rufus' eyes left Hawk. And he continued on. "Only problem was, is that Sioux and his boys was right behind us." Coughing a bit and wiping again at his face, Rufus looked hard at Moroni and Sarah, "I figgered it was over, I did. There was only me and old Hans and I knew we couldn't hold that ugly cuss and his men off forever. So old Hans, he gives me the reins to his pony and tells me and White Spring to ride. Well, I didn't know what he was talkin' about for a bit. Then he says to me, 'Rufus you got a family to care for. Now get on them horses and ride. I'll try and hold this bunch off for a spell.' I'll tell you, I was about fit to be tied. There was no way I felt like runnin' off and leavin' my pard. But he was insistin'. It was like he made me. And, may the Lord have mercy on me, I left him there."

His voice cracking, Rufus hung his head down and began to sob.

Going to Rufus and putting her arm around him, Sarah asked in a quiet voice, "What happened after that?"

Shaking his head, Rufus replied, "I don't know. We heard more shootin'. But the Indians never did follow."

"Your wife?" asked Sarah.

"Ah," said Rufus looking up and rubbing at his face. "We had twenty good years. The only regrets we ever had was that she never could have children."

"But you had each other and you had love," said Moroni quietly.

A faint smile cracked through on Rufus' face. He nodded, "Yes, we did have that. So now you know."

Giving Rufus' leather-clad shoulder a squeeze, Sarah said, "Thank you, Rufus. I believe you are one of the most lucky men I know."

"How do you figger that?"

A gentle smile on her face, she replied, "You had a wife that loved you very much and a friend who was willing to give up his life for you."

"What more could a person ask for?" agreed Rolf.

With a wan smile, Rufus replied, "I reckon you are right. I just been having bad dreams of late. And the closer we get to that pass the worse off I get."

For a moment all were silent. Then Hawk knelt next to Rufus and put his hand on his shoulder, "My friend, you will have peace. If you but trust in God he will give you the peace you need."

Closing his eyes for a bit, Rufus looked up and said softly, "I reckon I ain't had nobody since White Spring passed on. And you all have been like family to me. I thank you for that. Now I got me this strange feelin' we are going to meet up with your son right shortly and when that happens we best be a gettin' back to home."

Her blue eyes meeting the old grey eyes of the mountain man, Sarah nodded, "Thank you, Rufus. I have had the same feeling myself for the last day or two."

"Then we must prepare," said Hawk. "And rest."

CHAPTER 34

Riding their horses at a slow lope, Sam, Gal, and the remaining two Sioux warriors covered the wide prairie at a mile-eating gait. Ahead of them the outlines of the timber on the ridges of the Bighorns came into sight. Soon they would reach the mountains and there, hopefully, find a measure of concealment. Following the ice storm that had cost the party five horses, Gall had seemed nervous and more watchful than usual. When Sam had asked, his reply was, "I have a bad feeling."

Pausing on a low rise, Gall shaded his eyes and carefully scanned the surrounding area.

Still riding the roan, Sam stopped beside Gall. His own eyes looking for anything out of place, Sam asked, "What do you search for?"

A grim smile coming to his lips, Gall replied, "My eyes search for something I never thought I would see in my own country."

Following Gall's gaze, Sam's eyes riveted on the forms of at least twenty horsemen coming their way. At over a mile away, Sam could not make out who the riders were, except that they were Indians. "Who are they?"

"Pawnee," the word came as a hiss from Gall's lips.

For some time, Sam had known not to question Gall's word. So even if he couldn't make out the riders, he believed Gall without question. Knowing the Pawnee were the sworn enemies of the Sioux, Sam asked, "What do we do?"

"We run."

Pointing his horse toward the ridges and canyons of the

Bighorns, Gall led off at a gallop. Sam and the other two warriors were right behind him.

* * *

During the morning hours, Moroni had led the party along the faint trail they had started on the previous day. As he let the appaloosa walk on cat feet along the faint trace, Moroni was amazed at how carefully the trail followed the contours of the steep ridge. Never would he have believed that it existed if he had not seen it. From nowhere down on the flat nor the ridge above could a person see any hint of a trail. And every so often there was a place where one could stop and survey the whole of the prairie below them. Seeing what he assumed to be another lookout just ahead, he urged the stallion to a trot. Coming to the vantage point, he stepped from the saddle and looked out over the wide, grassy vista.

"Quite a view isn't it?" Sarah commented as she came up beside him.

For a moment, Moroni didn't reply. He thought he had seen something down on the flat. There it was again. Just spots moving rapidly. Going to his saddlebags he pulled out his treasured field glasses and put them to his eyes.

"Four horsemen," he said softly.

"Who are they?" Sarah inquired.

"Looks like Indians. Wait! There are about twenty more not far behind them and coming fast."

"Probably a raiding party of Crow being chased by a passel of Sioux or Cheyenne," Rufus offered.

"Sounds likely," commented Rolf as he led the packhorses onto the sheltered spot on the trail.

Staring hard at the four horsemen moving swiftly toward the safety of the mountains, Moroni felt an odd flutter inside. What was it about the four that caused him to pause? Shifting his gaze to the larger group in pursuit, he sucked in his breath.

"Those in the rear are Pawnee."

"Cain't be," grumped Rufus. "This be Sioux country." Then stopping himself he added, "Wait a bit. Didn't Connor have a bunch of them with him as scouts or somethin'?"

"That's right," Sarah replied. "When we left Laramie there were about a hundred of them waiting to go with the army."

"Well, about twenty of them are just about to corner and wipe out those four Sioux down there," Moroni said, still staring through his field glasses.

"They will, unless we do something," Hawk said, speaking softly.

Pulling the glasses away from his eyes, Moroni was about to ask why he should get into a fight with a tribe that was supposedly allied to the whites, when he looked into Hawk's eyes. Just for a second he saw something there. Then putting the glasses back to his eyes, he gazed at the four riders again.

* * *

Their horses beginning to labor, Sam, Gall and the other two warriors unslung their bows in preparation for a fight. Casting a glance over his shoulder at the first whoops from the Pawnee, Sam had a feeling it would be a very short fight. None of the Sioux were armed with rifles, but all of the Pawnee sported a rifle or a carbine. Smacking the roan with his bow, Sam hoped to get just a little more speed from the horse, but even with the stamina the little horse always seemed to possess, it was beginning to lag.

Then one of the warriors accompanying them swung his pony about and shouted, "It is a good day to die!" And brandishing his lance, he charged straight at the oncoming Pawnee. For a moment, Sam thought the Pawnee would veer off and slow down. But several rifle shots cracked, and the warrior and pony went down in a cloud of dirt and dried fall grass. Then as the main body of the Pawnee swept by the inert warrior and his pony, several of the enemy warriors dropped to the ground to finish the job. The rest swept on.

Gritting his teeth, Sam cast a glance at Gall, and in return the famed Sioux warrior shouted at Sam, "Show yourself to them. They are friends of the whites and maybe they will not harm you!"

Shaking his head violently, Sam yelled back, "No, I cannot leave you!"

"Then we will die!" said Gall.

"Then I will die at your side!" Sam shouted.

Just then he heard the reports of several rifles and the hum of the bullets as they passed by. A fierce expression on his face, Gall waved his bow and howled at the Pawnee as did the other warrior. His mouth suddenly dry and feeling slightly giddy with the wild chase, Sam shouted out in English, "You are going to have to do better than that!"

Again there were more sharp barks from the rifles of the Pawnee, and this time, Sam felt a tug on his sleeve and a sudden warmness. Looking down at his arm, Sam nearly fainted. Through a slit cut in his deer-hide jacket by the Pawnee bullet oozed a trickle of blood. His lower lip in his teeth, he nearly cried out. But instead, he began to pray.

* * *

For half a second, Moroni stared hard at the fleeing four horsemen. Then with his face pale as death, he looked at Sarah, "One of them is Sam." Without further comment he urged the stallion over the edge of the steep ridge and into the thick trees and brush. Not questioning her husband, Sarah plunged ahead after him.

His eyes wide in bewilderment, Rufus asked no one in particular, "Are you sure?" But by then no one was left on the hidden trail as Hawk and Rolf had followed Moroni and Sarah off the side of the ridge. Biting back a cuss word he ducked his head and followed.

With the appaloosa sliding and skidding on its massive hindquarters, Moroni clung to the saddle and attempted to avoid the worst of the branches and limbs slapping him. Reaching the bottom of the steep ridge, Moroni had to urge the stallion out of a dry wash that lay at the bottom of the ridge. Once out of the wash he searched to see where the four horsemen were just in time to see one of the four go down from a volley of gunfire from the pursuing Pawnee. A hard set to his face, Moroni yanked the Henry from the scabbard, dropped to the ground, and, trailing the reins of the appaloosa, sat cross-legged on the slight rise. Then, catching his breath he willed the remaining three fleeing riders to make it just a few hundred yards closer.

* * *

When the breath of the roan became more ragged, Sam felt the beginnings of despair. But then at the base of the tree-covered ridge that was still a quarter of a mile away he saw a faint plume of dust. For just a split second he feared a trap—a cunning trap laid out by the Pawnee. But then a whispered voice urged him toward where the dust was now dissipating.

"Follow me!" shouted Sam at Gall and the other warrior as he turned the roan slightly to take him on a straighter course toward where his heart now led him.

Once again he heard the reports of the rifles from behind him, and cringing, he expected to feel the thud of a bullet—but he was spared.

Drawing abreast of him, Gall yelled, "What do you see?"

Catching his breath, Sam motioned to where he had seen the dust and shook his head, "I don't know. But my heart says to go there."

An odd look on his face, Gall said nothing but looked ahead to where Sam suggested. Just then the spot blossomed with rifle smoke.

* * *

Taking a shallow breath, Moroni waited until the Pawnee were just over two hundred yards away. Then he placed the front sight of his rifle on the leading Pawnee warrior. He was so intent on the advancing riders, he hadn't noticed Sarah, Rolf and Rufus lined up beside him.

His heavy Sharps rested over a nearby tree branch, Rolf said quietly, "I can take them anytime."

Looking up, Moroni caught his wife's eye.

"Hawk is with the horses," she said, cocking her own rifle.

Giving her a quick smile, Moroni took careful aim again and said, "Now."

As one of the four rifles shattered the silence out on the prairie, four Pawnee warriors and their horses went down. Knowing he had to stop the charge of the Pawnee, Moroni levered shot after shot into the advancing horde of Indians. Beside him he heard the reports of Sarah's rifle as well as that of Rufus', then the deeper boom of his father-in-law's buffalo rifle. Cut to pieces by the steady rifle fire, the surviving Pawnee tried desperately to rein their horses around and flee. Seeing the now-panicked warriors attempting to run, Moroni held his fire and reached over to Sarah. But she had already mounted the appaloosa and had spurred him into a run toward a blond-haired boy riding between two Sioux warriors.

* * *

As the rifle-fire erupted from the base of the ridge, Sam cringed, half-expecting to be riddled by bullets. But instead he heard the screams and shrieks coming from the Pawnee behind him. Again and again the hidden rifles cracked and more of the Pawnee fell. Then, with howls of rage, the few surviving Pawnee whirled their ponies and fled. A shout of relief escaping his lips, Sam was doubly amazed to see a woman with long blonde hair, mounted on a big appaloosa, emerge from the brush from where the hidden rifles had fired from. She was riding toward them at a gallop.

Tears began to flow down Sam's face. "Ma!"

Closer and closer he rode toward the figure he knew to be his mother. Never taking his eyes from her, he feared that if he did, she would disappear as if in a mirage. Thundering close to his mother, Sam threw himself from the roan and ran toward her.

"Oh Ma, are you all right?" Sam shouted as Sarah dropped from the stallion.

Her tears bathing her sons sun-bleached hair, Sarah clutched him to her and whispered, "Yes, Sam, I'm all right."

* * *

Staring balefully at the rude stockade his men had built here on the banks of the upper Powder River, General Patrick Connor seethed inside. He had been recalled—ordered home! Smacking his fist into the palm of his hand he ground his teeth and pondered at what he had done wrong. Everything had been against him from the beginning. First the late start, then the mutinies by some of the troops, then the bogged-down supply trains. Cole and Walker had gotten themselves lost, and they nearly starved to death. And an ice storm had killed or maimed most of their mounts. He remembered when North's Pawnee had reported the mounds of half-burned saddles and other tack along with the hundreds of dead horses. At first he had feared the worst, but a week later, Cole's and Walker's footsore and starving troops had straggled into his camp here at Fort Connor. A disaster! Now he was ordered to leave two companies of infantry here at Fort Connor and take the others home to be mustered out. Savagely he glared at the mountains and plains before him and wondered if he would ever return.

CHAPTER 35

Marveling at how Sam had grown, Moroni stood back and watched as he clutched Sarah, shedding the tears that had been pent-up for so long. Catching up the reins of the appaloosa, he looked at the warrior he knew as Gall. Seeing the flicker of a smile on the warrior's face, Moroni walked over to where Gall stood next to his winded pony.

"We meet again," Moroni offered, holding out his hand.

His eyes leaving Sarah and Sam, Gall's face broke out into a wide grin. "It is a good thing. We were up against it out there."

Not sure of how to reply, Moroni shrugged, "You gave Sarah her life once. It is a debt I was glad to repay."

Gall was about to make a reply when they heard Sarah exclaim, "What has happened? You're bleeding!"

Turning, Moroni looked to see Sarah examining a bloody gash on Sam's upper arm.

"It's nothin', Ma. It's just a scratch."

Wiping at her tears, Sarah held onto Sam's arm and looked at Hawk who had just ridden up followed by Rufus and her father. "Hawk, Sam has been shot, can you look at his arm?"

Hawk nodded and replied, "Of course. But I believe we should seek shelter. There may be other enemies about."

Tying a cloth around Sam's arm, Sarah agreed. "Yes, you are right."

Taking Sarah's horse to her, Moroni looked at Gall and the other warrior who sat his horse looking somewhat nervously at the whites. "Come with us. We will talk."

Shaking his head, Gall replied, "We must go. One of our

brothers is back there in the grass, dead. We must care for his body." Then holding out his hand, he took Moroni's. "A safe journey to you." Then, looking at Sam, he grinned and added, "You have grown. Someday you will be a great man. Do not forget what your Sioux fathers, Gall and Killed His Horse, have taught you."

His lower lip quivering, Sam waved at Gall and replied in Sioux, "Thank you, my father. Tell Killed His Horse and Bear Man that I have found my white mother and father and that I am well."

Flashing a smile, Gall waved back and replied, "I will!" Turning his pony, he started back out across the wide plain with the other warrior.

Watching the two warriors ride away, Moroni took Sarah's hand, "Come, let's go home."

The next morning, as Moroni and Rolf began packing up the horses, Rufus came to them.

"I got a crawly feelin' on the back of my neck."

Facing the mountain man, Moroni asked, "What is it?"

Pulling at his beard, Rufus shook his head, "I don't know for sure."

"Could it be we are getting close to that pass?" asked Rolf.

His eyes widening a bit, Rufus shook his head, "No, I don't think so." Then looking off in the distance, he added, "Maybe so. I'll take a look around, though."

Nodding in reply, Moroni watched Rufus swing into the saddle of his horse and ride through the scattered trees to scout the wide valley once more.

His attention back to the horses, Moroni saw Sam putting the rough saddle on the roan he seemed to show affection for. Smiling, he couldn't believe how much the boy had grown. Far into the night Sam had regaled them with his exploits among the Sioux. When he told them of killing the grizzly, Sarah had gasped and clutched at Moroni's hand, and when he told them about the horses he had stolen from the Crow, Sarah had with a scowl on her face expressed her displeasure—even more so when Rufus and Rolf had roared with laughter.

Sensing Moroni was watching him, Sam grinned and asked, "What do you think of my horse?"

Chuckling, Moroni replied, "I think it's about the ugliest beast I have ever seen."

"And a temper to match," offered Rolf. "I tried to touch him last night and he about took my hand off."

A wide smile on his face, Sam replied, "Well, we didn't hit it off too well at first, but now we are the best of friends. He can go all day long on nothing if need be."

Just then the jug-headed roan turned its head and tried a bite at Sam, causing Moroni and Rolf to chuckle.

Packed and ready, Moroni looked around for Rufus, "We need him to guide us to the entrance of that pass."

Pushing his horse forward, Hawk said, "I know the way."

Studying Hawk, Moroni could detect a subtle change in the man. A certain aura had surrounded him and Moroni wondered if he should say something. But without waiting for a reply, Hawk led off.

For an hour, Hawk led the party at a mile-eating pace. Several times, Moroni thought they would be stopped or turned aside by dead-fall timber or other obstructions, but Hawk was always able to find the way around or through to the other side. Pausing for a moment, Moroni looked back. Where was Rufus? He had said he was going to scout around and return.

"What is it?" It was Sarah at his side.

"I'm worried about Rufus," Moroni answered, looking back over the faint trail they had been following for the last ten minutes.

"He said he knew where the pass was," offered Sarah.

"I know that, but I have had this odd feeling for the last little while. Like we are getting close to . . ." Rubbing at his eyes, Moroni shook his head. "I can't explain it but I have this feeling."

Looking at her husband, Sarah knew better than to question his feelings. "Should we go back for him?"

"He will come," Hawk had dropped back beside them now.

His eyes filled with questions, Moroni asked, "What is it?"

With a gentle smile, Hawk said, "You feel it, too."

Without replying, Moroni nodded.

"Where we are about to go is sacred ground. It has been consecrated with the blood of righteous men."

"I don't understand," Moroni said, looking into Hawk's eyes and trying to find the answer for his feelings.

"You will. Have patience," answered Hawk. Then, his eyes lifting to the trail, he added, "He comes."

Looking along the steep ridge, Moroni and Sarah saw nothing for a moment. Then they heard a hoof fall and saw a flicker of movement. Finally, from the trees Rufus came riding his horse at a gallop. At once Moroni knew something was wrong. The mountain man was riding half bent over and clutching at his side. Closer now and Moroni could see the stub of a broken arrow sticking out of Rufus' upper thigh.

Drawing up, Rufus gritted out, "I done played hob now. There be a whole passel of Sioux right behind me."

"Gall?" asked Sarah, fear in her voice.

Shaking his head, his teeth clenched against the pain, Rufus replied, "No, that scar-faced old son from Big Elk's camp and he's got about fifty of his boys with him."

Filled with dread, Moroni looked for a spot to make a stand.

"You folks go on and I'll try and hold them off," groaned Rufus.

Pushing his horse closer to Rufus, Hawk said softly, "Not yet." Then grasping the stub of the arrow, he pulled it cleanly from the mountain man's thigh. "There, you should ride easier now." Turning his horse he said one word, "Come."

Riding swiftly, they overtook Rolf and Sam who had kept going toward the pass. Gaining in altitude, they soon broke out of the brush and thicker timber and were now riding into a narrow canyon. Suddenly from below them they heard the wild whoops of the pursuing warriors.

His eyes narrowing, Moroni could see just ahead where the pass narrowed to no more than fifty yards across.

"There! A place to make a stand," he called to the others. And a good place it was, no cover approaching the spot for several hundred feet. And in the middle of the pass sprawled a clump of boulders and massive tree trunks that must have slid from the sheer mountain above in some past slide or avalanche. Sliding the stallion to a stop, Moroni felt Rufus take his arm.

"Boy, you gotta' keep goin'," the mountain man said, his eyes wide. "I can hold 'em from here."

Beginning to shake his head, Moroni replied, "No, I'm not leaving you. . . ."

His hand digging into Moroni's upper arm, Rufus looked at him with changed eyes, "Boy, this here is the place. This is the pass—Hans' Pass, where he held off the Sioux for me! Now I'm doin' the same for you. You got a wife and a family and I'm all old and worn out." His eyes filled with fire, he finished, "Now you git, boy, and when the stories are told around the fire at night you tell 'em about this place, about Hans and Rufus and all the others what gave their lives so others could live!"

Moving back, Moroni wondered at the change that had come over Rufus. Then Hawk was at his side. "You need to go. Take your family to safety."

Looking at Hawk with pain in his eyes, Moroni wanted to ask a question, but Hawk added softly, "Do not worry. He is among friends."

Then Moroni noticed the sword slung on Hawk's back and the odd-looking bow uncased and strung.

"Not you, too?" Moroni groaned.

A gentle smile on his face, Hawk nodded, "Yes."

His voice filled with anguish, Moroni asked with one word, "Why?"

His eyes taking in the sweep of the land and Sarah, Sam and Rolf who were waiting, Hawk replied, "As I have told you before, you have a great work to accomplish, and your time is not done here." Then, with the old, familiar, gentle and knowing smile on his face, Hawk finished, "This is sacred ground. Here, men died to keep others free. I know you do not understand, but someday you will. Now, please take your family to safety and, as Rufus has said, always remember." Then reaching out, Hawk touched Moroni on the arm.

At the strange man's touch, Moroni felt as if a bolt of fire raced through him, and for an instant he saw Hawk in a different way.

Turning the appaloosa, Moroni gazed at Sarah and Sam. With tears flowing down his cheeks he whispered, "Come, let's go home."

CHAPTER 36

His face set in a grim smile, the scar-faced Sioux warrior pushed his more than fifty men up the faint trail after the small party of whites. He would get revenge on them for the slights and insults he had received in his own village. For weeks now he had trailed them and now he was going to catch them—and kill them all.

Closer to the pass, several of his warriors expressed their worry over this place. It was a haunted place, some said. A place where bad spirits lived.

Scowling at them he shouted, "What are you? A bunch of sniveling Big Bellies? I shot one of them with an arrow and he will die, I am sure. Come on, let us finish them and take what they have."

Whipping his war horse around he started up the trail toward the pass.

* * *

Propped up against a rock with his rifle lying over a rotting log in front of him, Rufus looked around for Hawk. Whispering, he called, "Hey, Hawk. Where did you get to?"

From back of him he heard the whispered voice of Hawk reply, "Do not worry, my friend, you are not alone."

Smiling to himself, Rufus knew that was true. He wasn't alone. In his mind he could see the grinning face of his old friend watching over him. Pulling the blood-soaked bandage tighter on his leg, Rufus said absently, "Well, I guess this be it."

Seeing the first of the Sioux stream out into the open a mere hundred yards away, he took careful aim and fired.

* * *

Hearing the first shot, Moroni stiffened in the saddle and nearly turned the stallion around.

Grabbing his arm, Sarah looked into his eyes, "Moroni, remember when you told me to go?"

His eyes filled with pain, Moroni nodded.

"I can still hear that first shot as you held off the Shoshone that winter day, and believe me, the hardest thing I have ever done was to keep riding."

Ducking his head, Moroni whispered, "I feel like a coward."

Taking her husband's hand, Sarah gave it a gentle squeeze. "You're no coward and you know it. Please! Let's go. If the Sioux catch us, their deaths will be in vain."

Relenting, Moroni followed Sarah and the others down off the other side of the ridge and into the timber as more shots echoed over the pass.

* * *

Reloading his rifle, Rufus wondered where Hawk was. He had dropped one warrior and two ponies and stopped the advance of the Sioux for a bit, but he was getting weak. *Probably from the loss of blood,* he thought to himself. His hard, gray eyes scanning the area in front of him, he detected a stealthy brown form crawling through the sparse brush along the edge of the pass.

"Oh, no you don't," he whispered to himself and took aim. At the shot the warrior reared up and fell back, clutching his chest. Fumbling a little, Rufus began reloading his rifle again. Then he found himself on his back. Blinking his eyes, he wondered what had happened. His thoughts jumbled, Rufus wondered what he should be doing. Trying to form some words, nothing came out. Then a feeling of despair came over him. He had failed Moroni and Sarah. He hadn't held the pass for long enough. Feeling the slow wetness of a tear as it trickled from his cheek and down the side of his neck, he was suddenly almost blinded by a white light. Blinking his eyes, he beheld rank upon rank of warriors in polished armor, shields carried forward and swords or spears in the other hand. Rufus had never seen such a sight in his life. Trying to speak, he felt a presence at his side.

Kneeling next to him, Hawk gazed softly into Rufus' eyes, "I am here, Brother Rufus."

Looking up at Hawk, Rufus was speechless. Dressed in the same manner as the hundreds of armored warriors drawn up across the pass, Hawk was smiling gently at Rufus from under his feather-crested helmet.

"You were the one?" asked Rufus. It took all his strength to say the words.

Nodding, Hawk's blue eyes flashed for a moment.

Wetting his lips, Rufus tried his voice again, "Make sure the young'ns get home."

"I will, Brother Rufus. Now rest." Then Hawk stood, and surprisingly Rufus stood with him.

Gazing upon the scene before him, Rufus was awed by the sight. Formed in long lines, the armored warriors stood facing the Sioux, who in their astonishment had fallen to the ground. Standing next to Hawk was a square-built warrior in armor bearing a banner. When he rested his eyes on the banner, Rufus couldn't make out the strange writing, but in his heart he knew the words.

Then Hawk spoke, "Rufus, behold."

Looking behind him he could see two figures in shimmering white coming toward him: White Spring and Hans! Feeling an odd sensation, he looked at Hawk with the unasked question in his mind.

His gentle smile still there, Hawk nodded, "Yes, go to them."

Feeling as if his heart would burst, Rufus ran to them.

Turning back and taking the standard from the warrior at his side, the man known as Hawk walked down to where the Sioux were huddled.

Fixing a stern glare on the scar-faced warrior, his blue eyes, cold as ice he said, "You will not go further. You will return to your homes at once."

Feeling as if the breath had been nearly snatched from his body, the scar-faced warrior turned and fled down the ridge, followed by the remaining Sioux.

* * *

Not having heard any rifle shots for some time, Moroni could stand it no longer.

"I have to go back. I have to know," he called to Sarah.

"Moroni," she protested, but he whirled the stallion and was gone.

Running smoothly, the stallion covered the distance in a matter of minutes. Reaching the pass, Moroni drew his rifle and proceeded more carefully. Before him, the pass was bathed with golden fire. Catching his breath, he couldn't believe the scene. Before him, filling the pass, were strong-looking warriors in polished armor. Bearing swords, spears and shields, they seemed to shine like a million glowing suns. Holding a hand up to shield his eyes, he searched for some sign of Rufus or Hawk. Then one of the brightly shining forms was at his side. Holding a banner aloft, the figure spoke to him, "Brother Moroni."

Batting his eyes, Moroni looked closely at the face under the polished and feathered helmet. It was Hawk! His mouth agape, Moroni tried to ask a question but nothing would come.

The familiar warm smile coming to his face, Hawk asked, "Are you all right?"

"I don't know," he stammered. "Are you . . . ?"

Hawk replied, "All is well here. Now you must return to your family. And remember what Rufus told you."

"These men?" Moroni finally managed to asked in a weak voice.

"They are warriors who once, long ago, held this pass against a hundred times their number so that others could flee to a place of safety."

His mind still awhirl, Moroni gawked at the banner Hawk held. Although the writing was odd, he knew what it was—the Title of Liberty. Then as if he were looking into a pool of golden water, the figures of the warriors became blurry. Then shimmering brightly once more, they were gone. Feeling faint, Moroni gripped the saddle with both hands. Several deep breaths later he looked around for any sign of the warriors or Hawk. Nothing. Then he spotted a form lying next to a fallen log. Dropping to the ground he ran to the body. It was Rufus. Kneeling at his side, Moroni discovered a bullet wound in the old man's chest. But even though his eyes were closed in death, a gentle smile was on his face. Tears coursed down Moroni's cheeks. He bowed his head. Then a soft and gentle voice came: "Greater love hath no man."

The shadows were long and the sun was dipping into the western sky when Moroni caught up with Sarah and the others. Seeing him coming, Sarah rode to meet him. Drawing near, she caught her breath.

"Moroni, what has happened?"

His eyes shining with a new light, he took her hand and asked softly, "What do you mean?"

Unable to reply, she just stared at him.

Then Sam was at his side. "Your hair, Pa, it's gone white."

Smiling gently, Moroni looked at Sarah, then Sam and Rolf in turn. "I guess I have a story to tell, don't I?"

A slight nod of her head and Sarah whispered, "If you want to."

Leaning over and holding her close to him he said, "Remember what Rufus said? That when story time comes around the fire, we will tell the legend of what happened here? The legend of Hans' Pass."

Holding tight to her husband, Sarah replied, "Only it's not a legend, is it? It's a true story."

"Yes."

* * *

Sitting on his bench on the corner of the log porch, Moroni gazed out over the meadow and toward the aspen-covered hillside. The shimmering of the golden leaves reminded him of a river of gold or of a scene he had seen not so long ago. His journal, bound in tanned elk hide was in his hands. *How do I put this story down in the words of a mere mortal,* he thought to himself? Taking up his quill, he started to write, then smiled to himself. Sarah was expecting again, and if it was a boy they would name him Rufus.

EPILOGUE

Deer hunting. It was always his favorite time of the year. Tomorrow was opening day and this evening was time for the campfire stories. Sam Stewart shifted nervously as his father Hans Stewart poked at the fire with a stick and called to the others.

"You said you were going to tell us a special story this year, didn't you, Dad?" Sam asked, trying to catch his father's eye.

"Huh? What?" his father grunted. A sly gleam in his eye, he looked up from where he sat in his chair. Poking again at the fire he winked and called to one of his cousins. "Sam here is getting awful worked up over this story I promised to tell tonight."

As the others came up to the bonfire and gathered around, one said, "This is the one I been waiting for, too!"

Another asked, "Is it a story about when you were in that POW camp in North Vietnam?"

"Dad!" groaned Sam, snuggling next to his father.

"Okay, okay," said his father, holding up his hands. Then growing serious, he looked around the assembled crowd and said, "Now what I'm going to tell you is a true story, and it's about your ancestors. In fact, Sam here is named for the boy that was kidnaped by the Sioux. . . ."

* * *

Rubbing his back, Sam Stewart looked over the map again. Nowhere on the multitude of contour lines was there any indication of a pass or even a narrow draw leading up onto the ridge. Stuffing it into a pocket of his Levi jacket he pulled out an old leatherbound journal and carefully opened the brittle

231

pages. Perhaps there would be something there that would offer a clue.

"How are you feeling?" It was his wife, Angela, riding up beside him on her horse.

"Okay, I guess," Sam replied, but the flat tone in his voice was unmistakable.

In the year since he had returned from the Gulf War, Angela had noticed a change in her young husband. At times he seemed withdrawn and morose. Then, several weeks ago, they had been camping in an attempt to bleed off some of the stress. And while staring into the campfire, he began a story, a tale of one of his ancestors: he had been named after him—Sam. Hearing the wild tale, Angela asked where it had taken place and he'd been unable to answer because he really didn't know. What followed was two weeks of research in what Sam called his *genealogy project*. Most of the members of Sam's family had heard the story, but none were able to tell him where it happened. Then, in an old dusty journal found in an old trunk that had been supposedly written by a Moroni Stewart, he found the answer. Packing supplies for two weeks and loading their horses in the trailer, Sam and Angela traveled to the area mentioned and began their search.

Pulling her honey-colored hair back and wiping at the perspiration, Angela wondered for about the twentieth time what her husband was really searching for. *Was it peace? Was it a release from the war?* Silently she hated the war and what it had done to Sam. Then as if on its own volition, her bay gelding walked toward what seemed to be a solid wall of rock. To her amazement a slim opening appeared.

"Sam," she called. "Come look."

Riding his own horse over, Sam could see what appeared to be a faint trail. At first his horse didn't want any part of the vague path, but then, bowing its head, he started on it.

For several miles Sam and Angela followed the trail. Then surprisingly the trail began to wind its way up. Up toward a narrow notch in the steep ridge.

Looking up, Sam breathed, "I don't believe it."

"It must be the trail you're looking for," said Angela, stopping her gelding beside Sam.

Pushing their horses further up the trail, they found themselves riding onto a spot where the pass leveled out.

Turning to Angela in the gathering darkness, Sam said in awe, "This must be the place."

Taking his hand, Angela nodded. But she made no reply. For several moments they sat on their horses side-by-side. Then Sam shook his head. "It's getting dark. We can come back in the morning."

Squeezing his hand, Angela looked into her husband's eyes and asked, "Sam, what are you looking for?"

For a moment he was silent. Then with tears flowing down his face he asked, "I want to know why there has to be war. I want to know why my family has always been beset by the problems of the world? Why do we have to suffer?" Then looking around him at the narrow pass, he shouted, "Why?"

The horses picketed on the sparse grass and their sleeping bags rolled out. Sam and Angela shared a meager supper of freeze-dried food. With their jackets on against the night chill, they now sat side-by-side looking into the flames of the tiny fire Sam had built. Taking her husband's hand in hers, Angela wondered what she could say or do to excise the demons that seemed to be haunting her husband. Then, without warning, a man squatted at their fire.

Recoiling, Sam and Angela pulled back, but then the man smiled and said, "May I share your fire?"

Hesitating, Sam nodded, "Yeah, I guess so."

The man's blue eyes twinkled in the firelight from a bronzed, chiseled face. He was dressed in jeans, hiking boots and a flannel shirt. Looking directly at Sam he asked, "What is it you search for?"

For a moment, Sam felt irritated, but then the stranger leaned forward, "Samuel, do you not remember me?"

Looking intently at the man, Sam's mouth suddenly dropped open, "You're the man . . . the man from the Bear River Monument!"

Smiling, the stranger nodded.

Grabbing Angela's hand and jerking on it, Sam said excitedly, "Remember a couple of years ago when we were down by the massacre sight! This same man was there!"

Not knowing if she should be afraid or relieved, Angela nodded her head.

His eyes narrowing, Sam asked, "What are you doing here?"

The smile still on his face, the stranger asked, "You seek something, do you not?"

"How do you know?" Sam wondered out loud.

"Because others have come to this place to heal as you have done. This is a sacred place. A place of peace and healing."

A quizzical expression coming onto his face, Sam asked, "My father?"

The stranger nodded. "As have others."

"But why didn't he tell me?" wondered Sam.

"Because you had to find out on your own." The stranger continued, "Brother Samuel, you wanted to know why there had to be war—the killing and all the other terrible things that befall man." Then his voice became softer, piercing Sam to the core of his soul. "And you wanted forgiveness for the lives you have taken in war." Reaching forward, the strange man took

Sam's hand in his. "Brother Samuel, God will not hold against you the lives you have taken, for you have taken them in defense of freedom. You, Brother Samuel have become one of the special brotherhood. You have given of yourself to defend the weak and helpless. You have become as a son of Helaman."

Then with a wave of his hand he called out, "Look!"

Before him, as if in a whirling pool of silver starlight, Sam could see ranks of soldiers, some in polished armor, some in other uniforms and costumes. Some of the uniforms he recognized, some he didn't. Standing ready, they looked into his eyes and he knew—he knew he had paid the price and would be forever changed, but for the good. Then the vision was gone.

Catching his breath, he looked into the stranger's eyes. "Who are they?"

"They are your brothers, and they stand ready."

At once, understanding flooded Sam's soul. Nodding his head, he asked, "When?"

A smile and the stranger got to his feet, "Soon, Samuel. Very soon."

Then he was gone.

Gripping Angela's hand he stared at her, "Did you see that?"

Tears streaming down her face, she nodded, "Yes."

About the Author

David J Hawkes was born and raised in a small community in Idaho. He attended Ricks College and served an LDS mission to Italy. He developed a love for reading early in his life, and has studied the works of many authors.

He published his first novel "The Tarnished Angel" in 1998, and it has become a treasured Christmas story.

Also, he published the first novel in this historical, adventure series "Shoshone Trail," in 1999.

David has a love for the outdoors and has experienced much of what he writes about. He enjoys camping, hiking, and horseback riding.

David has served in the Army National Guard, and has spent much of his life working in the outdoors for the Forest Service, the Idaho Fish & Game Department, and on his family's ranch in Idaho, where he currently lives.

To visit with David about his novels and get the latest information on his upcoming projects, you may e-mail him at Hawkpublishing@aol.com.

CEDAR FORT, INCORPORATED
Order Form

Name:_____

Address: _____

City: _____ State: _____ Zip: _____

Phone: (   ) _____ Daytime phone: (   ) _____

Shoshone Trail II: Hans' Pass

Quantity: _____ @ $14.95 each: _____

Shoshone Trail

Quantity: _____ @ $12.95 each: _____

The Tarnished Angel

Quantity: _____ @ $9.95 each: _____

plus $3.49 shipping & handling for the first book: _____

(add 99¢ shipping for each additional book)

Utah residents add 6.25% for state sales tax: _____

TOTAL: _____

Mail this form and payment to:

Cedar Fort, Inc.

925 North Main St.

Springville, UT 84663

You can also order on our website **www.cedarfort.com**
or e-mail us at sales@cedarfort.com or call 1-800-SKYBOOK